A TOUCH OF BRIMSTONE

MAGIC OF THE DAMNED

MCKENZIE HUNTER

ACKNOWLEDGMENTS

I'm living through a pandemic. Of the many things I thought I'd say in my life, that definitely wasn't one of them. I believe that adversity can lead to renewed appreciation. Before I acknowledge the people who made this book possible, I want to thank my readers. I appreciate you for reading my stories and following Luna's journey. I'll never be able to truly express the joy of producing a book and having people read it, join my group to discuss it, or email me about my stories. I'm able to tell my stories because you all read them. I truly appreciate it and want to thank you.

Thank you to my family and friends who force me out of my writer's cave and check on me to make sure my characters aren't running amuck in my head and take breaks.

Elizabeth Bracker, Márcia Silva, Robyn Mather, Sherrie Simpson Clark, Stacey Mann, thank you so much for being the best Beta readers an author could ask for. Your feedback allows me to create a better book, and thank you for it. Meredith Tennant and Therin Knite, my editors, I appreciate all your hard work with helping me tell a better story.

McKenzie Hunter

A Touch of Brimstone

© 2019, McKenzie Hunter

McKenzieHunter@McKenzieHunter.com

Cover Artist: Orina Kafe

For notifications about new releases, *exclusive* contests and giveaways, and cover reveals, please sign up for my mailing list at mckenziehunter.com

ISBN: 978-1-946457-18-9

*J*ackson, my ex, red-faced, doubled over and clutching his berries while lambasting me for "overreacting" while sprinkling in variations of "bitch" wasn't how I expected our three-year relationship to end. But there we were. One of my best friends—or rather one of my *ex*-best friends—cowered in the corner, hastily trying to dress. She was making a desperate attempt to keep the top sheet she'd swiped off the bed around her.

"Don't bother with discretion, Ava. I've seen you naked before and Jackson definitely has, too."

She hurriedly put on her shirt and panties, grabbed her pants and shoes, and scurried out of the room. Jackson was huffing and grunting in pain, his hands cradling his cheating stick.

Finding them in bed together was more than just shocking and enraging; it was a revelation about him and our relationship. My discovery made his confidence, which I had adored during our relationship, morph into something ugly. What was on full display when he rolled out of the bed was a cruel audacity that bordered on narcissism. Standing in front of me as naked as the day he was born, his Good and Plentys dangling, he showed no remorse or shame, and his eyes fluttered with annoyance as he mumbled something about it not being what I thought.

In a moment of awestruck incredulity, I was rendered speechless. *What?*

"Really? *It's not what I think.* So, you weren't just inside Ava with her moaning like she was making an upload for Pornhub. I can assure you; I know what sex looks like. This is exactly what I think."

He simply jutted out his arrogant, self-entitled jaw in defiance. "Luna, as usual, you're overreacting. It was an accid—"

"Accident? Did you trip and fall into her?"

His response, accusing me of being unnecessarily crass, led to me kneeing him in the groin. That wasn't an *accident.*

"Where are you, Luna?" Emoni asked, leaning across the counter of the coffee shop of Books and Brew, where I was seated. Her face was just inches from mine. I wondered how long she'd been trying to get my attention. Telling her I'd been thinking about Jackson was out of the question; she'd worry. Something she'd done often over the past few months. Concern had already etched a frown on her face. I flashed her a smile and tapped the book in front of me.

"Sorry. It's such an interesting read. One of those rare books where you just ruminate over the information," I lied.

Picking up the book, she grimaced at the title, *The Discovery of Magic*, then flipped through Post-its I'd used as placeholders, since it was a borrowed book.

"This is so you. You're finding yourself musing over witches, goblins, fae, vampires, werewolves, and all the freaky things that go bump in the night," she teased as she returned to restocking the cups. Her tone was light and playful, but I caught the furtive look of concern she gave me.

"No fae or goblins. They don't specify werewolves, just shifters."

Her brow hitched. "No." She pointed an accusatory finger at me. "Bad Luna. You will not try to pull me into your world of fantasy. It's not my thing and you can't make me."

"It reads like fiction," I told her, aware that nothing I said would change her mind.

"But it's *not* fiction."

"Don't knock it until you try it."

Working at Books and Brew was a reader's dream job, but of the many things Emoni and I had in common that made us fast friends in college, our reading preferences weren't among them. They couldn't be any more different. My tastes were less discerning; if it seemed interesting, I'd give it a try. Emoni loved fiction, biographies, mystery, and thrillers and rarely strayed from those genres. After a moment of silence, each of us giving the other half smiles and persuading looks that had never worked in the past, we ended at an impasse.

"What are you having?" she asked.

"Whatever will keep me awake for my shift." I worked more now and that hadn't escaped Emoni's notice. The humor drained from her eyes and unease crept back into them the way they always did when she knew the conversation topic was veering toward my breakup with Jackson.

It wasn't just catching Jackson cheating that hurt. It was how much *his* cheating changed *my* life. For a few weeks I was homeless, staying on Emoni's sofa until I made the move from the three-bedroom house we'd rented from his parents, below market value, into a one-bedroom apartment, just a few square feet larger than the bedroom Jackson and I had shared and in a questionable neighborhood. Money was tight and it was hard getting used to sleeping alone.

"Are you getting settled in your apartment?" she asked, her voice neutral, although her eyes couldn't hide what she felt. She wanted desperately to wish my sorrow and pain away.

My smile took more effort than I wanted to admit, but

the more I hurt, the more Emoni alluded to kneecapping Jackson.

"It's cozy."

Cozy and very tiny. But mine. There wasn't anyone to complain about the stack of books on the nightstand, me staying up too late to read, or, well, about anything. Over the years of living together, Jackson's complaints became plentiful. I thought it was a product of two very different people sharing a space. He was probably comparing me to Ava. I tried to find the humor in the irony of how much they disliked each other initially.

For a brief moment, I delved into the emotional rabbit hole, trying to pinpoint the moment she'd stopped thinking of him as being too pompous and aloof, a claim she'd made often, and started viewing him as someone she'd betray a friendship for. Or when he started to find her overly whimsical personality endearing rather than annoying.

I wasn't getting out of the rabbit hole anytime soon because I started replaying the moments when Jackson invited Ava over to watch movies, to join us for drinks, and for dinner. I mistook their change in attitude toward each other as the inevitable transition to tolerating each other for the sake of the person you both loved. He and Emoni had undergone a similar evolution, though a wall of wary distance always remained between them. There wasn't any doubt they'd tolerated each other for the sake of their relationship with me.

Emoni, the self-proclaimed barista extraordinaire, handing me a cup of coffee pulled me out of the labyrinth that had the potential of ruining my day. "Here you go. A finely ground Robusta coffee. If this won't get you through an eight-hour shift, I'm not sure what will."

The heat from it warmed my hands that were chilled from the Midwest balmy fall. I took an appreciative sip. "Ten hours today," I told her.

She frowned.

"Lilith called in sick. I never mind coming in or working long hours."

Working kept my mind from being idle and recalling the images of Jackson and Ava entangled in the bed. It didn't chase away the hurt but made managing it easier. The months had ticked by, but there was still an Ava and Jackson-size hole in my heart and life. Each day it got a little smaller. Getting over a three-year relationship and the loss of a friend I'd known since elementary school wasn't going to happen overnight.

"More opportunities to discover more of your weird books," Emoni said, her nose wrinkling as she gave my book a quick glance.

"I didn't get it from the store, it's a loan."

"Let me guess, Reginald?"

The tarot reader from the apothecary store next door had become my paranormal books reading buddy. During our book discussions in Books and Brew, Emoni always gave me her affectionate quizzical look that screamed, "How are we friends?"

"Well, we can't all have side gigs and hobbies as glam-orous as yours," I teased, keeping my gaze down on my coffee, fully aware that she was glaring at the top of my head. She always did when I made similar comments.

I lifted my eyes to find her nose scrunched. Being the lead singer of a band, she didn't consider it a hobby. To her, it was a job, her calling, what she called "her breath." And when she sang, it imbued her with something that transcended life. She enjoyed it and it showed in all her performances. What kept the look on her face was her modeling side jobs that she got from local artists.

A few months ago, she reluctantly admitted she enjoyed seeing paintings and photos featured on social media and in the artists' studios, but that was the extent of what she liked about it. "It's hardly a job. There's no skill in being born with anatomical features in the right size, shape, and 'definition' and 'sculpt' that appeal to the humanoids," was her typical response to any mention of it. "Humanoids" was the derisive term she ascribed to people who were obsessed with beauty and things that weren't in a person's control. I knew it was her response to being called "exotic" too many times.

African American, with enviable flawless deep-mahogany skin, full defined lips, thick-coiled midnight ear-length hair, umber-brown eyes, and an oval face came together to create what many people often called exotic. We cringed at the description, believing it was an umbrella word often used to describe people whose appearance was different from most of the people in the city. Our consensus was that "unique" seemed like a word you'd use to describe a person who had all the right features but somehow things went terribly wrong. Instead of being a Rembrandt, your features were a mishmash of shapes and angles, likening you to a Picasso. Talent and artistic contribution aside, there was an insult in being called a Picasso.

Modeling jobs were inconsistent, whereas our employment at Books and Brew was steady money. We counted ourselves fortunate to be original employees of the combination coffee shop and bookstore. Located in the art district, the store was one of the less eclectically decorated businesses in the area. Dark wood furniture filled the space. An oversized tan sofa took up the entire wall to the left of the room, and teal-blue painted chairs brought a splash of color to the mundane beige walls. The curved-back metal-and-wood swivel bar stools at the counter added some chic comfort to the decor. The color scheme was continued in the connected bookstore.

The New Age apothecary to the right of the coffeehouse was more of a catchall, selling herbs, vitamins, candles, oils, healing crystals, massagers, yoga cushions, and handwoven baskets. Reginald rented a space to do his readings. The shop leaned into the modern Bohemian look: soothing beige walls, rattan tables used for displays, hanging plants in the corner of the rooms, and large-leafed plants near the register. He'd accented it with shades of orange and terracotta.

A hookah lounge neighbored us to the left. Our little corner of the block catered to the artists, eccentrics, and people who viewed the world through a different lens.

I sipped on my coffee while Emoni went to the register to take an order. We had our regulars but this wasn't one. I sat back and watched in amusement as Emoni plastered on her friendly but rigid smile. It was a look I'd grown familiar with as she assessed new customers, wondering if they were going to order the coffees we were known for or one of Starbucks' famously trademarked drinks. It always led to Emoni's barely affable tight-lipped smile as she pointed to the menu of available coffee drinks and with great effort politely informed the person that Starbucks was two blocks over.

It was after someone ordered a Caramel Ribbon Crunch Frappuccino and then recommended we make something similar that Emoni suggested to Cameron, the owner, a way to deal with the fancy coffee crowd. First violation, they would be politely asked to leave. A second offense would be met by coffee beans being hurled at them until they ran out of the building, feeling rightfully shunned. Cameron didn't object firmly enough to the suggestion. In fact, her eyes held a gleam of mischief.

"If you don't love coffee and books, why come here?" Cameron had defended herself when I pointed out that she didn't seem to hate the idea of assailing unsuspecting customers with coffee beans.

"They didn't come in here to be pelted by dark roast beans by affronted coffee lovers either. First rule of business, don't chase away your customers," I teased.

Her response was crinkling her nose and making a face.

We'd been with the company since it opened five years ago, which explained the less than purely professional relationship she had with us.

With twenty minutes to spare before work, I divided my attention chatting with Emoni between customers and reading my book.

I was reaching for my coffee when Emoni took notice of the ring that spiraled midway over my finger, missing the joint to allow free movement. The ridges, waves, and intricate patterns made me think of the scales of a dragon. Where a head should have been on the body was a flattened triangle with a more elaborate design of markings.

"This is interesting," she said, turning my hand over to get a better look at it. After she released my hand, I admired the ring with the same appreciation I had when I found it near the dumpster in the alley two weeks ago. It was a striking ring; the owner had to be looking for it. I figured that if I wore it daily, its owner would certainly recognize it, but no one had claimed it yet.

"I can't believe I found it. It's unfortunate I won't be able to keep it if someone claims it," I admitted.

She gave it another quick look. "I'm sure you can have someone replicate it or make something similar," she said.

I hoped that wouldn't be the case. I planned to give it one more week before considering the ring mine.

I glanced at the clock, hopped off the stool, and gave Emoni a motionless wave before hugging the book to me and heading to the adjoining bookstore where I worked.

"Ristretto, please," requested a deep, distinctively accented voice as a man sidled close, startling me. I dropped my cup and book. Before I could save the book from being damaged by the spreading coffee, it was scooped up. Grabbing some napkins, I cleaned up the mess. Someone behind the counter came out with a mop and wet floor sign. When I stood, my eyes trailed up the man holding the book. He towered over my five-two frame by a little over a foot.

Too many beats of time passed as I tried to pull my gaze from his smoldering amber eyes with flecks of gold and the striking intensity of banked fire. Veiled by long midnight lashes, they revealed more than his indecipherable expression.

His eyes traced over the lines of my face, which Emoni affectionately described as a "Valentine" face opposed to the traditionally accepted heart shape. I shoved my hand through my loose auburn waves and became self-conscious of the light-blue ribbon I'd woven into the lone braid because I was bored.

The stranger's eyes moved from my face, to my white t-shirt with a cat reading a book, to my fitted jeans, to my galaxy-imprinted Chuck Taylors, and then to the book. He scanned the title and flipped through a few pages then locked eyes with me. His hesitant smile drew my eyes to his supple lips. The light shadow from his beard complemented his sharply defined features. Dressed in a black button-up and black slacks, he seemed out of place in an area where people adored color. If they were wearing black, it wasn't tailored clothing. My eyes dropped to the network of tattoos that peeked from under his sleeve.

"*The Discovery of Magic*," he said in a low, smoky voice before returning the book to me. The intangible energy that wafted off him caused me to stand far too close, violating all social norms and decorum.

"It's an interesting, eye-opening read," I offered.

"Is it?" His question was rhetorical. He inched his face closer to me, his fiery eyes inquiring as he took me in. Specu-lative. "You're a witch." The inflection left me wondering if it was a question, but his appraising look seemed like a reluc-tant accusation.

Is he screwing with me? Did he really believe in witches? And even worse, he thought I was one.

"It's fiction. No one's a witch," I said. "It's a loan from the tarot reader next door." I jerked my chin in the direction of the store next to the coffee shop. Reginald called himself a divinatory, and because of the accuracy of his readings, he'd been called a witch. Something he never corrected. If people thought he was one, it would be good for business.

"I've had a reading by him. He's *not* a witch," the stranger stated.

I know. Because no one's a witch.

His penetrating and searching eyes moved to my ring. I looked at his face for any sign of recognition. There wasn't any but there was definitely intrigue. His attention flicked to my face, auditing my features with keen interest. His lips pressed into a tight line. Without another word, he turned on his heels, dropped money in the tip jar, and left without his coffee.

Emoni looked into the jar then her eyes trailed after him. "He just paid forty dollars for the privilege of looking at you and skimming through your weird book," she pointed out. The wheels were working behind her ever-calculating eyes. "This could be profitable," she teased.

"I'm not sure there's a huge market for peculiarly intense people randomly walking into coffee shops." *And definitely not for ones who believe in witches.*

She grinned. "We can hope."

Whether it was random was questionable, as the stranger was joined by two other people, one of them a slight man, a little over five-nine, who surveyed the area as they walked away. His thick, coal-black shoulder-length hair obscured his profile. He moved with fluid grace. Whatever the stranger who'd asked if I were a witch said caused him to stop and turn, narrowed eyes on me.

The woman who'd joined the stranger stopped as well.

Turning around, she walked toward the coffee shop's window, her long honey-and-chestnut box braids swinging with her quick approach. Russet-brown skin with rosy undertones gave her a vibrant, welcoming look, which was a contrast to the severe, luminous violet eyes that bored into me. She had a medium build and was an inch or two taller than me, and she wore a simple black slip dress that wasn't appropriate for the cool weather. She stared with the same ferocity of the stranger. Canting her head, she frowned.

Abruptly, she whipped around to join the men, who hadn't made it very far. She said something and they all looked back at me. Feeling like a deer caught in headlights, I watched them watch me, unable to look away from the intriguing trio.

Finally pulling my attention from them, I shuddered, pressed the book to me, and headed to work.

2

*C*ameron was all smiles, as expected. Small crinkles had formed around her eyes that I suspected were from the toothy, wide smile she handed out freely like candy on Halloween.

Her wiry thick curls were pulled into a low ponytail. A few escaped curls framed her face. In her midfifties, she had a lively personality and contagious smile.

"New releases tomorrow."

For five years we'd had new releases weekly, and her face still lit up each time as if it were the first time. Her honey-colored eyes reflected a liveliness that would excite even the most apathetic person. Even if the books were releases I wasn't expecting, she stirred the anticipation and excitement that often led me to buy a few.

"And the shipment of Morrison's *Beloved* is in, too," she informed me. An influencer recently mentioned it as a book that "broke" her. As a result, we couldn't keep adequate stock of a book published over thirty years ago. Seeing classics revitalized and award-winning books reach the hands of *new-to-them* readers made me appreciative of the double-edged sword of social media and influencers.

A year ago, a *coffee enthusiast*, who had more followers than a person should, whose favorite coffee preparation was basically just creamer and sugar, recommended our coffee shop; it became overrun with new customers. We were overjoyed for the business, but with new customers requesting sugary specialty drinks, I was convinced the next post about us would be about our snarky barista. It was also during that time that Emoni revisited her suggestion about pelting people with coffee beans.

To our complete surprise, it didn't run people off. It actually became the draw: Come get your coffee from the surly, quick-witted barista. Instead of a biscotti, you'll get a thinly veiled insult and a lovely smile. It convinced me once again that pretty people get away with far too much.

"*Frankenstein*, *Ender's Game*, and *Lolita* should be in the shipment as well," Cameron informed me. Another surprising uptick in sales, but we didn't know the source of their renewed popularity.

We quieted when a tall body slid in next to us, his studious good looks belied by the off-putting set of his rigid frown. Pushing his wide-rimmed glasses up his nose seemed to have been done for theatrics.

"Pardon me, purveyors. Has my copy of Howard Zinn's *A People's History of the United States* come in?"

Purveyors? Seriously, Peter?

Cameron said that Peter was an eccentric old soul. Emoni and I were convinced that he also enjoyed being a know-it-all. Or perhaps it was a combination of the two. In his early thirties, Peter had the airiness of an aristocrat, but his tattered jeans that hung low off his waist, his shirt that played homage to Q*bert, and his disheveled flaxen-colored hair was diametrically opposed to his patrician demeanor.

Spending most of his days in the store, Peter divided his time between his work as a day trader, roaming the aisles of the bookstore, and sitting in the corner with a cup of coffee.

Typically, he was unobtrusive unless he was accosting some unsuspecting customer with his unabridged version of history. His wealth of knowledge was simultaneously impressive and off-putting. I admired his dogmatic refusal to tell history for the side of the "victor," but I believed unfiltered history needed to be administered in small doses. Something he had no interest in doing.

"I'll check," I told him. He excused himself with his customary bow and departed to the small table in the corner of the store that he'd claimed as his spot. *Be weirder, Peter.*

Heading back to the storage area, I wasn't able to intercept the unsuspecting woman who sauntered over to the table where he'd taken a seat. *Enjoy the free lecture—see if you can get college credits for it*, I thought.

Peter would always ensnarl some woman. When he removed his large glasses, he revealed expressive brown eyes. His tall, slender build reminded me of a runner, and he gave off a casual air of indifference while engrossed in a book. His studious good looks and quasi look of apathy alluded to a sexy brood that drew many women into being recipients of his informal and interminable lectures.

Usually, if I saw someone heading in that direction or unwittingly involved in his one-sided conversations, I would ask if they'd found the book they were looking for or remind them of our rewards program.

Searching through the boxes in the storage room, hoping to quickly get to Peter's copy of *A People's History of the United States*, my mind kept revisiting the situation in the coffee shop. The ominous way the stranger's partners looked at me, his scrutiny of me, his questioning me about being a witch, and the certainty of his words. *"He's not a witch."*

Was I missing something? Despite feeling foolish for giving this more than just a passing thought and not dismissing it as the ravings of a person who beliefs bordered on psychosis, I pulled out my phone, texted Reginald, and asked if we could talk during my break. Since he tended to be busier on the weekend, he responded quickly. His weekdays were spent on his phone, reading, and, if needed, bartering his help for a reduction in rent space from the shop owner.

I stumbled on the step and spilled into Reginald's office. He had a broad build, and his chocolate-brown hair was shorn close, showing a wave pattern. Biracial—Mexican and white —he was the kind of golden brown that people spent hours trying to achieve on a beach or tanning bed.

"Luna," he greeted me, extending his hand toward the seat on the opposite side of the small table where he sat. He moved his tarot cards out of the way. Immediately he caught sight of *The Discovery of Magic* and his face brightened.

"Are you enjoying the world of magic?"

"I am, there's so much wonderful information." I opened the book. "It's better than anything I've read in fantasy. A real immersive experience. Like the author was speaking from real experience. Witches, people who turn into animals—"

"Shifters," he offered.

"And vampires."

He nodded. "Have you got to the part where they all can be linked to one god and the eternal curse that extended to them and their descendants?"

I nodded. "Yes, but…"

I hesitated because when Reginald loaned the book to me, I got the impression that for him it was more than a fun fantasy read. If it was more, then that was just another fun quirk about him. Even when he alluded to the existence of the supernatural, it was a vague and abstract concept that tied in with him being a tarot reader. But discussing it, saying it out loud, brought a validity to it, for which I wasn't

15

prepared. But the strangers looking at me like that had weirded me out. I wanted this to be fiction. All fiction.

"This is just fun reading for you, right? You don't think this stuff is real?"

He looked at the closed door and leaned toward me. "Are we speaking in confidence?" he inquired in a low, conspiratorial voice.

No, because depending on what you say, I'm staging an intervention. Is an intervention what I need? Do I call a therapist? A psychiatrist? Your parents?

My heart was pounding in my chest, my fingers becoming increasingly clammy. I'd honor our confidence because for the three years we'd worked next to each other, I'd considered him more than just a business acquaintance. He was my friend. If I swore to it, then that was that. We were in a trust circle. But was I ready for any conversation that would follow us discussing this book?

I nodded, unable to put words to it.

"Of course I believe in this."

I pointed at the bookmark on the open page. "You believe in witches, shifters, and vampires?" Leaning closer to him, I looked around the empty room. "Do you see them now? In this room?"

He threw his head back with a peal of laughter. "No, they're not here. But they exist, Luna."

"Okay, they exist and they came from one source." I flicked through the book, skimming the pages that discussed them, looking for the source.

"It's not in there," he said. "It's rumored that all magical beings came from one source and how they changed was a result of a curse. Experiment, maybe? But I'm so glad I ended up with the good curse."

Was there such a thing as a good curse? Wait, what? He'd ended up with the good curse? Silence stretched taut as I debated the incivility of me placing the book on the table, walking out, and never speaking to Reginald again. But curiosity overrode all.

"Good curse?" I finally said.

"Yes," he whispered. "I'm a witch."

"A witch?" Surprisingly, my skepticism sounded like curiosity.

He nodded, his face alight with pride.

"Casting spells type of witch?"

"You saw in the book that there are different types. Witches born of witches are stronger. And we all have different magical abilities."

"Yes." I flipped through the parts of the book where I'd stuck Post-its. Reading the book as fiction, they were just interesting passages I wanted to revisit, not study the way I would nonfiction. "Elementals, necromancers, and spell casters, who are said to be the strongest and able to perform spells and manipulate the world." The book focused so much on them because they were the strongest and the most abundant.

"My magical ability isn't listed because so little is known of it. I suspect because it's so fluid," he admitted.

"What's your magic?"

"I'm an influencer," he said cryptically, his smile growing wider.

That's an Instagram job.

Committed to not closing my mind to any possibilities, I kept my opinion to myself and from my expression.

"It's very nuanced," he added.

Also sounds very made up.

"I make things work in my favor. I guess it would be considered… probability magic. If the odds are close, I cast a spell to move things in my favor."

My mouth dropped open. He took it as intrigue.

"That's amazing," I said. "Do you ever feel like you're cheating? Making yourself so lucky?"

"I try not to use it. We all have laws we must abide by, and one is remaining hidden from humans." He leaned forward, taking my hands in his. "You must keep this between us."

Believe me, buddy, you do not have to worry about that. If I tell anyone about your fake-ass witch power and this world you believe in, I'm going to get some looks. I glanced at the clock on the wall.

"I have to go, but you have my word. Thank you so much for this and for trusting me with your secret."

He was so full of crap, but still a nice guy. I'd give him that. Mr. Not-a-Witch had to see the absurdity in what he just told me. If he could change the odds in his favor, why not go to Vegas and make a killing, or at least make enough to just tarot read and not have to work a second job? Reading, which he seemed to really enjoy, could be his full-time job.

Before I opened the door, I turned. "The tarot reading, is that linked to your magic?"

He gave me a coy look. I had no idea what it meant.

"No, that's taught, but I do believe my magical gifts help me be more skilled with it. And perhaps occasionally I cast a spell to ensure the accuracy of my reading." He was a talented tarot reader, but I suspected it had nothing to do with his *alleged* magical ability.

"Thank you," I said again. There was a small part of me that wanted to live vicariously through him and his belief in magical worlds of spell-casting witches, people who shifted into animals, and eternal beings of the night.

But realism and pragmatism reared their heads and I was back to regarding tales of witches, shifters, and vampires as nothing more than fiction and the stranger in the coffee shop as one of the peculiar people who populated this section of the city.

Our unconventional area seemed to be the catchall for the weird, nontraditional, and self-identified outcasts. There were the night owls, who'd created a small club named the People of the Night. Despite it being in reference to people who performed better at night, some of the members took it to the extreme, usually sporting midnight-black or platinum-white hair and dressing in dark colors, the scent of weed or patchouli oil wafting off them announcing their presence from some distance. It was quite obvious they were going for the noir of the modern vampires from television and movies.

Other than Reginald's recent revelation to me of being a witch, we had people who identified as Wiccan. With Wicca becoming more mainstream in our area, where eccentric was a sport and everyone was going for gold, these people decided to be a little extra. If someone was dressed as if they were on their way to a Steampunk or Renaissance festival, they were most definitely *our* Broad Street Wiccan.

In need of a breath of fresh air, instead of using the doors that connected the stores, I took the longer route outside. Just before I reached the bookstore's entrance, I thought I caught a glimpse of the stranger. Hugging the book to me, I stopped to take another look. There were pedestrians walking, but not him.

Get it together, I scolded myself. Had it been that long since I'd been with someone that I couldn't get this particular handsome stranger out of my head? Or was the Broad Street weird just getting a little too weird?

3

---

*I*t had been three days since my encounter with the man in the coffee shop and Reginald's confession, and despite my best efforts, the information still consumed my thoughts. I was fixated on it. Work had become the distraction I desperately needed to get my mind off the supernatural world. I hadn't returned the book to Reginald, but I was too reluctant to read more.

Work. I focused ardently on it: cleaning, stocking, making sure there wasn't a single book unshelved. Two more hours before I was scheduled to leave, I grabbed several boxes I'd broken down and headed for the dumpster, saving the cleaning crew the trouble of having to take them at night.

Snorting and chuffing made my head snap up, and my breath catch at the sight of the shimmering diaphanous wall behind the dog that stalked in my direction. The dog had the face and body of a Xoloitzcuintli Quetzal, but its height wasn't anything like the small dog I knew about. My attention moved between the shimmering illumination behind the creature and its approach. Tall enough that its head would meet my waist. A shiny gray coat covered its long, sleek, muscled frame. It was built for speed and agility, so me running away would be a terrible idea. It moved with an off-putting determined fluidity, its head swiveling back and forth surveying the alley. A humanlike intelligence lurked behind the dark eyes as they fixed on me.

I pressed against the side of the building and held my breath, as if that would render me invisible. The only weapon at the ready was the box cutter in my back pants pocket. Slowly, I retrieved it. With the size of the animal, would the cutter be enough to ward it off? It was baring its dagger-sharp teeth that looked capable of ripping apart anything it encountered. I stilled and melted against the building.

Even if it couldn't track me by scent, my pounding heart would make me easy to find. Coaxing myself to take slow, even breaths, I pressed even harder against the wall. It came closer, sniffed my hand, and licked. With swift and precise movements, it stood. Its heavy paws pressed on my shoulders. I strained to hold its weight. Tilting its head as if to study me, it inched its nose closer. Then it dropped down to all fours and ran in the direction it had come from.

I doubled over with relief. By the time I'd slowed my breath and calmed, there was no sign of the dog or any sign of the illumination in the alley.

Retrieving my phone from my other pocket, I looked up the number for animal control. What would I say? "Hey, be on the lookout for a dog. What type of dog? Imagine one that looks like it would guard the gates of hell in every movie."

Instead, I called, told them about the dog, and explained that it wasn't aggressive but might be perceived that way because of its size. After giving them all the requested information, I stayed in the alley, looking out into the emptiness of it as I started to second guess what my eyes had clearly seen. It felt so surreal, I wanted to attribute it to restless nights and long work hours.

I spent the walk time to the store convincing myself that my eyes had deceived me.

Instead of immediately going home after my shift, I made a detour to the alley again, walking the length of it, phone in hand, recording my traipse down it.

Nothing.

No strangers inquiring whether I was a witch, no massive dogs who deserved an appearance in *Supernatural*. Things spiraled into the bizarre when I sniffed the air, remembering the stranger's intoxicating scent. It had lingered in the coffee shop long after he'd left, so why not in the alley?

Could the stranger and the dog really be two unrelated events? There was no evidence that they were.

"What are you doing?" Emoni's voice came from behind me. She must have seen me poke the air where I'd seen the shimmering wall.

I whipped around, embarrassment flushing my face. How do you explain poking the air?

"Nothing," I said with a strained frown. It wasn't good enough to fool a stranger, let alone the friend I'd known since undergrad.

Her brows inched together. She grabbed a tuft of her hair and coiled it around her fingers, still watching me. Finally, she blew out a breath. "Luna, I hang around with musicians, writers, photographers, and artists. I can't have any more weird or"—she air quoted—"eccentric as they prefer to be called, friends. So get it together, girl." She beamed, her long legs swallowing the distance between us in a few steps. She gave me a quick hug, wrapped her arms around my shoulders, and guided me back to the store. Her demeanor was light and airy but I didn't miss the glint of concern in her eyes.

"I have exciting news. Guess who's playing at the King-makers tonight!"

Emoni's news did wonders for chasing away the encounter with the man from the coffee shop and the dog. Joining Emoni and her band's last-minute booking was exactly what I needed: strong liquor, dancing, and supporting my friend while she played in one of the most successful and swankiest bars in the city.

Her excitement at playing at that bar was contagious. I was buzzing with energy. After only three years, the King-makers had become popular and known for showcasing up-and-coming local artists but more notably for when two chart-topping artists, to show the owner gratitude for giving them their first break, made several surprise visits to perform. As I looked around the crowd of people, my cyni-cism got the best of me, suspecting most of the patrons visited the club on the off chance they'd see a major artist for the cost of a watered-down rum and coke.

Emoni's band, Night Ravage, was humming with excite-ment that I could sense from my seat at the bar as I sipped a Negroni.

"This is a surprise." Jackson, a whiskey in hand, slid onto the stool next to me. My eye roll followed. It wasn't a surprise that he was here, and he had to know I wasn't naïve enough to think otherwise. He followed the band on social media and knew the chances were high that I'd be anywhere Emoni was playing. As usual, I'd arrived with the band and helped with setup as needed.

"Really?" I asked with a sigh of exasperation. "It seems like it's about time for your bi-weekly request for us to work things out. Tell me, how does one work through you appar-ently *accidentally* falling into Ava's cooter?"

To Ava's credit, after her betrayal, she had the basic decency to leave me alone. She'd scuttled away and the one time we crossed paths, our eyes met for a brief moment only.

She jerked her gaze from mine the moment they met. I wasn't sure why. Was it difficult seeing the echo of pain that her betrayal had caused? Did she feel the need to hide her shame and remorse? Perhaps I was giving her too much credit. Seeing her was a sucker punch to the gut. But at least I only had to endure it once.

He laughed. "Cooter. You're adorable."

In that moment, I wasn't enamored by his wide, charismatic smile or his lush mass of chestnut curls tapered at the sides. Or his round face with the pronounced dimpled chin and hooked nose. The combination of features worked for him, gave him character. Jackson was aware that his unconventional but striking looks drew women to him. It worked and he knew it.

"Obviously adorable isn't what you want, which is why you looked elsewhere." I smacked my palm against my head. "I forgot. You didn't look elsewhere. What did you say? Oh yes, it was an accident. You *accidentally* slept with my friend."

He huffed a sigh. "I've told you a number of times, that was a bad word choice. It wasn't an accident. But a mistake. We all make them, and I think it's something we can work through."

"Does Ava know you're here trying to 'work things out'?" At each of his attempts, I wasn't sure how I had ever loved such a self-absorbed, unrepentant jackass. I'd been seeing him through rose-tinted glasses. They were off now, though, and his personality was being seen through an unfiltered lens.

My knowledge that he was still involved with Ava didn't faze him.

"Let's say that I entertain this idea of working things out."

Why not? I had time to kill. "What happens to Ava? Or do I become the side woman?"

His jaw clenched and he looked contemplatively into his glass of whiskey. "Not at all. You two are friends—"

"Were."

"*Were*. But you're no longer friends because of me," he started out slowly. Emoni had stopped fiddling with the microphone to give him a narrow-eyed look. It eased slightly when I smiled in her direction. Her brow rose in response, a nonverbal inquiry to ask if I was sure. At my slight nod, she returned to adjusting her microphone and preparing for her set.

"She really hates me, doesn't she?" he asked.

"Hate is being kind. You have no idea what she wanted to do to your man chops."

He frowned, took another sip from his glass. "As I was saying, you were friends and the situation with her—"

"The 'situation' being you cheating on me with her," I corrected again. He didn't get to minimize the situation.

"Cheating or whatever. We all used to hang out and have a good time. I don't see why it can't be like that again. But more *involved* than before."

I choked on my drink once I realized what he was insinuating. This jackass thought his cheating should be rewarded with a what? Three-way? Throuple? "Hey, I can't keep it in my pants so let me have both of you." I had no idea if he'd discussed this with Ava or if he thought that if I was on board, it would be easier to persuade her. "I'm a good guy. I think it's selfish of you to not want to share."

My head nodded as I took things in. He took it as consideration. This was beyond appalling. He wasn't suggesting it as a lifestyle he wanted to explore but because he didn't want to be accountable for anything. I wasn't convinced he could be faithful even then. His arrogance and entitlement were boundless.

"I've never been in a bar fight before," I informed him. "To be more precise—a fight. Period."

His brow furrowed in confusion.

"I plan to change that stat if you don't get the hell away

from me. First, I'm going to throw my drink in your face. *Then* I'm going knee you in your giblets. While you're whining about your throbbing crotch, I'm going to punch you in the face. Take this as your *one and only* warning."

Rage was rising in me at a pace that I couldn't control.

Deep breaths. No violence. You're here for your friend. But I wanted violence. I wanted to act on my threat.

I had to remove myself from the situation. I wouldn't ruin Emoni's show. "Stay away from me," I demanded and moved to the other side of the bar. I was farther from the band but Jackson was no longer in view. Within a half hour, the number of people in the bar had doubled. It was full but not packed and every so often, I'd look in the direction I'd left Jackson to make sure he was staying on his side of the bar.

Through the crowd, I got a glimpse of his slow migration toward me. As he lingered in one spot, the low lights in the room hit his frown of consideration. I hoped he would reconsider and turn around. He didn't and weaved through the crowd toward me.

I looked away, hoping he got the message. Drawing my attention from Jackson was the warm body that sidled up next to me. My eyes lifted to catch the stranger's eyes before his gaze moved to my approaching ex, whose attention had drifted from me to the stranger. A smirk lifted Jackson's lips while his eyes narrowed. He rounded his shoulders in a show of defiance and raw aggression.

"Go away." The man from the coffee shop's deep-edged voice hinted at something ominous. His command earned him a look of shock and irritation from Jackson.

"What did you say?" Jackson ground out through clenched teeth after the shock wore off.

The man stepped in front of my ex. The stranger's imposing presence overwhelmed the area. Jackson put noticeable effort into maintaining his composure and insolence. But the hubris remained; he had tons to spare.

26

"Believe me, you don't want me to repeat myself," the stranger told him. His breezy tone sounded menacing. With a viper's strike of movement, precise and swift, he was behind Jackson, giving me an unobstructed view of his hand as it wrapped around Jackson's throat. Jackson's face blanched and he managed to let out one strangled gasp before his words were cut off. Mr. Ominous whispered something in Jackson's ear.

I should do something. Scream. When you witness an assault, you do something.

The stranger released Jackson. Jackson shuffled back, glaring at the man, then he sneered at me before backing away. Leaving his drink on the bar's counter, he headed for the exit.

The stranger's amber eyes showed an unsettling level of indifference for someone who'd just wrapped his hand around someone else's throat. He eased closer to me, leaving just a few inches. The light cascaded over the sharp angles of his jaw and cheek, over the bridge of his nose and the outline of his full lips. Looking into his intense eyes was like staring into a fiery abyss. His presence: coiled violence. If I'd seen someone who emanated such intensity and bound danger, I'd cross the street to avoid them. Here in the crowded bar, I was in his crosshairs. Steely curious eyes regarded me with interest.

My side eye wasn't as inconspicuous as I thought.

"You wanted him to leave." He said it so matter-of-factly, I choked out an inappropriate scoff of laughter.

Fully aware of his lethality, I took several steps away from him. He inched forward. I inched away. He stopped, giving me space, a bemused gentleness moving over his features. It was disarming but not enough to keep me from being guarded. If necessary, I'd redirect the course of action to him that I'd planned for Jackson.

"Yeah. But I tend to just ask. I guess choking a person out

is an option, too." I smiled. I thought he'd mirror it. Isn't that what normal people do?

"Give me your name," he ordered.

I hadn't seen him move, but the new distance between us was noticeable. Stifling the air around us, his all-consuming presence made the people surrounding us seem miniscule.

"Dominic," he offered when I didn't respond. "I'm Dominic."

We were definitely closer. There wasn't enough room between us to extend my hand to greet him. Shaking his hand: too formal. Was nudging him in the chest to give us space an acceptable greeting?

After several moments of stony silence, I offered my name. "Luna."

He repeated it in a low voice. Slowly enunciating each syllable. Tasting the word. Seemingly turning it over in his mind, trying to place it.

When he spoke again, he leaned in, right against my ear. Heat radiated from his body, enveloping me. I inhaled his scent of sandalwood, my hand going to his waist, my thumb brushing over the hard muscles of his abs. Damn. My mind wandered to a place it shouldn't.

"Are you still enjoying the book?" he asked.

There was only one book he was inquiring about. I nodded, trying to read his expression. He'd asked me about being a witch, and I was curious as to how far down the supernatural rabbit hole he was.

"It's more detailed than I expected. I've read my share of fantasy books. But the author presents it in a manner that leads me to believe it's nonfiction."

"In what way?"

"The detail. It's very specific, especially when he writes about shifters and vampires. It's very reminiscent of Anne Rice's *Interview with the Vampire*, a gothic supernatural tale that draws you in so much you feel like you're reading a biography. *The Discovery of Magic* reads like I've been made privy to someone's journal about their experience with the supernatural world. Very introspective."

A dark cast fell over his eyes as they bored into me. Lips set into a tight line. Had I offended him? He believed in magic and witches, so were vampires and shapeshifters a leap? Like Reginald, would he claim to have his own dubious magical ability? "Luna, my magic is making vodka disappear faster than anyone else. When I ease it to my lips, it just disappears."

"You have no beliefs in the occult?" he asked.

"No."

His tongue slid across his lips, moistening them as he leaned in. I tried to make out the words he whispered. The air thickened around us, and I sucked in a sharp breath when the heat of our closeness was replaced by wisps of coolness that slithered over my skin and wove around my skin, constricting around me. The tightness then loosened and breezed over me like a brush of wind. His eyes were pools of darkness, submerging me, leaving me unable to look away. The sensation abruptly stopped. I yanked my eyes from his.

"Tenebras Obducit," he hissed. "Impossible." He grimaced and was gone.

Scanning the crowd, I looked for him. A glimpse. Nothing.

More people had flooded in. It wasn't packed. Navigating was difficult but not impossible. It wasn't crowded enough for him to completely disappear. But he had.

What the fuck was that?

Putting aside the weirdness was difficult and I had to force myself to focus on Emoni's performance. But my attention kept being pulled to Dominic's parting words. Was he insulting me? Possibly, based on the sneer. He definitely wasn't complimenting me. Taking out my phone, I wrote the words out, spelling it phonetically despite not knowing exactly what he said—or called me. I'd search it later.

Night Ravage now got my undivided attention. Emoni did. No matter how many times she performed, like the audience, I was captivated by her powerful and hauntingly elegiac voice and her undeniable stage presence. The audience had succumbed to fluid mesmeric movements, ensnared by her. This was her element. Despite her saying that music gave her life, I believed it was the opposite. She infused vitality into the lyrics like no other.

Night Ravage's music was a delightful mélange of R&B and Rock, with hints of Tina Bell's influence in the lyrics. Despite her contributions being overlooked by most, she had an everlasting fan in Emoni.

After the performance, as usual, an hour or so was spent talking to the audience, networking, selling merchandise and music. Once it was over, I helped the band take their equipment to the band's SUV. Once everything was stored away, we stood outside the vehicle debating if we were going to go for waffles. At this point it was just pro forma. After each show, we debated this and it always ended with us at an all-night diner, eating waffles. Gus, the guitarist, draped an arm around Emoni and pressed his cheek to hers.

"That was madness! They loved us. They really did... well, they loved you." His face was ruddier than normal, a burnished red, similar to his hair. He gave Emoni another squeeze before releasing her. "You were amazing. I told you that you had the vocal range for that song. I can't believe you almost didn't sing it." He moved toward the driver's side. "Have we decided? Waffles?"

Of course it was waffles. It was *always* waffles. Emoni would devour her food and eat his, too. Buzzing from the high of a show, Gus was never hungry, just looking for a reason to spend more time with Emoni.

"You know he likes you, right?" I informed her for the

umpteenth time. If she sounded like a foghorn, he'd still compliment her on having the foggiest of horn voices.

She shrugged it off. "It'll pass. He knows there's no chance. I mean, seriously, the lead singer hooking up with the guitarist. Why not the drummer and make it even more of a cliché?" She tutted. "You're one to talk. Tell Jackson to go away in no uncertain terms and be done with him."

"I've tried."

"You want me to talk to him?" she asked, her eyes glinting.

"No, because I don't have bail money," I teased.

Before she got into the SUV with Gus, I gave her an abridged version of the encounter with Dominic, discussing his curiosity about the book and how I thought he believed in witches. I left out the shift of energy between us, the cool air that grabbed me in a bear hug then relaxed into a breeze that flitted across my skin, and the whole weirdness of it. She would have simply dismissed it as a strange version of attraction between two obviously peculiar people. I couldn't blame her. What other explanation was there?

"He asked me if I believed in the occult. Supernatural stuff! Why don't you seem surprised?"

"If he lives around here, it's not bizarre for him to believe in the supernatural. And he did see the book you were reading," she pointed out. "He probably thought you were into that, too."

"Are you kidding me? You wanted to pelt people with coffee beans if they put cream in their coffee and think people who order a frappuccino should be on a government watch list, but the man who believes in supernaturals and thinks I'm a witch gets a pass?"

"Well, one group is dangerous and should not be allowed near the general public, and the other believes in the occult. That's quirky."

When she flashed me a smile, I wished Reginald hadn't

31

sworn me to secrecy. There had to be a best friend clause or something to promises. Despite thinking his professed magical ability was utter BS, I was starting to wonder if there was something to his believing in magic.

Looking up what Dominic said to me was at the top of my list of things I wanted to research. I would do more research on magic and make a concerted effort to keep an open mind. I had a feeling the latter part was going to be really hard. For years I'd read about magic and considered it just fantasy; seeing it as anything else was going to be difficult.

4

———

As I rushed into the bookstore the next day, it was no surprise to find Jackson waiting for me at the table near the employee lounge, flipping absently through a book. When he caught sight of me, he placed the book atop another book instead of returning it to its original spot.

"You never struck me as one who went for the tall, broody, menacing type," he said with a pout. After my late night with Emoni and her band, the three hours I spent trying to decipher Dominic's words, and the sleepless night caused by his accusation, my tolerance was low.

I hadn't had nearly enough coffee or sleep to deal with him.

"Usually, I'm not," I said. "I usually go for the boyish good looks, coltish build, average height, and tendency to accidentally fall into bed with my friend type. You know, the guy who is just arrogant enough to suggest a three-way after being caught cheating."

He winced, but not at the part he should have. Being described as coltish and average height struck a nerve. By intentionally hitting the two things he wasn't overly confident about, I hoped he'd just stalk away in a huff, calling me an insensitive bitch under his breath. But he let the insult roll off him. It was still a wonder how a person who thrived on unearned arrogance about everything had complex height issues about being five ten. Well, five ten and a half. He'd never let me forget that *ever so* important half inch only *he* cared about.

He rolled his eyes. "I never said a three-way. Monogamy is just so traditional and boring. It sets unattainable rules and limits on people like me. I am aware of what I have to offer and who I am. Doesn't seem like something you should reject so flippantly." He extended his arms to the sides, allowing me a full view of what he must have deemed impressive. "Share the wealth."

My mouth dropped open, and I quickly snapped it shut. This was one of those times when I wished there were onlookers so I could turn to them and say, "Can you believe this asshole?"

"Why are you here?"

"Because I'm concerned about you, Luna." His faux worry was the last thing I wanted to deal with.

"You don't like Dominic, and this should concern me why?"

"Because he's a complete psycho. He quietly speculated how long it would take him to choke me to death. And then openly wondered if I'd go easy into death or struggle. Who says things like that! A man like that is speaking from experience. I didn't want to make a scene and ruin Emoni's show, so I left. I should have kicked his fucking ass."

Nothing about the last part was true. Emoni tolerated him during the relationship; after it ended, she had no reason to pretend to like him. Their dislike for one another was mutual. At the sight of him, I knew pelting him with coffee beans was the nicest thing she thought about doing to him. Her glare could be classified as a weapon. And if he thought for a moment that he could have kicked Dominic's ass, he would have.

"Apparently him trying to choke you out in a bar wasn't psycho enough, because here you are."

"Damn, Luna, is this what I've reduced you to?"

On the off chance there was some sincerity to his concern, I turned to him.

"I'm not seeing Dominic. It was a chance meeting. You weren't respecting my boundaries. Like now. I'm not interested in you or him."

Hopefully the witch accuser was done with me. If he came around again, he'd get a similar rendition of this speech. I made a show of picking up the haphazardly discarded book and placing it in its proper place on the shelf, just a few inches away from him, while still under the pressure of his gaze.

"Good, because I'm better than that brute."

This conversation was over.

"Better? You're a cheating, narcissistic, arrogant, unrepentant jackass. Better? You flatter yourself."

He inched closer to me as he ushered a look of faux concern onto his face. "I made some mistakes. You made some mistakes—"

"What was my mistake? Coming home early or *not* being okay with the cheating?"

He huffed out a frustrated sound. "Luna, I'm growing tired of this game. Are you really willing to toss *me* aside for a few indiscretions? Seriously, be practical for once. We get back together and you can move back in with me. Because you live in a crappy neighborhood and I'm sure your apartment is just as bad. That guy last night isn't right for you, Luna. I am."

"You're right, I really should be more practical. And the first step to doing that is owning up to my flaws. My first flaw: I have *terrible* taste in men. The worst. Can you believe the last guy I dated was a total asshole on the highest level? I don't think he knows. Should I tell him?"

He scoffed and glowered. "You're being ridiculous."

"Jackson, let this be the last time you approach me. Leave me alone and go be with Ava and whatever other unsuspecting person you want involved in your relationship. I don't want you back. If housing is your selling point, you already lost the argument."

His lips were pressed into a tight line, eyes full of vivacity —I knew he was running a number of arguments through his mind. He was still not getting the hint to go away, so I pushed past him and went into the employee lounge to put my things away and drive home the point. *Go away and don't come back.*

Jackson was gone when I returned.

I welcomed the mundanity of my day, the highlight of which was ordering a list of obscure history books for Peter. While I placed the order, he studied my ring.

"What does the writing mean?"

Studying it, I shrugged. "I have no idea."

He seemed to find it amusing. For all I knew, it meant the wearer of this ring was shallow as fuck and that might be true. Since it was obvious that no one was going to claim it, I wore it because it was unique and cute. Peter made a face, likely because he'd never do that.

You want your books, then stop it, Mr. Judgy.

In a rush to get home to finish *The Discovery of Magic*, I was quick with closing down the store: I reshelved the books and closed. *Keep an open mind*, I reminded myself as I waved goodbye to Lilith, who went through the door before me while I gave the store another sweep to make sure things were in place. When I stopped to grab a book left out on the counter, Lilith paused. We never left anyone alone in the store.

I urged her to go. "I'll just put this away. I'll only be a sec."

She hesitated, frowning at the book.

"I'm fine. It won't take long."

With a reluctant nod, she agreed.

The weathered book was definitely not ours. No ISBN number on the back and just sigils in place of a title. This was left behind for me. I just knew it. Being asked if I was a witch, the odd way the strangers with Dominic had looked at me, and his accusation the other night were not coincidences. I was positive Reginald hadn't left the book. He wouldn't have just left it.

Dominic. It had to be from Dominic. Maybe this would explain what he'd said to me. Witch. This was definitely a case of mistaken identity. As I hugged the book to me, I admitted I was just as bad as Reginald, enticed and seduced by the mystique of the occult. This book would be akin to *The Discovery of Magic*. It was exciting.

The fifteen-minute walk to my apartment seemed like miles with me anticipating what I'd learn.

A bag of popcorn and a poorly assembled sandwich was my dinner. I placed the book on my lap, thumbing through it between bites of sandwich and handfuls of popcorn.

Disappointment flooded through me. Unlike *The Discovery of Magic*, which read like a meticulously detailed journal, this book seemed like it was written between shots of tequila. A jumbled word salad: "Death eludes the walker of night. *Taballuh*. Lifts the veils of thrall. Light and darkness align. *Acostmias.*" I read it over and over, trying to make sense of it. Riddle? It didn't make sense. Code. Perhaps. Flipping through the pages only revealed more coded language and meandering storytelling.

Curiosity dwindled to boredom and I flipped a few more pages. I started when a page sliced my finger, blood welling up and staining the tip of the page. The metal of the ring on my finger warmed.

I tried to push the book from my lap, but it was stuck to me. Line by line, the words disappeared from the page as I split my attention between the book and the ring that had reshaped itself around my finger. The interlocking design was gone, and in its place was now a simpler rendition of itself.

I finally managed to push the book from my lap. It landed on the floor, open to the page I was reading, all the words gone.

The ring had tightened on my finger. It took me almost ten minutes to get it off. Under it, on my skin, were markings identical to the initial version of the ring.

My breaths came in slow clips, the anxiety overwhelming. I forced myself to gulp a deep breath because otherwise I was going to pass out. I focused on the wall, but my eyes kept returning to the book and the markings on my finger.

What. The. Hell? It became a mantra on repeat.

---

5

*M*y day off started how the previous night had ended, with me trying to remove the indelible markings on my finger, which was raw and painful from all the scrubbing. Eventually I gave up.

The book had been relegated to the kitchen counter. I refused to get anywhere near it. The page was still blood-stained, but it and the adjacent page were blank of text. My ring was barely recognizable and I now had symbols tattooed on my finger. There were so many things wrong with the situation and my mind was a mess trying to make sense of it.

My first instinct was to contact Emoni, like I would with any problem. But I decided against it. This wasn't just a quirky incident. It was so much more, and while I was trying to wrap my head around it, I didn't have it in me to usher someone else into the mess. Actually, it would be less ushering and more like plunging her into icy water.

Reginald believed in the supernatural. It wasn't just something eccentric that people believed, like thinking if you go on enough camping trips, you'll eventually run into Bigfoot.

Although I had a hard time keeping an open mind about it, he didn't. Reginald had suspended all logical belief. This required outside-the-box thinking and an abeyance of everything practical.

After leaving yet another message for Reginald to call me, I went through another series of failed attempts to remove the markings on my finger, watching my phone expectantly.

"What's wrong, Luna?" Reginald asked after I rushed out a quick hello.

"We need to talk," I whispered. As if someone could hear me.

"What's the matter?" Concern was clear in his voice.

"I need to show you rather than tell you."

"I have a couple of clients, but I can come by your place around one," he told me. "Is that okay?" He seemed so disquieted that I made an effort to sound calmer, more assured when I responded.

"That's fine."

I used the time waiting for him to arrive to scrub at my finger again and look up what Dominic had said to me. Nothing came up. It was another language and I was probably spelling it so incorrectly that even Google gave up.

Minutes before Reginald was to arrive, I shored up the courage to open the book again. I handled the pages gingerly, cautious to prevent another page attack. The book was sentient; no matter how illogical and ridiculous it sounded, the book nicked me—no, it *bit* me. This wasn't a simple paper cut.

When I opened the door for Reginald, his face was flushed from what I assumed was a quick run up the three flights of stairs in my garden-style apartment. He looked around my place appreciatively. It was much smaller than the home I'd shared with Jackson and definitely on the other side of quaint. Now that it was decorated, he found it far more appealing than when he came with Emoni to visit me two days after moving in.

With the help of intensive bargain shopping, furniture

consignment shops, Craigslist, and Facebook Marketplace, I'd created a cozy home. Rust-colored sofa and a large print chair that looked better than it felt. A worn ottoman—one of the pieces I took from my home with Jackson. Reginald smiled at the abundance of plants throughout the living room. The greenery did make me feel like it was a new beginning. A new life.

"What's wrong?" he asked.

I wasn't sure what to do first, show him my finger or the book. My words rushed out like a broken dam and it felt like I did both at the same time. Waving my hand in front of him, I held the mangled ring, showed him my finger, and told him that the book bit me. At that moment, it seemed like a perfectly fine thing to say. Of course, the book bit me. That's what they do. Nick people and erase words. Move along, nothing to see.

He examined my hand first, then the ring that was now a sheet of metal, something I'd never consider picking up off the street.

He picked up the book, hissed, and dropped it. His hands and fingers were bright red. It was the words quickly disappearing from the page that made me grab my phone and start to capture it, recording just seconds of video before the entire book was nothing more than weathered blank pages.

"What. The. Fuck," Reginald hissed from the sink where he was running his hands under cold water. From his vantage point, he was able to see that there had been words in the book and now the pages were blank.

"Yeah," I breathed out, shaking my head. With apprehension, I lightly touched the edge of the book, without any problems. I was still hesitant about picking it up. After a few more preliminary safety measures, I picked it up.

Checked each page; all blank.

"It's a spellbook," Reginald informed me. That came as no surprise.

Reginald didn't have the same look of excitement and intrigue as he had when he gave me *The Discovery of Magic*. His face was strained by the emotions playing across it.

He asked more questions, urging me to remember the phrases I spoke while reading the spellbook. It felt like an interrogation. But the words had all jumbled together. If they made sense or there was some rhyme or reason to them, it would have been easier to remember.

"I don't know how to help you, Luna," he admitted, rubbing his hands over his face.

Please don't let this be the time he confesses he's not a witch. He needed to be a witch.

Frowning, he looked down at his hands.

"How're your hands?" I asked.

"Just a little tender. It was a deterrent, not meant to injure," he said with enough confidence that it reignited my hope in him being able to help.

"I've heard of magic like this, but the witches in my coven don't possess it."

"Coven?"

He nodded. Screw it, I was all in. Coven, shifters, witches, vampires, magic, books that bite and self-destruct. Yesterday, dammit, I saw a hellhound.

My head pounded and I became increasing lightheaded. I held the counter for support. The lightheadedness wasn't from the plunge into the unknown, but hypoglycemia. I hadn't eaten since dinner the night before. And it hadn't been much of a dinner. I needed food.

"I'm going to fix a sandwich. Do you want one?"

He nodded, taking the same care I had as he flipped through the book. There was nothing to gain from it since all the pages were blank, so he laid the book face down and studied the patterns on the front and back covers.

"I don't know what these sigils mean," he said. "The spell, was it in English?"

42

"Everything was," I told him, quickly making us a turkey and cheese sandwich with a side of a pickle and chips. Giving him a glass of water, I studied him. He looked like he needed something stronger.

"You have a coven of witches like you?"

"I only know of witches like me. We don't have strong magic." He waved his hand around the apartment. "Whatever happened here was strong magic. Out of my wheelhouse."

"Do you think someone in your coven knows witches who might have experience with magic like this? Maybe they can help?"

"I'll ask but"—he looked contemplative between the bites he took—"we're supposed to be discreet. If I bring this to them, I risk being tossed out because they'll know I told you I'm a witch."

"I don't want you to risk that." I didn't but I needed someone with magic that didn't seem like an Instagram job.

"No, I'll do it. There just needs to be some discretion," he said.

After we finished lunch, he took several pictures of the markings on my finger, the sigils on the book, and had me send him the video.

After he left, I couldn't stop thinking about Dominic and his role in this. I needed to find him.

Without a last name, finding Dominic was nearly impossible. I searched Facebook first, scrolling through pages and pages of names, viewing profiles for someone who looked remotely like him. But what would happen next? Did I friend him? Send a message? What was I going to do, search hashtags? I couldn't even imagine the rabbit hole that would have sent me down.

After two hours of searching Facebook and Instagram, I

was so desperate, I contemplated roaming the streets and just calling out his name. It would have yielded the same results. He had found me, twice. Could he be looking for me?

It wasn't long before I found myself at the scene of our first meeting, in Books and Brew, sitting at the counter people watching and sipping coffee under Emoni's questioning gaze. Secrets. I now had them from her. Did I tell her? The coffee shop was busy, which diminished my guilt about keeping yesterday's events to myself. I couldn't burden her with it until I knew what was going on. *Come on, Dominic.*

Increasingly restless, I went to the bookstore. Nothing says you're living your best life than hanging out at your place of employment on your day off. After perusing the newly released and books on my to-be-read list, I purchased five books. It took effort to ignore Lilith's "Really?" look as she rang me up. It was less a look of incredulity than more along the lines of a "you're a pitiful loser" look.

With a weak smile, I paid. It wouldn't seem odd to her that my purchases included an epic fantasy, a psychological thriller, and a YA coming of age book, along with books about Wicca and witchcraft. My taste was rather eclectic.

"You changed your ring," Peter acknowledged, his head tilted to the side as he examined it with a frown.

I nodded, the urge bubbling in me to say, "No, a book bit me, a lot of strangeness happened, and now I have this plain-ass ring covering marks on my finger. And now I have to play amateur sleuth to find the person I think is responsible."

He closed the thick hardback in his hand to get a closer look. "Same style. This one fits you better." He gave me that half curl of a smile that had entrapped so many people into unrequested history lessons. His eyes dropped to my bag of books. He took a look at me in my Converse, jeans, Baby Yoda t-shirt, and messy ponytail that displayed the minimal effort I put into styling it.

"If you're not in a rush, do you want to have coffee?" He

flashed me his wayward smile, which I quickly realized wasn't as unintentional as I'd previously assumed. He was setting out bait. Not today, Mr. History Man. Not today.

"Maybe another time. I have a ton of errands to run. I just needed something to read tonight," I lied. Although listening to Peter's lecture would have been a good distraction to keep me from looking at my phone and waiting to hear from Reginald or pursuing my quest to find Dominic.

Blind determination, wariness, and obstinate curiosity led to me trawling the area where I'd seen Dominic. I even went back to the bar where he'd threatened Jackson. Desperation wouldn't allow me to rule out any possibilities. I wished there were dark, dangerous, and broody Bat Signals I could deploy. Maybe if I left a trail of ristretto…

Standing on the middle of the sidewalk, I was planning where to search next when a hand girded my waist, pulling me against a firm body. Coolness wove around me, engulfing me.

"Close your eyes," the stranger ordered.

I didn't. Dropping the bag of books, I clawed at the stranger's offending arm and stomped indiscriminately, aiming for his foot, until the building that surrounded me and the distant view of people several blocks away disappeared. I was plunged into darkness.

When the arm released me, I doubled over until my head stopped spinning. When it eased to tolerable, I straightened up to find four people seated at a semicircular conference table, watching me.

"I told you to close your eyes," someone said from behind me. "You never really get used to it unless you're the one zoning."

I spun around to get a look at my abductor, who honestly should have been cast in stone and placed in front of a museum. Tousled umber-brown hair, parchment-colored skin, aquiline nose, broad pronounced cheeks, and generous rose-tinted lips. My eyes fixed on the unnatural contrast of his opal-colored eyes.

He was too close. When a person abducts me off the street, they aren't doing it out of politeness. I shoved him back. "Personal space."

His taunting smile widened, exposing sharp canines. Vampire. One hard blink. I convinced myself that when I opened my eyes, he'd be gone.

He wasn't. Standing just a few inches from me was a vampire.

A vampire.

"I like her. Perhaps a taste before we proceed."

A *perverted* vampire who wanted to *taste* me. There wasn't time to process it. My only goal was to protect myself. Come out of this alive. More optimistically—unscathed.

"Try it and you'll never taste anything again," I shot back, demonstrating a bravado I didn't feel and touting abilities I didn't have. How would I stop a vampire? If he tried to get a "taste," I'd do what I could to make good on my threat. The only weapons I had were my knees, which were going straight into his groin, and my fingers into his eyes. Damage be damned, I was going to smack him across his head with the phone in my back pocket.

He dismissed me with an exaggerated flourish of a bow.

I looked around. The creepy vampire wasn't the only person I had to worry about.

"I see the appeal. But as you know, the fiery ones tend to cause the most trouble. And this one has caused a great deal," said the woman seated at the middle of the semicircular table.

The vampire was still too close for my liking.

"Kane, step away from her," the woman instructed.

After he moved back several feet, her calculating hazel eyes homed in on me. Her narrow face took on a more severe appearance and her lips thinned into a tight line. I was willing to bet the lines that crinkled as she drew her brows together weren't from excessive smiling. Warm ivory skin was a stark contrast to her cool and aloof countenance. Her dark hair with hues of purple was coiled into a crown braid and the back in a low bun. Dressed in a blue suit complemented by a pearl silk shirt, she seemed to be in charge—or perhaps the role was self-appointed. The cool discernment in her eyes led me to believe she was older than she looked.

It felt like I'd been dropped into the middle of a conversation and couldn't figure out the right questions to ask. Whatever they were convinced I was guilty of had made me their enemy. I divided my attention between the people, the room, and the view of the city, compliments of the floor-to-ceiling window that took up the entire back wall of the room. I wasn't on the main floor. Maybe the third or fourth.

When I pulled my attention back to the people, I found the woman who'd called me trouble looking down her pert nose at me. Hazel eyes that bored into me with revulsion came from the younger woman to her right. Maybe enemy was being optimistic. The man seated to her left had the same luminous violet eyes as the woman with Dominic that day at the coffee shop. A colorful sleeve of tattoos covered each of his arms. Through his teal V-neck t-shirt, I could see the outline of more ink. He observed me with a gentler look as his fingers twined around strands of his ear-length reddish-brown hair.

"What do you wa—"

My question was cut off by the light padding of feet. Slowly approaching me was a lion. A *lion*. A *huge* lion. When he licked his lips, I began calculating how long it would take to make it to the door. The occupants of the room appeared totally unconcerned that an unbidden apex predator was just traipsing into the room as if it happened every day. Maybe it did. Sitting down for lunch, bam, a lion walks up and takes the steak off your plate.

I tensed as it moved around me, its nose brushing along my leg and then along my balled hand. Before I could gather a plan, it shuddered, and a man—a *naked* man—was on all fours at my feet. He stood, his lips quirked at my effort to hide my shock, which was something he definitely expected and wanted.

I needed to get away from this den of freaks.

"Lance, must you make a spectacle of yourself at all times?" the regal woman chastised. With a wave of her hand, a gust of wind pushed in my direction, followed by a swirling of golden lights that ensorcelled the human lion, and when it disappeared, he stood before me fully clothed in a fitted t-shirt, relaxed jeans, and flipflops. Unruly chin-length sandy-colored hair, his skin coloring just a few shades lighter. Predaceous, emotive golden-brown eyes and a long oval face. He was his animal incarnate.

He cast a look over his shoulder at the woman who'd clothed him. "Madeline, this isn't a witch," he announced.

Thank you. Listen to the shameless man who—oh dear fates— was a lion a minute ago. It hit me like a brick. He was a lion just moments before.

All eyes went to the man with the violet eyes. "She is the one I saw," he confirmed. He leaned forward in his chair; his elbows rested on the table as he steepled his hands. Wary interest entered his kind eyes. "She tasks me. This is the one I envisioned before seeing the empty Perils. How can this be if she has no magic?"

Madeline's frown deepened. "I thought she was shrouded in a cloaking spell, which was why I couldn't sense it." She directed her attention to Lance. "But a cloak doesn't work on shifters. You're sure she's human?"

It wouldn't be hard to determine that I wasn't a witch, if everyone with magic gave off such foreboding dynamic energy. It prickled at my skin, plucked at my nerves, and made it very apparent that I was in the presence of something other. With all of Reginald's declarations of being a witch, nothing about him felt like this. Surely, nothing about me hinted at it, either.

"Yes, I am human," I offered before anyone else could. "So there's no need for me to be at… whatever this is. I don't know, the Meeting of the Weird and Scary?"

No one seemed to find me amusing.

I started backing away, but the shifter's sharp predatory scope stopped me in my tracks. A warning. "She's human," Lance confirmed.

Madeline looked unconvinced. "But does it make her innocent?"

"As far as her role in the Perils being compromised, she is," confirmed a deep, rich, commanding voice.

"Dominic." Madeline's eyes snapped in the direction of the voice, as did mine and everyone else's. The vampire's lips furled, displaying fangs.

"You can put those away because you're definitely not going to use them on me," Dominic told him, as he and the two people who were with him at the coffee shop moved toward the table. Speckles of blood stained the sleeves and front of Dominic's white shirt that clung to the muscles of his chest and arms.

The man whose face I hadn't been able to see at the coffee shop was in full view. Fawn-color complexion; I guessed Middle Eastern descent. His light-hazel eyes appeared to have undertones of green. The angles of his face were diamond sharp and he had a strong, well-defined jaw and cheeks. The roil of danger that came off him made holding his gaze hard. Initially distracted by the sword secured against his back, I eventually let my eyes trail to the scar that ran across his cheek.

As they moved farther into the room, two things became overwhelmingly apparent. The cadre behind the table didn't like Dominic, and he was wholly unconcerned by that.

"You have no reason to be here," Madeline asserted through clenched teeth.

A smirk flitted along Dominic's lips as he cocked a brow. "Yet here I am." Once standing next to me, he fixed Madeline with a hard look. There was a fine line between admirable confidence and unrepentant jackass, and from the cocksure look on his face, he precariously straddled that line.

"Were the sentries to entertain me or stop me?" he asked with a darkly amused smirk.

Anger swept over Madeline's face. "Are they alive?"

"If that was a concern of yours, you shouldn't have ordered them to stop me," he countered, returning her glare.

I took that as confirmation that I needed to get away from him and this hot mess as soon as possible, but curiosity had me too intrigued to run at that moment. Desperately needing to find out what was going on and how I had mistakenly been pulled into it, I remained for an explanation.

Madeline stood, leaning into the table. The magic roiling off her changed the pressure in the room, stifling the air with minacious energy.

"You tell us that the Perils has been compromised, the prisoners escaped, and the worst of our kind are at large, and you expect us to do what? Sit around and wait for them to exact their revenge on us—the people who allowed them to be incarcerated there?" she barked. "Our seer confirmed that she is involved."

"I expected you to take the necessary precautions for you and yours to stay safe. To lie low and not impede me while I remedy the situation. And I damn sure didn't expect you to try to stop me from attending meetings. Tell me, what are your plans for this human?"

Not loving the wording of that comment, but I'd ignore it if it got me out of there.

Madeline's jaw set as they held each other's gaze. I was wrong; they didn't dislike him. They hated him with a fiery passion that was amply displayed on all their faces but more profoundly on Madeline's.

"The seer informed us that she's the one involved. We plan to handle the matter."

Before Dominic could respond with something that I guessed would further agitate Madeline, Dominic's violet-eyed companion directed a question to the man whose eyes resembled hers.

"What did you see, Callum?"

His gaze slid to me. "Her, empty cells and…" He picked up the phone, unlocked it, then turned the screen to her. I moved with her to get a glimpse.

Damn. It was so similar to the markings on my finger. I was thankful that they were hidden by the ring. Not similar. Exactly the same. My breath hitched.

"You plan to kill her?" Dominic concluded.

"That's the spell that freed them. Obviously, you weren't able to break it or you wouldn't have been placed in the position of telling us our lives are in danger. We're being proactive. Defending ourselves. Kill the caster, break the spell. She is the caster."

Murder is proactive?

"Ah," Dominic mused, a little too casually for a discussion of murder, in my opinion. "She's not a witch. We can all see she doesn't possess any magic. I can assure you not one time were you at the forefront of this matter. I've met Luna twice before." He waved a dismissive hand in my direction while I made an attempt to hide my finger without looking suspicious. "Nailah"—I assumed he was referring to the woman with the odd violet eyes—"was presented with the same. I performed an *ostendo* spell on Luna to disarm any cloaking spells and she is not a witch and does not have the ability to cast such a spell."

My heart raced. Technically he was right but… I was involved. However, in a room full of people whose game plan was to kill me, I wasn't going to disclose that. Taking slow easy breaths, I waited for things to unfold.

"Madeline," Dominic drawled. "Do you still plan to kill her?"

Stop suggesting that. It's not an option. What about: Hey, she's innocent, let her go? Has that not crossed your mind?

"Situation like this, it is best to err on the side of caution."

It was irritating how casually they were discussing my murder, like they were deciding whether to sprinkle a little salt on their avocado toast.

"Murder of an innocent human? Isn't that the very thing that you all sentenced others to the Perils for?" Dominic offered.

Kane growled. "You said the Perils is nonfunctional, that it had a global spell cast on it that won't allow even you to use the same spell on another confinement. The most ruthless and cruel of our kind who can't be subdued or imprisoned with basic magic are free, and you're asking us to let you handle it. Three days. Your handling isn't efficient enough. Don't you dare lecture us. We will do what is necessary to protect ourselves and right this."

Dominic's lip lifted into a cruel smile. "And I'll do what I need to punish you for that. Perhaps we'll return to our old ways, the ones you all perceived as too barbaric. Torture then murder—a seemingly appropriate penalty for killing an innocent." His eyes darkened in warning.

Is this some type of murder cult? Why is murder Plan A for these people?

Screw this, I was out. Inching back slowly, I hoped I'd be undetected while they discussed murder in the casual manner of sociopaths.

"If she's so innocent, then why is her heart beating a mile a minute? It wasn't before," said another man who could only be described as silver. Grayish-silver hair despite appearing to be in his early thirties, fierce platinum eyes, and a sinewy lean body that put me in mind of a greyhound. His eyes possessed Lance's predatory keenness.

"Do you think it has anything to do with you all casually discussing murdering me?" I huffed.

He looked unconvinced. Eyes narrowed as he leaned back in his chair, hands clasped behind his head. The black t-shirt stretched over lean, taut muscles. "Are you a witch?"

"No."

He licked his lips but not in a seductive way. Rather, in the manner I'd seen predators do before pouncing on some poor unsuspecting prey. I swallowed and squared my shoulders, refusing to be intimidated, especially by a lip lick. How weak was that?

"Were you responsible for the destruction of the Perils?"

That I couldn't answer with complete certainty. None of this was coincidence. Me finding the book, the pages biting me, the spell I must've unintentionally evoked, or the indelible markings on my finger. I took his question to mean did I actively and knowingly do it. And I absolutely did not have anything to do with that. I was a passive participant and therefore not responsible.

"No."

I wondered if the next question would be about the sigil Callum showed us. It was shock that kept me rooted in place when I was faced with a man one second and a massive wolf with bared teeth lunging at me the next, allowing me just enough time to shriek and try to ward off the attack with my arms. Out of reflex my eyes closed. When I managed to pry them open, there was a flash of movement from my left and then a thud. Dominic's scarred companion was straddling the wolf, one hand around the wolf's throat, the other holding a knife at the jugular.

"Anand, let him live." The "for now" was laden in Dominic's voice as he scanned the room. "Leave me with Luna. If she is to be questioned, it will be by me."

I wanted no part of his or any of their questioning. Based on every spy thriller movie and book, I was very aware of the "questioning process." Images of brutal interrogations rushed to my mind. I definitely wasn't going to be interrogated by a man who had just implied he murdered guards for attempting to stop him from coming to this hostile freak show and casually suggested returning to the old ways of torture and murder.

To hell with this. I darted for the door at full speed, pushing myself as fast as I could go. Anyone in my way would be plowed over. Finding a safe place was my only goal.

Within inches of the door, an arm encircled my waist and jerked me into a hard chest that felt like slamming into a brick wall. Kane's deep throaty laugh taunted me. Thrashing my head back, my only goal was to hit something: nose, cheek, chin. I didn't care. The impact was bound to stun. Once his grip loosened, I pounded the heel of my foot into his toes. Grabbing my phone out of my back pocket as I spun to face him, I smashed it into his face.

I bolted.

I hadn't made it a foot before I was yanked back and slammed into the wall. His face inches from mine, coolness from his body enveloped me as he held me immobilized with an iron grip. Making it painfully obvious that the success of my initial escape attempt was because I had the element of surprise and he'd underestimated the human woman. Fangs were displayed as he inched toward me. I twisted and jerked my head, refusing to give him an easy target.

In a swift, practiced sweeping movement, Kane had me pressed against his chest, my arms bound to the side by his body and my head turned, exposing my neck.

A shallow ragged breath escaped when I felt sharp fangs press into my neck. They grazed against my skin. His enjoyment from my fear was apparent. He taunted me with it. Fangs pressing hard enough for pain but not enough to puncture the skin. Then they did. Pain made tears well in my eye as they sank deeper.

The hold on me eased and I tore away from him, pressing my fingers to the pierced skin. I pulled back blood but the puncture wasn't deep. He was just playing with me. Finding a thrill in the terror he invoked. Sick bastard.

Dominic held a sword to the back of Kane's neck.

What are you doing? That's not how you sword—or whatever. I knew nothing about swordsmanship but I figured wielding one was similar to swinging a bat. There had to be distance between the sword and the target to allow for momentum to drive in the blade. But maybe he didn't need that. Malicious intent dwelled in Dominic's eyes. Unfettered violence showed in his refined movement as he held the sword steady, gliding around to face the vampire. If looks could kill, Kane would have been eviscerated.

"Make no mistake, Kane. They"—Dominic's gaze flicked toward the others—"may not have believed you deserve to be in the Perils, but I do. This will be just as satisfying."

Kane's eyes slid to me. His expression contained the disgust of looking at something that needed to be wiped off his shoe. He was a fickle one: one minute he wanted to keep me like a trophy, the next I was crud on the bottom of his shoe.

"She was seen by both our seers. Whatever her involvement, she is a threat. One that must be remedied."

"You only confirm how much you should be in the Perils. You've convinced them you're not a monster, but I believe no such thing."

"Then this must be as if you are looking in a mirror. Monster to monster." The hostility between them intensified, thick violence lingering in the air. They pinned each other with merciless glares.

"Shall we see which monster survives?"

There was no fucking way I was staying to see what

violence could be perpetrated by these self-identified monsters. Nor did I want to continue watching their casual banter about wanting to end each other.

I shoved my phone back into my pocket and headed for the end of the hall. There wasn't an elevator, not that I would have chanced it.

Taking the stairs two at a time, I crashed through the door leading to the main floor.

Safe.

I released a deep sigh of relief too soon.

Anand stood in front of the exit, wielding two knives.

6

*I*f I learned nothing else from Marvel movies, I knew this was the time to run at him full speed, leap into the air, and scissor my legs around his neck. Hammer pound his face and head until he was dizzied and disoriented. Bring him to the floor by using my positional advantage and shifting my weight. With my super powerful thigh muscles, I'd choke him out.

A woman can dream and have lofty goals. That plan wasn't rooted in any form of reality since he'd subdued a massive wolf in the time it took me to gasp a breath, and the week before I'd tripped over my own feet. I didn't possess the agility and mastery of fighting to go hand to hand with this man and be remotely effective.

My best defense was to get the hell away and figure the rest out later. Giving me a taunting look of menace, Anand twirled the weapons with practiced precision before storing them in the sheaths at his waist.

I backed away and ran in the opposite direction, which I guessed was the main exit.

Fuck.

Dominic stood between me and it. Steely eyes, coiled

danger, and raw power radiated from him in waves. Whatever transpired between him and Kane had ignited something vicious in him. I scanned the area for an escape route. Nowhere. This building served one purpose: a meeting space for them.

"Go away," I ordered.

"No." In an ominous wave of movement, he was close and circling me. Scrutinizing me with narrowed eyes. I turned, following his every movement and returning his considering look.

"I have questions for you." He bristled, accusation heavy in his voice.

"What?" I wanted to sound challenging and confident, but my words came out in an uncertain squeak.

"How did you do it?" he demanded. "I thought we had rid the world of such magic. Yet here you are."

"You know damn well I'm not a... witch." It still felt ridiculous saying it, despite knowing witches and other—worse—things existed. I didn't understand how he could defend me so ardently to the group and then make such accusations.

"No, you're not. You're far worse." With narrowed eyes and a hard jaw he regarded me.

Fire blazed and encircled me. Heat licked at my skin.

"Reveal yourself," he ordered.

My arms tucked to the sides and my hands shot up to protect my face. I pressed my thighs together, trying to minimize myself to prevent further injury as the flames inched closer and closer. He was going to burn me alive.

I wailed each time the flames brushed my skin. Pain rampaged through me, tears blurring my vision. I couldn't die like this. I refused to die like this. Squatting down, I readied to spring through the flames in a manner that would only cause minimal damage.

Before I could act, Dominic made a sharp command and

the flames disappeared. It was as if they'd never existed, leaving the ground unmarred. But they were real; my blistering skin was proof of that.

"You're not a witch—not a Dark Caster," he said, stepping closer to me.

"That's what I've been trying to tell you!"

He reached for one of my burned arms. I jerked it away. Tears spilled. I was so close to a torturous death. Anger rampaged through me, tumultuous and unfettered.

When he reached for my arm again, I punched him. Hard. His head snapped back. Not bad for my first punch. But I wasn't expecting it to hurt my hand as much as it did. There must be an art to it. And I planned to learn it. Despite the pain, my burned skin hurt more.

Punching him felt good until a smile feathered across his lips. His amber eyes lit up with amusement, the flecks of gold dancing with delight.

Oh, you want another? I put more power behind the next strike. It evoked a bark of laughter from him. I never thought punching people better would ever be a life goal, but here I was, making it one.

Maybe he was a lifelike robot. Vampires, shapeshifters, witches, seers. Why not impeccably lifelike robots? No one laughed when their crotch was being kneed. Before I could execute it, his finger sliced through the air and a strong force smacked into my leg, collapsing me to the floor with a thud. Dominic knelt next to me; his hands covered my red, blistered arms. His uncompromising eyes held mine.

Coolness crept up the length of my fingers, hands, and arms. The pain receded along with my anger and anxiety. Coaxed into calmness, my body relaxed and I lay back on the floor, my head dropped to the side. Was it my imagination or could I smell lavender and vanilla? I was lulled into a somnolent state as my body healed. Peace. The world didn't seem so overwhelming, my life not a calamitous crapshow.

This is not real.

Yanking my arms from his hold, I jumped up, looked at my healed arms and then at Dominic who was on his feet, too, just a few inches from me. He was giving me a knowing look, baleful delight curling the corners of his lips.

"What the fuck did you do to me?" I spat out.

"You needed to be calmed and healed. I didn't have time to deal with your petulance."

"I wouldn't have needed healing if you hadn't tried to burn me alive," I shot back.

"Yet you stand here, alive and well, in all your tedious insolence." All emotion had drained from his expression. His cool indifference spiked my anger even more.

"Believe me, I'm more than happy to take my insolence elsewhere and get the hell away from you." I backed away, watching him carefully to make sure he wasn't moving closer. When he stayed put, I quickened my pace toward the exit.

"That is your choice. I predict your death will be within the next day. Hopefully it will be painless and quick."

I scowled. "Is that a threat?"

His dark chuckle eased through the room. "You have no idea who I am, do you, and what I'm capable of. I can assure you, if I wanted you dead, it would be as I wished."

Not something to brag about.

"Then who?"

"Luna." There was a musical note to the way he said my name. A rich, sultry drawl. "The seers have connected you to this situation. Desperation to return the prisoners to the Perils will cause people to react to the slimmest of leads. You are the face of the spell right now. Their only lead. They're convinced that getting rid of you is the only way to break the spell. The only thing standing between you and death is me. What you saw upstairs is nothing. How will you survive it?"

He inched toward me, slowly, taking in how attentive I

was to his words. How would I handle people who could perform magic, shift into animals, teleport—or zone or whatever—and effortlessly call on fire?

The slow breath I took had little effect on my panic.

"Tell me, Luna, what is your role in this?" This time my name was said with the disdain of a curse.

"I don't understand any of it. I'm not part of it and you know it," I said, lying through my teeth. I was certainly tangentially involved; I just had no idea to what degree. But since the murder cult upstairs was prepared to kill me because of it, I had no intention of confessing. It was something I needed to work out later, but it wouldn't be with Dominic or the others. I wanted to get as far away from them as possible.

"Oh, but you are. I just need to figure out how." He took hold of my hand and slipped off the ring, revealing the markings.

My chin jutted in defiance to show my innocence despite the evidence. His brow furrowed as he gently bent my fingers back to show me the markings, as if I hadn't seen them before. He had to know I'd seen them before.

"I saw the way you responded to the picture Callum presented. You balled your hands to hide your fingers, which is when I noticed the ring was different."

Borrowing a page from his playbook, I gave him a look of cool indifference.

It brought a dark smile of interest to his lips. "At first I thought you were a powerful witch who managed to get access to forbidden spells. That is the way of the witch, always pushing boundaries, thirsting for power and ways to leverage their privilege. When my spell didn't uncloak you, I knew you had to be more. Stronger. A Tenebras Obducit—a Dark Caster. If you were, the Conventicle need not be involved. I wanted to handle you the way I handled the others."

61

Hearing the brutal edge in his voice, I could imagine the way the others were handled. I swallowed. After a long, considering look, something vaguely empathetic showed on his face.

"Great power that can't be checked or reined in leads to chaos and the wielder of such power feeling omniscient. That can't be allowed."

"You seem to have a great deal of power and no one upstairs seemed to be able to rein you in."

A smirk tugged at his lips but he forced it back into a cruel straight line. "I'm never to be reined." It was a simple response that spoke volumes. He'd stepped over that line of confidence. The man was a certifiable jackass.

"Luna, Luna, Luna."

My name came from him in a low, deep, melodious sound. A draconian chorus with a dangerous harmony. He circled me again, watching me carefully. My heart pounded and everything in me screamed to run, but Anand guarding the exit made that impossible.

"What mess have you gotten yourself into?" he whispered.

I swallowed and shook my head. "I don't know." The statement escaped before I could stop it. What *had* I gotten myself into?

Again, he was in front of me, studying me with avid curiosity. He spoke softly, as if to himself. "You're not a witch or a Dark Caster, but you are responsible for releasing the prisoners from the Perils. How was it done?" His gaze slipped to my finger again.

I had no response for him.

He sighed. "Tell me what you know of the Perils."

Dominic was trying to discover a link where none existed. What I knew of it was only what I'd gathered from the conversation upstairs.

"A prison for supernaturals. Where you keep your worst."

I couldn't imagine anyone worse than the ones upstairs, but obviously I was wrong.

His head barely moved into the nod. "Perils of the Underworld, where I am its guardian."

Whenever I watched a show where a person passed out after getting terrifying information or horrifying news, I always called BS. No, double BS. *What? You forgot to breathe?* To do the very thing so intrinsic to your body's survival that you hold your breath to deprive it of oxygen, but the body's like, "Nah, bitch, give me the good stuff. Give me oxygen." And forces you to breathe.

Now I felt the need to issue a formal apology. Because my body seized. All the things that seemed automatic, essential, a necessity just felt foreign. My mouth dried, my breathing was ragged, shallow, and definitely not enough to survive, and fight or flight was simply nonexistent. I stood there for what seemed like eternity trying to get my body to respond appropriately. To react. And to participate in anything that would remotely be considered self-preservation.

"What?" I eked out.

"Luna, you've released my prisoners from the Underworld. You may not have been the weapon, but you were the tool."

Believe me, you're a tool, too.

Oops. Didn't mean to say that aloud.

With a wry smile he started pacing around me again, his hands behind his back, my name said over and over but not in the alluring, sultry way. It was a rough, disparaging string of words. Nearly excruciating in its execution.

"Tell me, Luna," he said behind me. I whipped around to face him. "Should I destroy the tool for a short-term solution, or find the weapon?"

Fighting with the guardian of the Underworld wasn't going to fix my problems. In fact, it would probably make them worse. I was moored to this. Despite my protective responses rearing in overdrive and telling me to run like hell, this situation wasn't going away. But if I was going to be a player, I wouldn't be intimidated into my decision.

Squaring my shoulders, I looked him straight in his fiery amber eyes. Despite the hard intensity of them, I held his gaze. "If you were interested in the short-term fix, you wouldn't have intervened."

His face remained impassive, his head canted slightly as he continued to listen.

"I've been pulled into something that I definitely don't want to be in, dealing with people I hope to never encounter again. I want it to be over. I want to have nothing to do with this situation or you dreadful people." I lifted my hand, presenting the markings. "If working with you is the only way, then I'm in. If we are working together, no more threats. I don't care how thinly veiled they are. You will not bully me. Are we clear?"

His expression changed but it was still indecipherable. Understanding? I didn't think that was it. Amusement? Definitely. Portentous? It better not be.

His lips curled slightly into a small, tight, mirthless smile. He looked over his shoulder at Anand, who flashed a grin. "I've been commanded to behave," Dominic said to him. The laughter in his voice made its way to his eyes.

"Little Luna."

"It's just Luna," I shot back.

"Luna. You are correct. I want to find the person behind this, especially if it is a Dark Caster. I know their history and the chaos and destruction they enjoy. It needs to be stopped. And to do so, we will have to work together."

I'd been abducted and attacked by a vampire, sniffed by a lion, interrogated by a witch, and nearly devoured—or whatever his intentions were—by a wolf. I had every right to be overly cautious and I didn't like the subtle undertones in his response. A limited alliance.

"I want to help." *Biggest lie ever.* I *had* to help in order to get out of this mess. My face must have betrayed that because he looked smug now.

"You are the little fish. I want the whale. You are the means to the whale. As long as I need you for that, the others will never touch you." Everything he said possessed an implicit "but" and I didn't like it.

Our interests aligned. As long as he wanted me alive, the others wouldn't touch me. For now, it was my best hope.

A slow smile moved over his lips. He handed me back the ring and I slipped it on my finger. "It seems like we are in this together, Lit—" He bit the word off. "Luna."

Several moments of tense silence passed, then he extended his hand to me. "Would you like to see what you've done?"

Not really. Did I really need to see an empty cell? Definitely didn't want to see one in the Underworld.

There were many reasons to say no—one being Mr. Personality in front of me—but I needed to know exactly what I was dealing with.

I was unsure whether, when I analyzed this in the future —if there was a future—this decision would make the list of the things that made this situation infinitely worse.

Despite the high likelihood, I nodded.

"*Y*ou won't be able to enter the Underworld without me," Dominic explained after several minutes of my contemplative staring at his hand. My internal debate continued long after his explanation. It took a lot of pep talk and coaxing for me to fully give in to my decision and take his hand.

I was going to the Underworld.

His lips quirked into a half-smile. His warm fingers entwined with mine.

"What?" I asked.

"I'm glad you agreed. This way is far more preferable. I don't believe you would have liked the alternative."

"What was the alternative?"

I took the flicker of menace that shadowed his features and the trace scents of amber, gold, and burnt orange that arose as indications that the alternative was probably more barbaric. Something along the lines of me getting tossed over his shoulder and carried away. I frowned.

I tugged slightly to loosen his grip on my hand. It was hard to relax around him. He'd saved my life but had caged me in flames. I shuddered at the memory. What would have been my fate if I were a Dark Caster?

His mouth barely moved as a diaphanous shimmering wall appeared. There was a moment of hesitation before I allowed him to lead me into it and then we were plunged into complete darkness. Heat poured over me and needlelike prickles flitted over my body. It wasn't painful but a discomfort I would be happy never to feel again.

When the darkness lifted, it was no longer midday; the moon offered a muted melon glow over the stone castle-like mansion. The palatial building couldn't be fully taken in. Neatly manicured bushes surrounded the home and lush forestry lay on the outskirts. Instead of verdant green, the leaves were variations of dark grays and deep currant. The air was inundated with notes of pepper and sage. The light from the moon hit a large lake off to the right.

Intricately carved decorated columns surrounded the home, supporting the balcony above. Thick curtains covered the windows. This wasn't at all what I expected from a supernatural prison.

At Dominic's arrival, the doors swung open and six guards greeted him on each side. They were dressed in black button-downs and slacks, a small emblem on the chest. Daggers sheathed at their waists and swords sheathed at their backs, each stood at attention, relaxing to ease once Dominic had passed. Their furtive looks of discomfort and intrigue stayed on me, and I felt them continue as we headed along the marble floor through an entrance the size of my apartment.

Abstract art and sculptures on pedestals. The number of winged creatures on display was astonishing. Angels? Was this irony? One sculpture of a copper-winged person on its knees in what looked like supplication—its wings fanned together behind its back—seemed to be a statement piece. I slowed to give it a better look.

It wasn't me being distracted by the sculpture or being several feet behind him that placed a wary frustration on Dominic's face. "That is all," he told the guards. "No need for such formality at my arrival. At ease. Always."

He looked at me, I assumed to tell me to follow. Before we could continue down the long expansive entryway, one of the guards responded.

"But your father—"

"You're my guards. You answer to me, not my father." He made an attempt at a smile, but it seemed to be too much effort. "I will talk to him about it. For me, this is unnecessary."

You don't get a twelve-guard welcome if you're just a glorified babysitter of misbehaving supernaturals. Dividing my attention between the infinite gray of the outdoors offered by the large picture windows, the guards at the door, the palatial home, and the spiraling dual staircases we'd passed, my attention finally returned full circle to Dominic. His brows rose.

"Have you forgotten the reason for your visit, Luna?"

With the mildest change of inflection, lilt, or modulation he managed to say so much with just the simple use of my name. I hated it. A sharp emphasis on the L made it a chastisement. I took a few larger steps to catch up with him. To match his long strides, I had to take double steps. He seemed to be all legs.

"In my world, guards usually don't live in a mansion, and I'm sure they don't get such a reception whenever they go home. I'm willing to bet at work they probably just get a simple wave, maybe an unenthusiastic nod before going through a metal detector," I pointed out, leaving an opening for him. Which he didn't take, simply responding with a shrug.

"You're more than just the guardian of the Perils, aren't you?"

He ignored my question.

This guy.

"You're…" I prompted, letting the word linger.

"Dominic."

"Oh, all Dominics are greeted with a military welcome?"

He stopped abruptly. His depthless dark eyes, which always had a flicker of a fading fire in them, studied me in contemplative silence before he resumed his rushed long-strides.

"Why are you guarding prisoners? It seems like you're in a position to have others do that." It would be a lot easier to continue with my questioning if he was more forthcoming and not power walking.

"I have help."

"You do most of it?"

A tiny nod in response.

"Is it a micromanagement situation? Do you feel like you're the only one who can handle it?"

He sped up, forcing me to jog and ignore the rows of closed doors we passed just to keep pace with him. We turned down a long hallway. At the sight of the library, I stopped. Seeing it lifted my mood even if for just a moment.

Floor-to-ceiling bookshelves, a rolling ladder, vaulted ceiling with gilded trimmings. In the corner, there were oversized plush chairs in pairs with a small table between, and a circular ottoman in front of each. On the other side of the room, a semi-private area boasted a cognac-colored leather chaise. Warm yellow walls made the room so inviting. The only thing that would complete the paradise would be a coffee/tea bar and a snack station. I couldn't imagine ever wanting to leave it, even for food.

I stepped in, inhaling the scent of leather, vellum, aged paper, and the faint scent of oak that lingered in the air. It was like being hugged by a book. It took effort not to just stay there, but I turned around to find Dominic regarding me with a smirk.

"Sorry," I said, backing out.

We returned to our journey down the never-ending hallway. After another turn, he unlocked beautiful double doors, but when I pressed my hands against them, they were heavier than expected and more difficult to move than Dominic made it look.

The doors led us to another section of the house that seemed as if it didn't belong. Dull beige walls, unimpressive flooring, and no evocative art, beautiful décor, or beautiful libraries. This area was functional. Dominic stopped at a heavy door that I assumed led to the prison. To my surprise, there wasn't a lock or any other barrier to entry.

"You sure magic released them and they just didn't walk out?" I mumbled.

He turned to face me, studying me, his expression indecipherable, but the intensity of his gaze could not be ignored. When he moved closer, the heat of his body wrapped around me, his fiery gaze held mine, and pulling away didn't feel like an option. He studied me with interest, while I just gawked at him like a person oblivious to the social contract of not staring.

"You are quite the peculiar human, aren't you?"

In my book, peculiar was right up there with exotic. Definitely on the wrong side of normal but not interesting enough to be considered quirky and not unique or winsome enough to be weird.

He whispered something; the door illuminated and opened. I followed him down the spiral stairs, holding close to the rough stone walls of the stairwell faintly lit by warm yellow sconce lights that ran along the walls.

A dungeon. Significant parts of the footage were dedicated to the supernatural prison. My expectations were squalid conditions and minimal amenities. A stone-walled antechamber with harsh unforgiving lights and what looked to be poorly cleaned bloodstains on cement floors led to a large room, divided into two rows of twenty-by-twenty smaller rooms, each with a full-size bed and a small door that I assumed led to a bathroom. The front of each room had frosted glass instead of bars.

It was far better than any prison I'd seen on TV, but for occupants who spent their days causing chaos, killing, and pillaging, a mundane existence in a small room must've been torture.

"This is where you keep the worst of the worst?" I asked, still surprised by the decent conditions.

"The only sentence in the Perils is life."

"Once they're sentenced, they die here?" I frowned. "Aren't vampires immortal? And shifters and witches can live to be close to two hundred. This is where they stay for whatever infraction landed them here until they die of old age? What happens to vampires?"

He seemed surprised by my breadth of knowledge.

"*The Discovery of Magic*," I reminded him.

Nodding, he frowned. "I obtained a copy. That book is grossly inaccurate and I urge you to be very wary of the information within it. The only thing that was correct was the information about the existence of vampires, shifters, and witches. Vampires can only be killed with a stake through the heart. It failed to mention that if they feed before they meet true death, they live. Best way to kill a vampire is to subdue them with a stake to the heart and take off the head."

I took a shuddering breath. As detailed and explicit as the book was, I wasn't disappointed with that being left out. I'm sure if it were included, pages would have been dedicated to ways of murdering a vampire. "Shifters?"

"In that book, magic is underestimated and everything about shifters is wholly incorrect. They don't require the moon to change—as you witnessed during your encounter with the wolf. They heal extremely fast. Silver weakens them, but to kill them, other than beheading them, silver must puncture the heart and remain there until it stops beating. Their dominant magic is their ability to shift into animals and advanced healing, which makes them particularly dangerous. They are immune to magic but have the ability to sense it, even through cloaks. The immunity to magic also prevents them having it. Or so we thought. One anomaly exists. Vadim—the wolf shifter you released—"

"I didn't release him," I interjected, refusing to be assigned culpability to an offense in which I was made an unwilling participant.

He continued. "Vadim has proven to be immune to silver and to possess magic. When one possesses such power, they don't believe they must adhere to any rules. He didn't. I tracked him for decades. He escaped twice until we found a way to contain him." His eyes flicked to me. "Until he was released." There wasn't any accusation in his voice but it was potent in his eyes: whether or not it was intentional, he held me at the same level of guilt as the person truly responsible for the spell.

Despite needing to figure out how much disinformation was in *The Discovery of Magic*, I was in desperate need of a small break. I moved toward one of the enclosures to get a better view of the markings on the wall. Up close, they looked exactly like the ones on my finger. There were no grounds for denial. This was proof of my link to the magic that released the prisoners.

"What happened the day they were released?" I asked.

"I felt the magic. It was hard to miss, but by the time I got down here, they were gone and in their place were the sigils from this casted spell. It broke all seven spells we had on each cell to keep them restrained."

"Seven?"

"Yes. That one spell broke a myriad of magical spells that took decades to perfect. When you are dealing with the most powerful and ruthless of the supernaturals, it's prudent to be cautious."

"I don't have magic. I didn't cast the spell."

"You were used as a conduit. This magic resembles the work of a Dark Caster. One who is smart about going undiscovered, which is why they used you."

"I'm still confused as to how I can help." Magicless and used as a conduit, what exactly could I do?

"You are the common link." His eyes dropped to my marked finger. "The magic needs to be removed from you. Once it is, I will be able to trace the location of the Caster without it being skewed by you."

A dark delight flitted across his face. Although this was problematic for him, he held the look of a man who found exhilaration in the chase and the mystery. Or maybe it was the promise of reprisal. I was pretty sure the Dark Caster's punishment wouldn't be a stay in the Perils. Dominic's earlier comments about their old ways of torture and murder haunted me.

This made me think of Peter's constant affirmation of Winston Churchill's adage "History is written by the victors." Were the prisoners as bad as Dominic and the others wanted me to believe they were, or was I getting my information from the victors? I was willing to concede that among the supernaturals, there were their own degrees of awfulness, present company included.

I couldn't afford to delve into this philosophical minefield, I thought as I touched the wall with the sigil.

"Undo," I whispered. Then I said, "Stop it. Bring them back." It devolved to me just tossing out any words that I thought might reverse the spell. How could it hurt? The spell that I invoked was just a mishmash of senseless words, so my hypothesis wasn't necessarily ridiculous. Or at least I didn't think so until I turned to find Dominic with a look of bemused incredulity.

"You are an odd one, aren't you?" He frowned and turned toward the stairs. "Come," he ordered.

It was said with such indomitable coolness that my instinct was to follow. Until I decided that this was a perfect time to set boundaries for a man who seemed to expect full compliance without challenge. He needed me just as much as I needed him. We were partners in this. And even if we weren't, *Learn some damn manners.*

I didn't move. He'd walked several feet before realizing I wasn't with him.

He looked over his shoulder. "Luna, come," he demanded.

I'm not your toy poodle.

"It's 'Luna, please follow me' or 'Will you follow me?'. Things between us will be a lot more pleasant if you learn the words *will*, *please*, and *thank you*."

The smile had returned, with a dark, dangerous undercurrent. He approached me with the measured grace of a predator. Glints of amber and gold glowed intensely in his eyes.

He looked at my arms crossed over my chest.

It took several moments before he spoke. "Luna." There was a coarse edge placed on my name. "Thank you for that advice. Will you please understand that if I kill you now, the spell will be broken and the prisoners returned?"

I swallowed hard and shored up resolve that was hard earned. If things were that simple, he would have done it. With that knowledge I stood my ground.

"Possibly, but I'm almost positive it will happen again. The next time the Dark Caster may be cleverer and you won't even find the person they used. It's them that you really want."

A muscle ticked in his jaw. As his eyes continued to bore into me, it was clear he was a man who was never defied or challenged.

"Killing me might be the easy way out, but as you said, it's only a short-term solution. You want the Caster and to find out their motive." I shrugged. "The way I see it, the Conventicle seemed really upset and scared that the prisoners are at large, and with the possible exception of two or three people in that group, they're awful and have a questionable moral compass. I'm going to include you in the questionable moral compass."

He didn't seem to find my comment insulting. In fact, he seemed pleased by it.

"It's safe to assume that the people they deemed worthy of being imprisoned are worse." I stepped closer, meeting his intense gaze. "You and I both know the Caster unleashed them all, and I suspect it was for one person. You have to be curious as to who and why."

This was just my theory—an educated guess. Perhaps they wanted to sow chaos. Or it was a giant screw you to the arrogant domineering guardian of the Perils or the Conventicle who sent them there. But my gut was telling me there was more to it. I had no idea what, but if I was the only link, Dominic needed me more than he was willing to admit.

The taut muscles in his neck relaxed. There was a hint of a smile, but he quickly relaxed it until his expression was indecipherable.

"Come with me, please," he said, and without another word, he led me back upstairs to the library. Tamping down my excitement became harder the farther we walked into it.

I wanted to open my arms wide and spin around, though I knew there was no spinning allowed. But how could I not in a library that rivaled the one in *Beauty in the Beast*?

"We're going this way," he directed, leading me to the far left. As I inched farther into the smaller room off the main library, leather and sulfur inundated the air. The room felt sentient. The thick air clung to me and wrapped around my limbs as if trying to determine if I belonged. I didn't. Nor did I want to.

Despite the warm, gentle hues from the overhead lighting, the calming mint-green walls, the plush oyster-colored leather seats, the room was cold and shrouded in darkness. It teemed with an unsettling and ubiquitous toxicity. A fustiness that overtook my senses and coated the air with a thickness that made breathing a challenge.

"Spellbooks?" I pointed to the wall of weathered leather books in the tall bookcases that reached just a few inches shy of the ceiling.

He nodded, appearing unaffected by the room in the manner I was. If anything, he seemed calmed by it. He inhaled, taking in the room, the two floor-to-ceiling shelves filled with books. The expansive wood table in the middle of the room held three large binders. Papers dulled yellow with age peeked from them. A worn, comfortable chair was in the corner, but it was not as plush as the ones in the main library.

"What happened when you evoked the spell that marked you?" Dominic finally asked.

"Can we discuss it in the main library?" There wasn't anyone in it, if privacy was his concern.

He nodded and I rushed past him to the clean air and a space that didn't reek of bad intent.

It was obvious to me that magic or any variants of it unnerved me. Supernatural people—with the exclusion of Reginald, who still had not convinced me of his supernatural status—were violent, unscrupulous, and possibly sociopathic. Magic and spells were chaotic and portentous. My short experience with it showed it to be foreboding and destructive. This incentivized me to do whatever I could to undo the spell and return to my normal, uncomplicated life. I'd never considered my life to be a simple one, but with the soot of the spellbook room still on me, it was blatant that it was.

Dominic waited patiently as I settled into one of the chairs. Remaining standing, he crossed one arm over his chest and rested the other arm's elbow on it as he ran his thumb languidly over his lips. I couldn't help but watch him do it.

Leaving out any conversations with Reginald, I told Dominic about what at the time was an uneventful moment of finding the ring, me wearing it, and no one claiming it. When I got to the part about me seeing the weird dog, his brow furrowed.

"Oversized dog?"

"Maybe the Dark Caster sent it after me. I don't know, but a dog who looks like he should be guarding the gates of —" I stopped before saying "hell" because I was, unbelievably, actually in the Underworld, speaking with a supernatural jailer… guardian… or whoever he was. The "man with a military welcoming committee" who lived in a mansion absent a sun or any greenery. Saying hell in this place seemed blasphemous. No, not blasphemous, but maybe a smug reminder of where we were. Either way, it was definitely apropos.

There was a hint of humor in his eyes. He said, "Zareb," and moments later there was the clicking of nails along the marble floor as the massive dog made an appearance. Gasping, I jumped to my feet and shuffled away from the animal.

"I sent him," Dominic informed me.

"Why?"

"Your scent. Once he has it, he can track you anywhere. He's a better option for scouting."

"You think a horse-dog is less inconspicuous and better at scouting than you would be?"

"Yes," he said.

With a small tremor the terrifying creature disappeared. If I hadn't just seen him, I wouldn't have known he was near.

The only hint of his presence was the feathery touch of warmth that flitted across my skin. Dominic moved toward us and reached out, his hand stroking the air. The dog reappeared, revealing that Dominic was rubbing the top of the dog's head.

With Dominic being the only one who could see him, Zareb was indeed a better scout.

He made a tick sound with his tongue and the dog padded away.

"Is he the only one?"

Dominic shook his head. "But he's the one with your scent. He can track you anywhere."

The hint of warning wasn't missed. Instead of commenting on it, I asked, "Can they track down the escaped prisoners? Surely they can get a scent from the cells."

Dominic frowned. "This spell is strong, like a scorched earth scenario. The spells we had that neutralized their magic, strength, and ability to teleport were all destroyed. The binding spell that kept them tethered to the room is broken. And there's no scent to detect. Tenebras Obducit—Dark Caster—magic is immense, their spells nearly insurmountable. And this particular spell was so meticulously engineered, it will be difficult to find them."

Despite what he'd just admitted, he didn't seem hopeless, which I couldn't claim. Despair was slowly engulfing me. Optimism about getting out of this situation was slowly dwindling.

"Then how will they be found?"

"You. Once we are able to unravel the spell, its owner's signature will be revealed. I can use that to track them as long as it is unlinked from you. One thing that your little book, I'm sure accidentally, got right is that each of us comes from the same source. Depending on how you view it, we bear the mark of a curse or gift. Each and every descendant bears the mark. If I find a new vampire, within his signature,

I'll know his creator. The same with shifters. No one can hide from me, because I can find their signature."

"Not everyone's. You're having a hard time finding this Tenebras person. They've managed to elude you." I immediately regretted pointing that out. A wave of heat sweltered the room. The glow of his fiery eyes blasted me.

Sorry. Got it. Don't point out Dominic's shortcomings.

"True. They've never performed magic around me to be traced. Once the magic is pulled from you, I can track the source." He took in a slow breath, the room cooled and returned to normal, and his eyes held his normal look of dying fire.

"Continue," he urged with a faint look. "Please." He was trying, but he wore the effort on his face along with the remnants of his ire.

I continued with the story. By the time I finished, his smile had been replaced by a rigid frown.

"I performed magic." It was the first time I'd said it aloud. It had been in my thoughts, but I was too busy trying to distance myself from it.

"No, you were used in order for the ring to perform magic. It's bound to you and your life energy is what's fueling the spell. You're blocking me from finding the owner."

A look passed over his face that I wanted to ignore, but it was too telling. One sweeping act of violence would break the spell and return the prisoners. Swallowing my fear, I tried to inconspicuously put more distance between us while I furtively looked around for a weapon. My phone was still in my back pocket, but it wasn't much help without the benefit of surprise. And my punches had very little effect on him.

"So, I'm a magic signal jammer?"

"To put it simply, yes. Once unraveled from you, it can be tracked."

"Dominic."

His name came in a deep, throaty purr from the woman

who swept into the room. Although she was a deeper olive than Dominic, there were obvious familial similarities. The same dark hair—hers pulled back into a chignon—amber eyes with flecks of gold and orange that looked like fading fire, striking sharp features, and captivating beauty.

A broad smile remained on her face as she hugged him. She was clearly the affectionate one of the two; his squeeze in return was stiff and obligatory. She pressed a kiss to his cheek before she turned to me. I studied her flowy maroon V-neck bohemian maxi dress. A long slit revealed her legs and lace-up sandals as she moved. She linked her arm through his and the other she shoved in her pocket. That was the moment I envied the stylish woman. Her dress had pockets. I was sold, I needed it.

Her eyes appraised me and snagged on my finger with the marking. "This is her? She's the one?"

Dominic's head barely moved into the nod.

"I don't sense any magic. How can this be?" She moved closer, inspecting me like a peculiar creature she was attempting to name. She ran one finger from my forehead down to the tip of my nose. Then pressed it like it was some strange face button that would reveal my secrets to her.

Boundaries! I thought, taking a small step back while Dominic explained everything to her. The distance I placed between us was quickly swallowed as she continued to scrutinize me with amusement. An amiable smile settled on her lips. I eased into it, relaxing some and ignoring her blatant disregard for social norms and acceptable social distance. Suddenly, her hand cuffed my neck. It was such a gentle touch that I didn't feel threatened.

"Do you want me to kill her?" she asked in such a gentle, melodic voice it was like she was trying to ease me into acquiescence. I jerked from her hold and moved away. The genteel smile she gave me was unacceptable.

No, psycho, I'm not okay with any part of this discussion.

"Helena, no," Dominic said firmly.

Her eyes dropped to my finger that bore the markings. "Do you think your way is the wisest tactic?" she challenged, looking over her shoulder at him. "Perhaps alternatives should be explored." She turned back to me, her smile and countenance far too kind, easy, and welcoming for a person discussing murder.

I hated this world. I hated it so much.

She shrugged at his stern look. "Her finger. Should we re—"

"Helena," he snapped. "She is protected. You won't remove her finger, nor will you kill her. You have no business in this. Are we clear?"

She frowned, her mood dampened, but I was very confident it was only because he raised his voice and not the censure that accompanied it.

"Very well, we'll do it your way. I'm off to have an early dinner." She turned to me again. "Would you like to join me? We're having roasted duck with beet salad and mashed pumpkin. I think you'd enjoy it."

Is she serious? Moments ago, she was requesting permission to kill me or sever my finger; now she wanted me as a dinner date. Nothing about this world was acceptable.

Stunned into momentary silence, I just gawked at her. All the fear, frustration, confusion, and annoyance at being pulled into this abhorrent situation erupted.

"No, you sociopathic bitch. I do not want to eat with you. What is wrong with you?"

Unaffected by my outburst, her face remained chillingly pleasant as she gave Dominic another smile and quick peck on the cheek. "If she changes her mind, you will direct her to the dining room, won't you?"

"Of course," he said, returning her pleasant smile.

Our long silence was fraught with tension as I stared at him. Reaching into his pocket, he removed my ring and handed it to me. "My sister has a directness to her nature," he attempted to explain.

"The word 'directness' is reserved for people who are blunt and unintentionally rude, not for a person asking their brother for permission to murder or dismember someone."

"Her enjoyment leans toward darker elements. She finds a certain pleasure in murder and torture. She's quite good at them both," he said mildly, as if he'd just disclosed something mundane, like her favorite color was yellow. I wondered how different these siblings were. Was he okay with these behaviors but just didn't really enjoy them to the extent she did?

"What you call 'darker elements' is known to us mere humans as state's evidence," I tossed out before closing my eyes, inhaling the air, and letting the calm of being in a library wash over me. It was the only thing that kept me somewhat grounded.

When my eyes opened, Dominic was close and staring down at me. Too close.

"Are you afraid of me?" he asked.

"You just described enjoying torture as darker elements of amusement. How should I feel about that?"

He studied my lips, his face expressionless. Neither one of us spoke, just stood in the tension-filled silence. His eyes turned expectant as he waited for an answer.

"No." That wasn't entirely true but close enough. Even if I felt it, admitting it to him—to myself—would change the balance. For some peculiar reason, I needed that. "I'm afraid of the woman who offered me food after glibly suggesting killing me or cutting off my finger," I admitted.

His voice was low, rough, unyielding. "She'll never touch you as long as I wish for you to be safe," he assured me as his eyes roved slowly over my face. "Nor will the others. The consequences would be too great."

With that, he was moving with a relaxed stride as if he'd offered me some comfort.

He returned to the spellbook room's door and looked back at me. I guessed I wasn't going to get a *please* or *will you follow me*.

8

*B*ack in the spellbook room, I was unsuccessfully trying to get used to the atmosphere and becoming increasingly curious why it didn't bother Dominic. Did magic appeal to only magic? Could this room sense that I didn't belong and its eeriness was repellent, trying to force me to leave? It was working; I didn't want to be there.

Leisurely moving from shelf to shelf, I examined the books while feeling the full weight of Dominic's attention.

"What should I do here?" I asked.

"These books hold the strongest and most arcane magic known. Something in here should work."

I heard the hesitation in his voice and turned to him. "What else?" I asked.

"You'll be able to find it better than I can."

Lifting my finger, I said, "Because of this?"

He nodded.

Of course. It all came back to the markings on my finger. It was the beginning and the end.

"What do I do?" I asked again.

"Touch the books, go through the spells, and see if you feel anything. I believe antagonistic spells will respond to it."

"Spells that want to undo what's in place."

He nodded.

Find the books. Starting at the lower shelves, I ran my fingers over the bindings of the books, feeling sillier with each passing moment. Dominic urged me to continue but nothing happened. Then I took one off the shelf, slowly gliding my finger over each spell in the book. If another book bit me, dammit, I was going to bite back.

After ten minutes, there was no refuting his logic or the hard jolt and noxious feeling I got when my hand went over certain spells. I placed a gray, age-warped book on the table and took some Post-its that someone had placed in the middle of the table and marked them. It went faster than I imagined once I realized slow, deliberate movements weren't needed. The spells wanted to be found.

I found the spells, and Dominic added them to a notebook, placing them on different pages; I assumed in categories based on their designation.

Despite the phone screen having survived being used as a weapon, it wasn't working. No service in the Underworld. Oddly, the clock on my phone hadn't changed. I had no idea how long I had been searching. Hours had to have passed because my stomach was growling. Staying on task was increasingly difficult. But if the only option for food was to eat with Helena, I'd starve.

"We should take a break," Dominic suggested. "Let's get some food."

He had to have heard my stomach, too. Understanding my hesitation, he went on. "Helena's long finished with dinner. But we'll go to the kitchen. That's one place we'll never find her."

"I know she eats, so why don't you think I'll run into her in the kitchen?" I said, following him out of the room, through the library, and down the hall. Avoiding her was my mission and not knowing how much time had passed, it was possible I could run into her again, on her way for a snack.

"She eats but doesn't believe she should have to prepare it. She has a kitchenette in her suite so she doesn't have to come down for anything to drink." The sharpness of disapproval was heavy in his voice. She was a self-indulgent prima donna who enjoyed "dark entertainment." Helena seemed terrible on so many levels.

The kitchen was a chef's dream and larger than Books and Brew's entire store. Black stainless steel throughout, and a large marble island near the double oven. One of the counters displayed a variety of pastries, cakes, and cookies that made my mouth water. A well-stocked wine fridge was to the left, and from what I could see it contained an extensive selection. The other door near the refrigerator was undoubtedly the pantry.

Sitting on a leather barstool at the counter just a few feet from the fridge and the dessert display, I watched Dominic while he moved through the kitchen with familiarity. He opened the refrigerator and the pantry. When he finished, he placed an assortment of cheeses and breads, berries and grapes, prosciutto, summer sausage, and smoked salmon on a platter in front of me. He moved in graceful silence as he opened a bottle of pinot blanc and poured two glasses of wine.

"I'd like water, please," I requested when he placed one of the wine glasses in front of me. He nodded, took a bottle of water from the fridge, and poured water into a glass. "This should tide you over while I prepare something for you. Do you like steak?"

"You don't need to prepare anything. This is more than enough. I appreciate it," I told him, looking at a platter that could easily feed four people.

Nodding, he tilted the glass of wine he'd given me and

finished it in a few swallows. He drank the other glass more slowly.

Great, drunk research. Nothing can go wrong with that.

I slid the platter over toward him to share. He took some bread and a few pieces of cheese, which I believed was just to be polite.

Eating a few berries, I took in the view from the bay window. Moroccan-style lanterns provided ambient lighting for the mélange of flowers that managed to be simultaneously intriguing and disturbing.

Dominic leaned in, his head close to mine, glimpsing what drew my attention.

"Roses." He pointed at a section of the garden. I could feel the warmth of his skin, smell his alluring scent. *Focus, Luna, focus.*

He directed my attention to another section. "Black Forest calla lily, and those gruesome looking things are bat orchids, compliments of my sister's wicked inclinations."

I nearly missed the bizarre plant as I became increasingly aware of his closeness, his warm, wine-scented breath breezing against my face. The hint of pear, white nectarine, and faint notes of honey and apple lingered on it.

He didn't seem to mind our proximity. He left just enough space between us to bring the glass to his lips again and for me to become acutely aware of how savagely beautiful he was. After finding myself staring at him, I shifted back and shoved a piece of cheese in my mouth and concentrated on tearing off a piece of baguette.

Dominic leaned against the counter behind him and sipped his wine, looking through the window. But he didn't seem relaxed by the view. Pulling my attention from my food to him, I took in not just his beauty but also his blood-speckled shirt. It didn't seem to bother him. Maybe he was used to it. Blood on his shirt wasn't cause for alarm.

"You live here?"

"Yes."

"Are guardians of the supernatural prison typically greeted as you were and allowed to live in a mansion with their sibling?" I took a sip of water.

He met my gaze and nodded.

"You're not *just* a guard are you, *Dominic*?" I asked, trying to emphasize his name as he had mine.

Without entertaining my question, he gulped down the remainder of his wine. "I trust you can find your way back to the room."

With that, he was gone, striding quick and graceful down the hall.

Not wanting to chance another run-in with Helena, I devoured the rest of my food and returned to the spellbook room, where I found Dominic, who had changed into a blue shirt and midnight-blue slacks. His hair was slightly disheveled. A peppery, earthy scent of either soap or cologne broke through the other smells in the room. There was an icy edge to his mien. One that I was sure I couldn't thaw.

In wary silence, I returned to my search. I completed the rows of books I could easily reach and unsuccessfully pushed to the tips of my toes to reach the books on the second to top shelf. Who has bookshelves this high without a step stool or ladder?

Dominic sidled up next to me, his body warm, his scent intoxicating and preferable to the others that inundated the room. With a taunting smirk, he handed me the book.

"Thank you. If you get me a step stool or ladder, I can reach the rest."

"We don't have a step stool." His voice was light with amusement.

I huffed. "So, everyone who uses this room is a giant." My

height was a sore subject with me. It wouldn't have been if people didn't make a big deal of it. I wasn't *that* short. The average height for a woman was five-four. Just two inches below average and people were ready to put me in the same category as Thumbelina. And Emoni mocking me for having that information "in the chamber" only made things worse. She was probably right; knowing the average of anything to use in a debate did point to it being a contentious subject.

He shrugged, the quirk still on his lips. "Anyone who uses this room can reach the shelves. Until now." Based on everyone I'd seen, no one would have a problem. Even Helena was just three or four inches shorter than him.

With no desire to be more fodder for his amusement, I moved to the next shelf and worked on the books that I could reach and he continued adding spells to the notebook. The ones in languages I didn't understand, he translated into English on the paper. Based on the twelve books we'd gone through, the marks on my finger weren't very discerning. They had selected forty-nine spells.

"What next?" I asked.

He slid a piece of paper toward me. "These are the spells used to secure the prison. I've done a reversal spell and it didn't work." He moved closer, taking my hand in his. He removed the ring and studied the intricate markings on my finger. His hand was warm and his touch gentle as he moved my hand around to inspect each mark. Distinguishing the network, he used a finger to travel the various lines, pointing out the distinctions of the spells. There were seven spells that needed to be unraveled.

My hope began to peter out again. He evoked several spells, keeping a close eye on my finger for a reaction. When a golden outline illuminated one of the lines on my finger, we both breathed a sigh of relief. He made note of it and continued. One spell down. He invoked thirty spells out of the forty-nine and my markings only reacted to three. This was going to be a long, arduous task. And fatigue was setting in. I needed to sleep.

Standing, I stretched. "I get off work at three tomorrow," I informed him and then flashed a smile. "Maybe you can find a step stool by then."

His eyebrows inched together with confusion.

"Step stool or small ladder. They're everywhere. You can get one from Target. You have to know what I'm talking about."

He shook his head. "I know what a step stool is. Where are you going?"

"Home. I can't stay here." Based on the look on his face, that was exactly what was expected. For my life to be placed on hold and me to remain completely devoted to his cause until this was complete. "Dominic, I have a job. I have friends. If I go missing, things are going to get very complicated. Questions will need to be answered."

"Luna, things are already complicated. Do you grasp the severity of this situation?"

"If anyone does, I do. You have a single-mission focus. Find the Dark Caster. When this is over, I can't be jobless because of no-shows for work, and I'll have to explain going missing to my friends and family. And 'I was just hanging out in the Underworld with the Perils' guardian' isn't going to cut it."

"Tell them what you must when this is over, but you aren't leaving."

My heart pounded. Could he stop me leaving? How could I get out of the Underworld when he was my passage out?

"You said that as long as you willed it, I'm safe, so what's the problem?"

"This needs to be done quickly," he urged.

I waved my hand at the bookcases. "I've been here for hours and gone through shelves of books, you've invoked thirty spells, and we yielded three results... *three* spells." Frustration was getting the best of me. "There has to be an alternative plan. Hunt the prisoners and find somewhere to store them until we have this figured out," I suggested. Being locked away in the Underworld until this was over couldn't be the only option. With a bold and uncharacteristic show of bravado, I headed for the door.

"No." His firm response made me halt midstep. For several beats, I debated if I should argue then indignation fueled my reaction. This wasn't a *no* situation. He didn't have authority over my coming and going.

"No isn't an option. Take a few minutes to reconcile with that. I'll meet you at the front door." Marching toward the door of the main library, I waited in anticipation of his approaching light steps. When they never came, I headed for the front door of the house. The moment I touched the doorknob, there was collective whoosh sound from behind me. Turning around, I was faced with five swords and a crossbow aimed at my chest. I froze and locked onto Dominic as he sauntered slowly toward me, his eyes never leaving mine. Breezy self-assurance and a predatory confidence hardened his gaze.

Refusing to give him the pleasure of my fear, I squared my shoulders and stood taller.

"Are you ready to go?" I asked, ignoring the weapons.

A faint, cynical smile lifted the corners of his lips. He looked to his right, where stoic Anand stood.

Casually shoving his hand in his pocket, Dominic continued his advance, his face turning eerily expressionless. "It seems that we are at an impasse, Little Luna."

We're back to this crap again?

"Luna is fine. We don't need commentary on my height."

The woman holding the crossbow moved slightly to let Dominic pass. My sight fixed on the man in front of me, who seemed far more dangerous than the weapon-wielding people surrounding me.

91

His eyes traced my face with interest. "What do you know of vampires?" he asked softly.

"Probably not enough. Only the stuff in fantasy books and *The Discovery of Magic*. You already told me most of that is wrong."

"Who they were as humans is intensified by vampirism. Roman, whom you released, has killed thousands of people. Destroyed small cities. And created three other vampires who share his lust for violence and death. I put his sired down in their infancy and only caught him ten years ago. The witches and I have spent his existence cleaning up his messes and making sure that knowledge of the supernaturals remains hidden." He paused. "Tell me what you know of witches."

His jawline hardened as I remained silent. I knew very little of this world and *The Discovery of Magic* had given me a diluted version and a great deal of misinformation. I would not be an active participant in the castigation of my lack of knowledge.

"Luna," he urged me in a low voice, but I remained silent. "Some witches are stronger than others. Then there are those that are significantly worse."

Really, if you think I'm shocked by this information, you haven't been watching.

"The worst of their kind are Mors—witches with the ability to kill with a single touch." His finger slid languidly over my collarbone to drive home the point. "One spell, one touch, and you're dead. I've found and stopped all of them, except one. Celeste. By the time I got to her, she'd performed a spell that linked her to her bloodline. If she dies, so does everyone in her bloodline."

"So?" I said, making my voice hard and callous. "Witches aren't immortal. She's going to die anyway."

Amusement played over his sharply carved features. He wasn't falling for my act of indifference. "It gives them time to undo the spell. Madeline is quite resourceful. I do believe she'll find a way." Something lingered after the last sentence. He may have had an appreciation for that quality in Madeline, but there was uneasiness entwined as well.

Dominic's impassivity made it difficult to read his mood or decipher his thoughts. Unlike his sister Helena, who'd appeared from one of the rooms. Her dark, ethereal presence was alight with the anticipation of violence.

Anand was just as hard to read as Dominic. The guards hadn't lowered their weapons. With a deadly sword strike, this could be over for Dominic. I was very aware of that as he pondered the situation far too long for my liking.

Everyone appeared disquieted by the tension-laden silence, standing in anticipation. I struggled to keep my patience.

"I want this to be over as much as you do, and I'm committed to doing whatever I can. But when it's over, I still have a life. I still need my job. And my friends and family will want answers about my sudden disappearance if I don't make a showing. This is not my world. I was dragged into this fight. It seems the most pressing concern you have is the anonymity of the supernaturals. Others know about the book and what happened to me. I go missing, there'll be questions."

I took liberties with "others." One person, maybe more if Reginald consulted his coven, but I needed to press upon Dominic how me going missing would hurt the anonymity they desired.

His expression hadn't changed and I was forced to rely on Helena, who looked pleased. That wasn't good.

"We want the same thing," I rushed out after seeing Helena's expression. "What are you concerned about?"

"You are the sole link to me finding the Tenebras Obducit, and finding them is important to me."

"Fine, you want to make sure nothing happens to me"—I

waved my hand in Helena's direction—"let her come with me to work, make sure I'm safe. She can serve as my bodyguard."

The suggestion brought on a smirk. Helena appeared aghast with disgust.

Killing and dismembering a guest in your home is perfectly fine, but playing guard for a day is where she feels scandalized?

"I work tomorrow from ten to three and I'm off the following day. If we find nothing tomorrow, then I'll stay the next day," I offered, hoping this would make him more amenable. I wanted him to know this was a priority for me.

He regarded me in silence as time ticked by, and my hope that things would be handled amicably dwindled.

"You'll return after work tomorrow and stay the next day if needed," he confirmed. There was weight in his words, as if what I said was binding. Perhaps it was. My word. Possibly to test if I would honor my word.

I nodded in agreement.

"At ease," Dominic finally told the guards. Once they had relaxed their weapons, he dismissed them with a wave of his hand.

"Try not to die," he said.

Who's not choosing that option?

"Of course."

"Let's get you home," he said, extending his hand for me to take.

The shimmering wall appeared to his left, and we slipped through it.

We entered my world in the alleyway behind Books and Brew, where I'd first encountered Zareb. I checked my phone. It was two in the morning and I had to be at work at ten. There were several messages. One from Jackson, which I deleted without reading, and two from Emoni, that I would answer once home. Expecting Dominic to leave once I waved goodbye and started for my apartment, I was surprised when he fell into step next to me. He seemed content with the silence as we walked, but I decided it was an opportunity to find out more about him.

"You can get home from anywhere?" I asked, turning down my street. It was still discomforting to discuss the Underworld so glibly. Calling it his home made it feel somewhat normal.

He nodded but didn't elaborate. It was like pulling teeth to get any information from this guy.

"So why choose the alleyway next to Books and Brew and not closer to my home?"

"It's dark, not a high traffic area. Less chance to be seen."

"If you are seen?"

He shrugged. "Most people will convince themselves they didn't see what they did. If I think it's a problem, I'll manipulate their memories so they forget it."

Great, more horrific discoveries. There was truth to his comment. I had convinced myself that my eyes were just playing tricks on me, that it was the sun, a burst of sunlight, behind Zareb the hellhound, and not the shimmering diaphanous wall that I'd actually seen.

"I don't like to do it. The manipulation works on other memories as well. It's required infrequently. Humans want to believe they are the only ones who exist in this vast world. They're very imperialistic and self-centered that way. Unaware that they are the inferior of the species."

I scoffed. "I admire your modesty."

"Do statements of fact require some modicum of modesty?"

I shrugged. "No, but it seems like the polite thing to do."

"Politeness is overrated."

"Yeah, to rude people," I muttered under my breath.

He responded with a wry frown. "Our anonymity is not

just for our benefit but that of humans as well. Knowledge of us would change the dynamics of the world. Something humans aren't ready for. The ones who believe that supernaturals exist have a rather puerile appreciation for it. Not truly understanding the depth and nuances."

"It's violent and dark."

I could feel his assessing eyes on me. "It can be."

"It seems like that's all there is to it," I challenged, turning to face him once we were in front of my building. "This is my place."

He looked at the modest building. The entire complex wasn't as spacious as his home. It wasn't surprising when he followed me up the three flights of stairs to my door.

Despite me leaving the door open, he stayed at the threshold, awaiting an invitation.

He was rather selective in practicing good manners. Attempts to burn me alive, direct threats, and abduction attempts—no problem. But entering my home without an invitation was where he drew the line of impropriety? Maybe he couldn't. Like vampires in movies, he couldn't enter without an invitation. But once he was invited, could the invitation be rescinded?

"No, I don't require a formal invitation," he said with a grin.

My mother always commented about my expression speaking volumes. It made communication easy most of the time but rarely gave me the advantage.

"Nor do vampires," he added. "Something else that *The Discovery of Magic* got wrong." It seemed like the only information correct in the book was the existence of the supernatural beings. It was definitely a work of fiction.

"You can come in if you'd like."

He nodded, entered the apartment and surveyed it.

"It's you," he said in a neutral tone. His attention quickly moved to the book. He picked it up, flipped through it, examining each blank page as if it'd reveal something. Even my blood had been absorbed into the book. His long fingers traced the markings on the spine of the book.

"Do you know what it means?" I asked.

He nodded. More beats of silence. Damn, he was exhausting.

"What?"

"Awakening," he whispered in a breath. "A story for another time." And that was the only thing he offered. He returned the book to the counter. "What are your work hours again?"

"Ten to three." Before I could question him more, he plucked strands of hair from my head and was out the door. *Just so very selective about demonstrations of propriety. Who just snatches hair from someone's head without warning them?*

He knelt, allowing his fingers to glide just above the threshold, then he dropped the hairs over it. They ignited into a quick burst of flames. Upon his command, a rust-colored shimmer of light flared and disappeared.

"It's a temporary protective field. Once you cross the threshold, it will be disabled. No one can get in." There was a moment of hesitation. "The Caster may be able to break it, but it will be with great effort. You should be safe."

I went to bed but sleep didn't come easily. I had no idea what to do with all the new information. The most pressing thing: Could my life return to normal after this?

9

The next morning, I tried to be more optimistic. Dominic would find the Dark Caster, the prisoners would be returned, and I'd spend my life forgetting everything I'd learned, or at the very least pretending that people I passed on the streets weren't more than what they appeared to be. Which was what I was doing as I walked to work. Scrutinizing everyone I passed, wondering. Were they a shifter, witch, vampire, seer, or whatever Anand, Helena, and Dominic were?

Thinking about the people in the latter category tugged at my curiosity, but admittedly, there was comfort in not knowing. Every curtain pulled back revealed something more portentous, making the new world I was exposed to disturbing.

A man sidled up next to me as I hitched up the overnight bag I'd brought with me in case I stayed too long in… damn, in the Underworld. *I'm just hanging out in the Underworld, like it's an overnight trip to my Nana Reed's. Ugh, what is my life now?*

"What, Kane?"

"Such hostility," he drawled.

"I get that way when people abduct me and then attempt

to bite me. I'm so irrational that way," I snarked back.

"Perhaps my past action warranted your response."

"Perhaps?" I stopped to look at him, hoping to see some regret, shame, or basic remorse. Nothing. He held my gaze, his dark eyes narrowing, a hypnotic beat to them, pulling me to him. My eyes remained transfixed, unable to pull free from his.

"Luna." His voice was satin smooth and demanded compliance that I gave wholeheartedly. Pulled into the depths of his eyes, I was unable to do anything but look at him and be attentive to his commands.

"Do you hear me, Luna?" he asked, his voice a gentle caress.

"Yes."

Pleased, he gave me a small smile. "I need you to do something for me, Luna."

"Okay," I agreed, warming comfort wrapping around me, a contrast to the withering brush of wind just moments ago. This heat I desired to the point of necessity. Like breath. Pleasing him became a priority.

"Good," he whispered. "I want—"

His mouth gaped open. He tore his eyes from me and looked down at his chest, where the tip of a bloodstained stake peeked out and then disappeared.

He whipped around to find Anand baring his teeth.

"That's a bad injury. You're going to need to feed or..." Anand let his words trail off, providing an insinuating brow. The vampire looked at me and then back at the wound.

"The stake's made from Dracaena cinnabari, the dragon blood tree," Anand provided with a dark sneer. Kane looked down at his hand; it was drying and turning a grayish color.

A scream caught in my throat as I shuffled back. Anand had stabbed Kane in the middle of the street. None of this was normal. None of it. Instinct had me wanting to flee from the violence.

"Luna, don't run," Anand ordered, his eyes still on the vampire. There was a hint of warning in his voice. As quickly as he had attacked, the vampire would be able to track and subdue me. I placed my bag in front of me as if it could be used as an adequate barrier to protect me from Anand.

"I hope I am the one to kill you," Kane gritted out through clenched teeth.

"A fervent wish that many have made," Anand shot back as Kane clutched his chest and darted out of sight. Anand pulled a small vial from the pocket of his jeans, opened it, sprinkled it over the stake, and whispered something. The stain lifted from the wood and dissipated into the air. Placing the stake in his back pocket, he tugged his shirt down to conceal it and started walking.

Anand then turned back to me, the hardness in his face when dealing with the vampire ebbing away. I wouldn't allow him to get closer and kept a cautious eye on him as if he were an unpredictable predator—and I wasn't convinced he wasn't.

"You have no need to fear me, Luna."

That seemed highly inaccurate, but him waiting patiently for me to move toward him offered some comfort. My migration toward him was done with hesitation. Each step slow, measured, and cautious.

"I saved your life," he declared, sliding an assessing look in my direction. Still trying to process what happened, my mind was just a whirlwind of thoughts. "The older the vampire, the harder they are to kill. Ram a stake through the heart of a young vampire, and death comes rather quickly." He was heading in the direction of Books and Brew, just a block away. "With older vampires, the process is slow, giving them ample time to feed and survive. For supernaturals, age has its benefits. But staking an elder vampire with Dracaena cinnabari will hasten the death process."

"The older they are, the worse they are to deal with.

Great." Taking in the impromptu lesson in vampire slaying only cemented my theory that the supernatural world was driven by violence. It was doubtful I could ever get used to it.

"I don't consider it worse. I enjoy the challenge." Anand had a melodious deep voice with a hint of a rasp that I was sure was from lack of use. He struck me as a man of few words.

"And you're an old…" I waited for him to provide his supernatural denotation. I had to navigate this world, and despite my trepidation, knowledge gave me an advantage. I was curious as to what supernaturals occupied the Underworld. I assumed the only other options were demons. Or fallen angels. Anand's quiet beauty would easily be considered seraphic. Was he a fallen angel?

He stopped at the door, and I focused on the scar that ran along his face, fighting the urge of being all types of cringy and creepy by running my finger over it. Something that should have detracted and marred his appeal added distinct character.

"Never look a vampire in the eye, okay? That's how they compel you. I suspect Kane was about to instruct you to hurt yourself, walk into traffic, perform a self-inflicted injury, come to him and request he feed until he is sated. A vampire is never sated." He frowned. "If a vampire stares at you, gouge them in the eyes. If you don't want to use your finger, keep something long and sharp with you—knitting needle, pen, whatever, and use that."

"What!" I gawked at him. Was he trained by Helena? "Why is that option number one? What about not looking them in the eye? That'll work too, right?"

He nodded and lifted his shoulders in a shrug of indifference. Then he headed to the counter of the coffee shop, and I went to the bookstore, acutely aware that he'd never answered my question about what he was.

I'd have another opportunity to question him. I'd

requested Helena as a guard but got Anand. Although he struck me as a person who thrived on adrenaline, violence, and danger, it was still an upgrade. He'd only suggested gouging out the eye of a vampire who was trying to harm me; she wanted to murder me but had settled on just taking a finger.

The deep-seated frown brought on by thoughts of Helena relaxed when I caught sight of Cameron's toothy smile. It was the smile she gave when she needed a favor. Based on how wide her smile was, it was going to be a big request. Hopefully it wasn't a request for me to work later or the next day.

I wanted desperately to be done with Dominic, the supernatural world, and the lurking eyes. Where they excelled at being amoral, violent, and powerful, they totally failed at stealth. That failure was being demonstrated right now; the wolf who attacked me was perusing books in the corner of the store and obviously watching me. Another person sat at a table shooting me none-too-furtive glances. I had no idea who or what they were. The wolf shifter definitely had a look of discontent at the sight of me. Had he learned of Kane's failure or was he acting alone and disappointed that Dominic hadn't killed me? Who knew?

Anand walking into the bookstore had them all scrambling to get somewhere else, fast.

Cameron greeted me with an enthusiastic hi. It was times like this that Cameron reminded me of a hyperactive pup—and she evoked the same response. The smile that curved my lips widened despite knowing she needed a favor.

She finished up with the customer she was helping.

"I need a favor," she announced. Shocker. She led me to the gaming section of the store.

"Really? I never would have guessed," I teased.

"Reese had a family emergency and had to cancel and I was hoping Emoni could fill in. I know coffee shop music isn't Emoni's thing, but you know how much people enjoy our Wine-Down Thursdays."

Cameron enjoyed them, too. Maybe it was the music or the reduced-price wine or a combination of both, but the income she lost on wine, she made up for in book sales. Buzzed book buying was more lucrative than I ever imagined.

"I'm not Emoni's manager. Just ask her. She's not shy about declining things when she's not interested."

"I know, but I'm the owner and she might feel obligated to say yes just to appease me. I don't want her to do that."

"No."

Her eyes widened.

"See, I have no problem telling you no. Do you think Emoni is any less likely to do so?" I teased. Giving her arm a gentle squeeze, I told her I'd ask and headed off to help out a woman who looked as if she was searching the store for an employee. I looked over my shoulder at Cameron. "She's going to say yes. You're giving her an opportunity to do two things she'll never admit she loves: coffee house music and performing covers."

When Emoni arrived at work a couple of hours later, I was unsettled by Anand's presence at the counter. He was studying the pastries on display. Had he anticipated my move, heard our conversation, read our lips?

Anand and I hadn't spoken since he gave me his disturbing advice. He'd been inconspicuous in the store. Occasionally I got a glimpse of him leaving or moving but never knew when he had returned or how he managed to get close to me. When I saw him, it felt like he was allowing it. It was as if he faded into the nonexistent shadows of the store. Disappeared. I wasn't convinced he didn't. Employees typically commented on people who lingered in the store, but no one seemed to notice his presence.

As I eased my way closer to the side of the counter to talk to Emoni, I was staring at Anand until she cleared her throat.

"He's new around here," Emoni said. "He likes his coffee black," she whispered. Her eyes slowly traveled over him.

"You really need a more interesting kink because the no-sugar no-cream thing is weird. And not in the quirky way that people find adorable. It's just weird." I wasn't fooled by what drew her interest to Anand. If he poured out half his coffee and filled it with cream and added tablespoons of sugar until he was having a little coffee with his sugar and cream, her interest wouldn't have dwindled. Reluctantly pulling her eyes from him, she reached over the counter and nudged me playfully.

"What question from Cameron brings you to my little hub?"

"What makes you think I'm here on her behalf?" I asked.

Anand's migration to a seat in the corner tugged at Emoni's attention before it moved to the door that separated the coffee shop from the bookstore. Cameron had passed by, giving us a tight, overly wide smile and an odd finger wave.

"I feel like I'm Batman and she's devising a plan to destroy me and Gotham City," Emoni noted, waving at Cameron, who attempted to busy herself with the display, failing miserably at discreetly watching us.

"Reese cancelled this Thursday and you know how important Wine-Down Thursdays are to her."

"And it's great for business, too."

"That too," I admitted "She wants to know if you could fill in for him."

"Of course I'll do it. Maybe Gus will join me."

"Maybe? You wouldn't completely get the invitation out before he agreed. And you can stop with the eyerolls. I'm not wrong." I wasn't, despite Emoni wanting me to be. He loved performing as much as Emoni did, and the extra time with her would be a bonus for him.

To put Cameron out of her misery and ease the tight Joker smile, I nodded. She noticeably relaxed. We knew how important the store was to her; over the years it had its struggles and there was a period when it was at risk of closing down. With the addition of the coffee shop, events, and introduction of the wine bar, she'd saved the business. I chatted with Emoni a while longer, hoping Reginald would reply to the text I'd sent him earlier, so I could stop by his office before returning to work. He hadn't responded.

Suspecting that he might have missed the message, I went by his office. The door was closed and I heard voices, which was probably why I hadn't heard from him.

When I returned to the store, Anand was seated in the corner that Peter usually claimed. It earned him a glare from Peter when he arrived. Anand dismissed Peter's overtly dirty look and passive-aggressive attempts to crowd him out as they shared the table. Peter covered the table with too many books and slouched in his chair, swallowing up the space underneath the table with his long legs. I passed the table several times, finding Peter making attempts to "history" Anand away. They were having spirited debates, and Anand's detailed knowledge made his contributions sound like first-hand accounts. It was a slow day and I found entertainment in the simplicity of Peter's pettiness. It was rather humanizing. He was territorial, irrational, and trivial—like us average joes. Peter finally gave up, shooting Anand a searing look before he found another spot at the back of the store.

"I feel like I should bring you a cookie or something. Give you the title of Dethroner of the King of the Round Table," I said.

Anand was kind enough to reward my bad joke with a halfhearted smile. After Anand relinquished his claim on the table, I spent the remainder of my day playing my version of Where's Waldo with him.

Reginald had free time at three thirty. I'd given up on keeping up with Anand's whereabouts, and when he allowed himself to be discovered, I told him about the meeting, ignoring his frown of disapproval.

Although pessimistic that Reginald and his coven could help, I found some comfort in having a companion in this adventure we were unwillingly thrust into. I was pleased to be able to speak with him, even if for no other reason than to vent. *How much do I tell him? Everything? Do I go full-throttle? Will he even believe me?* I was living it yet several times I found myself waiting to wake from this magical realism.

Reginald's hollow look of confusion surprised and unsettled me when I suggested he speak to his coven about what had happened with the book.

"I told you about my coven?" His brows inched together in disbelief. Leaning back in his chair, he looked even more perplexed as I recounted his visit to my apartment after the book debacle.

Concern shrouded his face at my agitation as I repeated the scenario over and over. If he'd had a panic button to press to have me escorted out, he definitely would have used it. It wasn't agitation, it was desolation as panic rose in me. How could he not remember?

"Look at your phone. You have pictures, and I sent you a video." I strained to keep my voice level but failed. Raw panic was in the driver's seat. Standing, I leaned into him. Based on him going wide-eyed and rearing back, I must have looked feral. The semblance of calm and control I manufactured as I sat down was hard earned.

"Will you please look?" I asked softly.

"Okay." His smile pensive and wary, he fumbled to get his phone from the corner of the desk while keeping a cautious eye on me. Once in his hand, he split his attention between me and the screen as he scrolled. After several minutes, it was apparent he was reluctant to tell me what I already knew. There weren't any pictures. No video. I knew showing him the markings on my finger wouldn't have proven anything other than I now had a tattoo to match my ring. But I had to try.

"Remember the ring? Look at it now."

He looked at it and then at me with concerned eyes. "I told you before, I love it. I still can't believe you found it in the alley. It's so detailed, eclectic. Definitely handmade."

The alley. Where Dominic told me he could manipulate memories. Was this Dominic's handiwork or the vampire's? Reginald was seeing the ring as it had been and not with the magic drained from it.

I rubbed my hands over my face and forced a smile when I removed them. "Not enough sleep," I lied.

"I get it. When I don't get enough sleep, I'm in a fugue state. Reality and dreams mesh together. Sleep's important for a reason." His smile was grim and his voice taut and reticent. "I once had an argument with my sister over something that happened in a dream. It felt real. Make sure you get some sleep tonight, okay?"

I nodded, fighting without success to ward off the

abysmal feeling. For ten minutes we continued with our BS-fest, my trying to deescalate the situation and Reginald continuing to search for remnants of sane Luna. After we made our way through the tension-heavy conversation, there was a vestige of a smile fanning over his lips. Forced and fake, but considering the circumstances, it was all I was going to get.

My feet felt heavy walking toward the door and I glanced back at Reginald's worried expression, trying to figure out how to make him remember. I gave him a little wave of reassurance.

"I'm going home to crash. I'll be better on Thursday. Emoni is singing at the Wine-Down."

The glint of excitement in his eyes was the lifeline I didn't realize he needed. It was a brief moment of normality.

Who had wiped his memory? Dominic, the Conventicle, someone else? When Kane snatched me off the street, how long had they been watching me, and had I done something to implicate Reginald? I squashed any thoughts of telling Emoni; I couldn't get her involved.

I knew I wouldn't have to look for Anand. The moment I stepped out of the store, he found me. Emerging from nonexistent shadows again. He studied me for a long moment. If I looked as bleak as I felt, it had to be concerning to see. This was a game of survival and it appeared I was alone in it.

"Ready?"

Did it matter if I wasn't? An unenthusiastic nod was all I could offer.

Traveling with Anand was different than with Dominic, and although it only took a few seconds, I spent that time wondering if I'd spiral into an unknown destination, a place between my world and the Underworld. Anand barely touched me. Once we were standing in front of the darkened estate that housed the Perils, he snatched his hands away from me as if he'd touched a flame. With Dominic, I knew we'd end up in the same place; with Anand, I wasn't so sure.

In front of the gloomy house, devoid of the vitality of greenery and sunlight, I still found some comfort in knowing exactly where I was.

At our approach the doors opened, but we weren't greeted with a fanfare of guards. The moment we breached the entrance, Anand headed in another direction. Initially I stood waiting, expecting Dominic to greet me. After several minutes, I realized he wasn't coming. The large home was elegant and luxe but impersonal, making me feel even more alone since I no longer had Reginald in on it. Each step I made toward the spellbook room made tamping down my irritation harder. I was more determined than ever to repair the damage and sprint back to my nice, normal, magicless life.

No amount of encouragement or hype could prepare me for the feel of the spellbook room. I inhaled the comforting smell of leather, old paper, sandalwood, and hints of lavender that lingered in the air of the main library before stepping into the spellbook room. The feel and smell of it served its purpose as a staunch reminder of the dark and portentous world—and my new role in it.

As I dropped my bag on a chair, I took in the new changes: shorter bookcases, a juniper-scented candle on a warmer, a clock on the wall, and a bowl of fruit, individually packaged nuts, and chips in a bowl. The juniper couldn't overshadow the scent of potent magic that thickened the air. Or the nudge of reproach it inflicted on me. I was an interloper. Definitely someone who didn't belong, and the room made sure to remind me of that. The markings on my finger didn't seem to be enough grounds for entry. Despite that, I removed the ring.

Taking a seat, I pulled out the notepad and looked at the notes I'd scribbled last night once I realized insomnia had won. Seven spells from the markings needed to be disengaged. Dominic hadn't given me specifics, but I assumed they were spells that stopped shifters shifting, prevented vampires zoning, nullified magic abilities, inhibited preternatural strength, and bound prisoners to the cell. Two spells were missing; I wasn't sure what they were needed for. Examining the markings on my finger again, I wondered if the other two were overlapping spells. Or I might not know what the hell I was doing, which was likely the most accurate possibility. I was still examining the markings when Dominic walked in.

"I would consider it a work of beauty if I didn't know its purpose," he said.

I wouldn't go that far. It was unique and definitely a conversation starter, but not a work of beauty. Obviously, my views were biased.

Dominic looked at the notepad on the table with curiosity. My scribblings of words were in languages I wasn't familiar with, and I had spread books out on the table.

"I got started," I told him, keeping my eyes on my work. If I'd looked at him, it would reignite my anger that he might be the person who tampered with Reginald's memories. That anger would just distract me. *Stay focused and don't deviate.*

"As I expected you would," he provided in a crisp voice. Feeling the weight of his eyes on me, I flicked a look at him and returned to sorting the spells from the book I was working on. His baleful indomitable presence added a heaviness to the room that poked at my flight response. Working and shooting him furtive glances made productive work impossible. Even when he'd moved to the other side of the table, his presence couldn't be ignored.

"Luna." Command rasped in his voice.

I ignored him. He called me again; it demanded compliance. Something I wouldn't give. The stony silence continued, until I finally succumbed to it. My eyes locked with his.

"What the fuck did you do to Reginald!"

I was the only one surprised by my outburst. We watched each other with mutual skepticism.

"It needed to be done," he said, his tone cool and his expression flat.

Did it? It wasn't for Reginald's safety; it was for theirs. "Did you compel him to forget, like vampires, or manipulate his memories?"

He nodded. "I can't compel people, only vampires can. Manipulating memories is close."

"Can you do it from just a look, like the vampires?"

His head barely moved into the nod but his eyes showed knowledge. I was sure Anand had told him about my run-in with Kane.

"Anand said I should gouge a vampire's eyes out if they try to get me to look them in the eyes. What should I do to you?"

Moistening his lips, he fixed me with a roguish smile. "What would you like to do to me, Luna?" There was nothing innocent about his insinuating words or the look he gave me.

Heat ran up my neck and over my cheeks. I dropped my head to look at my book and hopefully hide my flush. If the warmth radiating on my face was any indicator, I wouldn't be able to hide the strawberry coloring.

His eyes were heavy and inquiring, making it difficult to return to the work in front of me. *Redirect. Discover what is necessary to survive in this world. I got this.* I repeated it over and over with no success because I was drowning and there wasn't anyone to throw me a lifeline.

"What do you think is happening?" Dominic's grave voice splintered the silence.

I didn't have an answer.

"Supernaturals have been living among humans for as long as humans have existed. But they do so with the agreement to stay hidden. It works to the benefit of all involved, but know that not everyone is happy about it. There are supernaturals who want to awaken the world to all that exists. They want to be known, to eventually have power. There aren't many and they are so inconsequential, they *were* regarded as just a fringe group. An insipid cult."

"The markings on the book," I guessed.

He nodded. "That's their mark. Fifty years ago, some supernaturals wanted the Awakening. Everything that is hidden to be brought into plain sight. The Conventicle is the ruling body of the supernaturals and represents the supernatural community. Staying hidden was decided upon. What is best? The Conventicle and I work together to make it so. You met the representatives, but the Conventicle comprises one hundred and twenty members. Awakeners are dissenters, believers of the Awakening. In the past they were a simple nuisance and were managed rather easily. Once in a while, there's a revival when new, ambitious members join."

Annoyance showed on his face. "The Conventicle is efficient and ruthless about maintaining their anonymity and dealing with the Awakeners. I assure you, manipulating Reginald's and his coven's memories was the most humane thing. It wasn't what the Conventicle wanted for them... for you. They wanted a permanent solution for all involved." He'd halted at the word 'coven.' Accustomed to dealing with actual witches and covens, it had to seem blasphemous putting Reginald and his friends in the same category.

Swallowing, I got a handle on my agitation. Why were the options they chose permanent? Did death always have to be the answer?

"I suspect the Dark Caster is part of the Awakening movement or will eventually become part of it. There's no doubt that the supernaturals you released will join as well. They were reckless for the sheer enjoyment of it, but it was also their unsubtle way of being discovered. If their existence becomes known, it will open up speculation that there are more out there. Although most supernaturals follow the way of the Conventicle, in any group there are those who are opportunistic or complicit. It's the opportunists that concern me. They will latch on to whichever side they believe will be the victor. If the Awakeners are a viable movement, then this will be a problem. I'm not just trying to retrieve the prisoners and discover the Caster; I'm preventing a war."

This wasn't about altruism. If the supernaturals were discovered, he would be, too. There were benefits to anonymity.

"So, there's an agreement between you and the Conventicle. That's why you warned them about the prisoners, right?"

He didn't respond. I looked up to find him scrutinizing me with suspicion.

There was honor among thieves, killers, or whatever the hell type of reprobates they were. It meant he honored agreements. Whatever oath bound him to the Conventicle, I needed that extended to my friends and family. Protect them the way he protected the Conventicle, despite them clearly loathing each other.

"We have a binding agreement." Suspicion was heavy in his tone. "What is it you're hinting at, Little Luna?" His full lips tightened into a rueful line. A stony expression and fierce intensity replaced his previously amiable demeanor. He relaxed back in the chair, his fingers clasped behind his head, causing his slim-cut hunter-green shirt to conform to the muscles of his chest and stomach. The folded sleeves revealed the taut muscles of his tattooed forearms. The muscles bulged and relaxed with the most minor movement.

"I want you to agree that my friends and family will be protected."

"Only Reginald and his coven were involved, correct?"

I nodded, happy that I hadn't disclosed everything to Emoni. He was looking past me at the new bookcases with a look of contemplation.

"He won't agree," Helena provided as she entered the room. She leaned down, wrapped her arms around his neck in a hug. Pressing her face against his, she gave me a full view of her cleavage in her slinky low-cut maxi dress. As it had before, her attire made everyone, including Dominic, look underdressed. Her presence unsettled the room. A shift that I couldn't quite put my finger on. It was as if her presence caused the room to recoil.

Even if she wished to, I doubted she could go unnoticed. I considered Anand's beauty quiet, whereas hers was flamboyant, intrusive. From the smoldering dark liner that highlighted her intense amber eyes, the bone structure that was carved to striking precision, the supple lips that formed a resting pout, to her wardrobe, everything demanded attention and required appreciation. I wasn't in the mood for either.

"Eventually you will become collateral damage," she cooed. Her tongue made a ticking sound like a clock counting down.

I held her gaze, refusing to let her rattle me. She peddled in fear and threats, and I wouldn't give her that. Her taunting smile widened as she stood, keeping an attentive hand on Dominic's shoulder.

"Perhaps it will be Dominic or someone in the Conventicle. Fear breeds betrayal. I wonder which one will sacrifice their life to take yours?" She looked delighted at the prospect.

The casualness of her words and her aloofness ignited a terror in me. But instead of prompting me to retreat, it triggered me to fend it off.

"Just what my day needed, commentary from Underworld Barbie complete with tacky Seductress of the Night wardrobe."

Dominic fought against a smile.

Her sharp gaze was fixed on me as she spoke to Dominic. "You find her entertaining. That surely can't be the reason she's still alive. Is it, brother?"

"Helena," he warned. "You are not part of this."

"But I will be affected. I have just as much say in this as you do."

"Perhaps, but you can't get involved. Nor will you. This will serve as your last reminder."

"It is part of your doing that I can't be involved," she pushed out through clenched teeth.

"I think you have yourself to blame for that. You were never able to abide by any established rules or basic tenets of diplomacy," he chastised.

"Penalized for making those remorseful of their bad deeds." She pulled her eyes from me and looked at him. With a dramatic flick of her hand, she waved his comment away as inconsequential. "How am I the villain in this story?" Her lips pushed out into a moue. "I've honed my skills whereas yours have become dull from disuse."

Helena trapped me in her gaze, granite hard and hinting at unspeakable violence. "Disuse doesn't make you strong, brother. It makes you vulnerable."

Moving with the fluidity of water and the speed of striking lightning, she was behind me with a hand wrapped around my throat. Not in the gentle way she had before, as if lulling me into complacency about my death. This time it was an iron grip. Her face sidled up near mine, her breath warm against my skin.

"Dominic, I understand your desire to play the long game and to find the culprit responsible for the prisoners' release. But the longer the prisoners are gone, the more havoc they will wreak. You believe diplomacy is the answer, but I can assure you the right choice is violence. Make it known that they cannot ignore us without consequences. Those who want the Awakening—we'll find them. The two of us. Eliminate people even tangentially involved. Destroy the movement in a mighty show of violence. If anyone dares revive it, we destroy it in its infancy. Every. Time. We'll make them fear the very word. Silence it and the movement." The anticipation of violence put a musical note of excitement in her voice.

"Helena," he cautioned in a low rumble. My breath caught as I watched his expression go flat. I wasn't sure if this was a battle of wills or wit. Was it a zero-sum game?

"Not just a long game," I said in a steady, even voice in an attempt to deescalate her anger. Her hold on my throat tightened and I eked my words out in a low whisper. "Violence won't do you any good. If you don't find the Caster, this will happen again. Violence can't be the answer every time it happens."

"Dominic," she coaxed. "One act, and the prisoners will be returned. We can make better use of our time by finding this Caster. And then *we* will make them pay for forcing you to coddle this *human*." Her voice hardened. "You are showing weakness now. Weakness that will not serve you well in the future."

A medley of anger, frustration, and disgust replaced my calm. The callousness and arrogance of this woman to lament my life as being inconsequential while she attempted to convince him to kill me. The sheer disdain in her voice as she said the word "human." Less than bugs, squashed under her feet at a whim. I hated the insufferable bitch.

My fist smashed into her nose.

She gasped, releasing me and stumbling back, covering her nose. Grabbing the thick magic book off the table, I smacked it across the left side of her face, then the right. Before she could recover, I drove it into her neck, pushing her back against the wall, where I pinned her. The pressure of the book against her throat was enough to make breathing difficult.

"This is the second fucking time you've threatened my life," I ground out through clenched teeth. "This will be the last."

Fire blazed in her amber eyes as she drew back her lips, baring her teeth like an animal prepared to fight to the death.

"Human girl," she drawled in a low, oxygen-restricted husky voice. "Do you believe you are a match for me?" Pain shot into my stomach at her touch. The sharp retaliation of magic sent me flying across the room and slamming into the bookcase. I slumped against it as books rained down. Tears sprang to my eyes from the piercing pain. I fought them back, refusing to give her the satisfaction of me crying. I hoisted myself upright. She straightened. Golden light skated around her fingers.

Dominic's flash of movement placed him directly in front of Helena, shielding me from her. He reached for her hand and his low voice carried throughout the room as he extinguished her magic.

"Helena." The razor edge of his voice snapped her eyes from me to him. "You started it and are quite deserving of her retaliation."

"Yes, I started it and I have every intention of finishing it, Dominic." No more cloying affection in the way she addressed him. It held the sharpness of a machete. Anger pulsed in every syllable. "Don't let her be an issue between us."

"It is not one because I have spoken." His tone was stern, his command absolute.

A slow, wintry smile curved her lips. "It seems that you believe your control as the guardian of the Perils extends to me. Brother, you are mistaken."

He shook his head. "I believe no such thing, Helena. I

know you well. Any attempt to control you is a foolish endeavor. I'm no fool nor do I waste my time with pointless tasks."

That was a troubling thought. Not even he could stop her? He promised my safety but how effective would he be against his sister?

"I want her unharmed." There was that unspoken "for now" that laced his words. "My objectives are no concern of yours. Stay out of this. Don't force my hand and make you honor my request." The threat lingered in the air.

Any sibling congeniality had been stripped away. Before me were just two magically powerful people grappling for dominance. I eased away from them, placing myself in a position where I could keep a careful eye on them both.

Helena's cold smile turned warm and honey sweet. "I do hate when we fight." She pressed her palm to Dominic's face before turning for the door. Dagger-sharp claws formed on her fingers and before I could shriek out a warning, they slashed across his face. Other than the quick jerk of his head, there was no other reaction. If it hurt, he did a hell of a job hiding it.

"I'm sure you do as well," she said tenderly before leaving the room.

If she'd do that to her brother, I had no intention of finding out what she'd do to me.

Rushing over to the table, I plopped my bag on it and started loading it, stuffing in as many of the books we hadn't gone through that would fit.

"Take me home," I demanded. "I'll do the research there." Fueled strictly by blinding anger, fear, and frustration, I didn't wait for a response before heading for the door. If he didn't follow, screw him. I'd track down Anand and ask him —plead, if necessary—to take me home.

I was met with a force so strong it rebounded me back several feet. I rushed to the door again, pushing into it with greater force, but it returned the favor, sending me sprawling to the floor.

"The books cannot leave this room," Dominic said, his tone indifferent.

I whipped around to face him. "Find a way to make it so," I demanded. "Because I can't stay here."

He sighed. "You aren't at any risk of harm."

"Really!" I stood and jabbed my finger at his clawed face. The pads of his fingers ran lightly over the gashes, closing them and removing the crimson lines of blood. When the healing was complete, there was no sign that his sister had mauled him. How many times had he healed injuries inflicted by her?

I sagged against the wall. No matter how many slow, measured breaths I took, I couldn't get a handle on the panic. Nailah easing into the room, breaking some of the tension, was the closest thing I was going to get to calm. At the sight of me, her violet eyes turned a gentle earthy brown that complemented her appearance. Watching someone's eyes change in a matter of seconds paled in comparison to the unsettling things I'd already encountered.

Acknowledging my presence with a genial smile, she immediately went to Dominic and whispered something to him. He blew out an exasperated breath and quickly left the room. Her presence was enough to redirect me to get a handle on the things I could control. Research. That was the one thing I definitely could do.

11

Find the spells, leave this world. That sentence played as a continuous loop in my head as I returned to the table and removed the books from my bag. Without Dominic to translate, I simply made notes for him and continued scrolling through the books to find the spells. My markings' response to the spells hadn't diminished, but it was still alarming.

"Helena's bruised ego often requires a lot of management," Nailah volunteered, taking a seat at the opposite end of the table near the door. Considering the heaviness of her voice, she didn't agree with the indulgence.

"What about her temper, how is that managed?"

Nailah huffed a sigh. "That, too, requires a great deal of patience and delicacy. Her propensity for violent overreactions has caused a great number of problems. Helena's last one nearly led to a war. Had the witches found a way to get to her here in the Underworld, it would have been a battle that I'm not sure Dominic would have been able to win. Despite Dominic's and Helena's considerable power, they're no match for a coven of Strata Three witches. She's made enemies of so many covens. They tend to only protect their own, but they would have formed an alliance to punish Helena. She causes unlikely people to unite."

Her fingers idly made designs along the table as she spoke. It felt like she was venting and I remained quiet, hoping to glean more information. "That's Helena. Her response to anyone who displeases her is to go for the jugular, literally."

"Strata Three?"

"Those are the strongest. Able to create spells, perform strong magic: manipulate time, telekinesis, advanced spell casting, magic mimicry by stealing another practitioner's magic, which is illegal. Necromancy—controlling the dead—and some minor shifting abilities.

"Strata Three witches aren't limited to simple magic, which makes them dangerous and unpredictable. Strata Two witches' magic is more limited: Elementals usually fall into this category, although they can do wards, basic spell casting, and illusions. Their talents lie in controlling elements. The same with techno-witches. Although their skills are highly sought after, they are still considered a Two. Except for Celeste, Mors have the limited magical ability of taking a life with a single invocation and touch, but they're classified as Strata Three. They consider themselves beyond reproach or rule," she added.

That may be why they were given a death sentence rather than imprisonment.

"Witches are watched carefully because they are so powerful and there's always the risk of abuse," Nailah went on. "Madeline is a Strata Three, as are most of her family. Their line is the strongest and most talented. Helena learned that firsthand, but despite the consequences, she still hasn't learned restraint."

I held my breath, hoping she'd continue. It yielded great information for me.

But maybe it wasn't about getting this information off her

chest. Perhaps it was driven by compassion. There was undeniable warmth and empathy in her eyes. I found comfort in her since that was the only place it could be had.

Leaning forward in anticipation, I realized how desperate I was for the peace that knowledge brought. She was providing me with information that would unravel some of the complexity of a world I didn't belong in. Tools for survival that I desperately needed. And what seemed to be basic humanity, in a place where it was missing. For all I knew, Nailah could be as cold and vengeful as the others. She could be offering me a deception, but I was willing to accept it because I was thirsty for it.

Instead of continuing, she leaned forward, picked up one of the books, and started perusing it.

Dammit. No. I need more.

"Consequences?" I urged.

She frowned. I couldn't determine if it was the return of our discussion about Helena or the consequences she suffered.

"Most supernaturals can be rather pedantic when it comes to their status as elite magical practitioners. Alpha shifters have an obnoxious sense of entitlement. Elder vampires feel worthy of an excessive amount of veneration—I guess for just existing for a long time." She shrugged. "And Strata Three witches feel deserving of reverence. From other witches, they receive it. But since shifters are immune to their magic, the witches get very little reverence from them unless they need the witches for a task. Strata Ones and Twos can meet their basic needs for wards, protection spells, and illusions. Vampires are strong and fast. Before the witches could perform any acts of magic against them, the vampires could kill them. They all believe themselves to be greater than they actually are." She punctuated her speech with a heavy sigh.

"Navigating the rules and tacit agreements requires deli-

cacy, diplomacy, and, when necessary, assertive coercion."
Her voice had lost some of its frustration. She delivered the
information in such a dispassionate manner it was as though
she was telling a story she'd repeated so many times that
she'd lost the desire to keep the listener interested.

Assertive coercion seemed like a pleasant way of saying
intimidation or brutalizing into compliance. I kept that
theory to myself.

Nailah inhaled a breath as if it offered some comfort.
There was nothing comforting about the stifling air. But she
exuded a tranquility that made things seem less overwhelming. Was that part of her magic? Lulling me into somnolence?
Her warm, earthy eyes were in contrast to Dominic's, which
were sharp with intensity and boundless in depth.

"No one is without their weakness. Something Helena
forgets often." She shrugged and frowned. "When your father
is Lord of the Underworld, it is easy to lose perspective.
Helena was beyond loss of perspective. She believed she
could do whatever she desired with impunity. History had
given her that false notion." The look that passed over
Nailah's face reminded me of the disapproval Dominic
showed when discussing Helena's indulgences.

It shouldn't have been shocking to me, but it was. The
signs were there: I was sitting in the spellbook room in the
Underworld. On my first arrival in the Underworld,
Dominic was greeted by guards and he displayed what I
considered hauteur born from sheer arrogance, displaying
the pride of a prince.

My life had irreparably changed. Not by a stretch could it
be considered boring any longer. Not only had I punched
both the Prince and Princess of the Underworld, I'd made a
deal with the Prince.

"There was a power struggle over who'd be responsible
for policing the supernatural world. The witches were the
most adamant about dealing with rule breakers." Nailah's

hand swept across the room in a dismissive wave. "Perhaps they were right. But, because of their biases, they are often more lenient than they should be. Powerful people require powerful punishment."

"They get it here."

"I've seen worse confinements where you live. The best way to punish the powerful is to render them powerless for the rest of their lives. That is their personal hell."

I questioned if she was intentionally veering the topic from Helena.

"What does this have to do with Helena?" This was information I desperately needed. Maybe it could help me deal with her. Best her in some way.

"Ah, yes. Initially, both Helena and Dominic guarded the Perils. As I said before, Helena handled the mildest of slights with extreme penalties, even where she had no jurisdiction. She involved herself in affairs that didn't require her intervention or judgment. Crimes against other supernaturals were handled by the denizens involved. Helena and Dominic handled supernaturals who violated crimes against humanity. That's what this is about. They shared a common goal, to stop the worst in the supernatural world and to ensure they remain hidden from humans."

"Their father is Lord of the Underworld and they are the Prince and Princess—aren't they the worst of your kind?"

Nailah's lips pulled into a tightly puckered moue of disapproval. How was I wrong for coming to that conclusion? I was sure the requisite for ruling the Underworld wasn't being a sweet cuddle bear. Helena and Dominic were born to this, but neither one seemed like victims of circumstance. I couldn't forget how the members of the Conventicle looked at Dominic. Disdain, fear, and abhorrence. No esteem or veneration. Whatever existed between them was a reluctant alliance.

"Cruelty must be handled with cruelty. Dominic is

capable of using fear as a tool of compliance." Nailah gave me a bitter smile. "It is necessary. Diplomacy and patience are required as well. Dominic has mastered them, Helena hasn't. It's doubtful she can. Since Helena's whims had been indulged for so long, it was difficult to rein her in. She killed Madeline's grandmother for not giving her the Trapsen—an amulet that allowed passage into the Underworld. Dominic had acquired and destroyed all but that one. If he'd handled that situation, I have no doubt he would have managed it through bargaining, not brutality. Of the three, Dominic is more diplomatic."

She was ascribing diplomacy in the same manner a person tries to determine who's less dangerous: a black mamba, a lion, or a grizzly bear.

"Helena doesn't... Well." She sighed and gave me a weak smile. "She doesn't believe in negotiation and has always responded to denials and rejections poorly. As a connoisseur of strife, violence, and havoc, she finds new and inventive ways to test her brother's patience, which has been stretched to the point of breaking. I suspect it won't hold for long."

A wave of fear washed over me. Her retaliation could have been worse if Dominic hadn't intervened. What would she have done to me?

Nailah relaxed as she exhaled deeply. "The coven's retaliation was swift and severe." A deep frown hardened her features. "I believe it was *too* swift, as if they had been waiting for a moment worthy of such retaliation. They performed a curse that restricted her magic and they refused to show Dominic or even their father how to reverse it.

"With the help of other witches, it took ten years for Dominic to discover a way to return her magic. But the curse was never completely removed. They found a workaround. And that help came with a compromise. Punishment of the supernaturals was no longer solely the domain of the Underworld. The Perils would handle only the worst of their kind.

Pursuing violators has to be approved by the Conventicle. Although Dominic and Helena were the sole proprietors of regulating and determining sentencing, it is now up to the Conventicle. The problem is, that is still a good faith courtesy that Dominic extends."

"Why is that?"

"Because he discovered another way to undo the curse that restricts his sister's magic. And a counterspell to keep witches' magic from ever affecting him. He can't be cursed, nor can they use any of their magic against him."

"Do they know that?"

She shook her head and smiled, bringing a finger to her lips. I mimed using a key to lock away the secret. It was hard to blindly trust anyone in this world, although something about Nailah seemed earnest and kind. But the bar was set pretty low. She hadn't abducted me, tried to kill me, or compelled me into harming myself. Things had devolved so badly for me that basic common decency earned my trust.

"You're able to see things that happened and the future, correct?" I asked reluctantly after several moments of internal debate.

She chuckled. "No. As with all magic, it has limits. I saw you, the markings. But I had no idea who you were. We had to find you. Some futures are shown to me, but like all things, it is susceptible to the butterfly effect."

"Am I going to survive this?" I rushed out before I lost the courage to ask.

She responded with a weak smile.

"Please tell me."

"There's merit and comfort in having the future be a mystery."

"There has to be some merit and comfort in knowing as well."

She nodded and closed her eyes, then opened them to reveal her peculiar illuminated violet eyes, which bored into me with such severity it felt like she was pulling the details of my life from me and taking part of me with it. Her body shuddered slightly and then she slumped against the chair. Minutes burned away without her speaking.

"Will you tell me how you got involved?" she asked.

It wasn't that I didn't want to retell the story, but I was sure Dominic had already discussed it with her. This was a distraction tactic. I gave her the unabridged version since Reginald's involvement was already known.

Her lips pressed into a tight straight line. "I couldn't see any of that," she admitted, shifting her gaze to my marked finger. "You were unwittingly pulled in—a victim of circumstances."

"And my curiosity," I provided with a wry smile. How different things would have been if I had left the ring or the book. Or both.

The sympathy on her face made me question if I could rely on anything she told me regarding her prophecy. "It's the burden of my magic. We can't lie about our visions. Even if I wanted to, it's not possible."

I really needed to work on keeping my thoughts from showing on my face.

Her adherence to truth was the reason she was delaying answering me.

Damn. I'm going to die.

12

No, death would not be the end of this journey. I refused to accept that fate. But Nailah wasn't going to give me a definite answer and seemed content with us remaining silent. I'd change whatever was necessary to give myself a new fate. I returned to my task of going through the books with a renewed determination and had finished all but three books by the time Dominic quietly returned.

Sliding into the chair next to me, he had a hard etch to his features. The deep brood in his eyes made holding his gaze much harder, and I was about to return to the books when I felt Nailah's eyes boring into me. Even without seeing her do it, I would have known. The weight of it flowed over me like I was standing under a waterfall. It couldn't be ignored. Her lips curved into a reassuring smile, uncoiling the tension in my chest at her evading my question.

"I don't see your death," she announced, standing. She and Dominic exchanged meaningful looks.

Even in my relief, I fixated on the ambiguity of her divination. She didn't see my death today? Tomorrow? Seven days from now? What was the timeframe of this sight?

She gave Dominic's arm a squeeze and exited before I could question her further. How did Dominic change my future?

"How far are you?" he asked.

"Just three more books."

With quiet determination, he reviewed the spells I'd highlighted and transferred them to the notebook he'd used the other day. After he finished, he hastily scribbled spells on a separate page.

Ignoring me, he continued to work with the strained silence he exhibited earlier. He was focused, on a mission. An hour later he walked to the corner of the room, retrieved a cylindrical container, and opened it, spreading out an aged piece of vellum on the table.

"This will contain the spell here and hopefully direct me to its caster," he told me.

Dominic had requested Nailah's return after the second failed spell. Her presence did nothing to ease his tension or improve our success. By the fifteenth spell, Dominic was pushing the invocations out through clenched teeth.

"I'm about to do this spell," he told her, pointing to a new spell.

"Like the other one, I don't see anything." She made another attempt to see the future success of the spell, then shook her head.

He nodded.

"I think there's a protection spell entwined in the markings," she informed him.

"I think so, too."

The next spell he invoked caused lines to illuminate in a cycle of pale colors that eventually changed to bright orange. My finger felt like it was in a vice. I sucked in a ragged breath, convinced this was the one.

"Keep going," I said in a strained voice when he hesitated. He continued. I'd never experienced acid being thrown on me, but I was sure it felt similar to this. Doubled over, I balled the other hand into a fist, waiting for the pain to subside.

It didn't, but the spell fizzled like the others and I remained marked.

My breathing was rapid and my finger stung. I cradled my hand against my chest, the slightest movement sending sharp pain as if there was a strain in the joint or a break in the bone.

Dominic's eyes lost some their intensity as he searched my face. His touch was featherlight as he took my hand into his. Coolness wrapped around my hand, and the pain lifted and receded. Tranquility overtook me, relaxing me to the point I could have slipped easily into sleep. The room no longer felt sentient. It felt comforting, airy, and cloudlike. I loved this easiness. The tension that had plagued me had uncoiled.

"You're okay?" he inquired in a hushed voice. He'd moved closer and I resisted the urge to rest my forehead against his.

I nodded.

"Want to continue?"

Why not? The pain before wasn't *that* bad. Before I could agree, Nailah intervened.

"No, that's enough for today."

I heard her but kept my eyes trained on Dominic.

"Luna, look at me," Nailah requested.

I dragged my eyes from Dominic's. The pain was gone. I was still feeling relaxed, although a smidge of tension resurfaced as the room's nudge of defiance returned.

"Good. I think you should take a break." Her eyes flicked to Dominic and narrowed.

"She agreed to continue," Dominic argued.

"Take a break." The assertion in her tone made Mr. Prince-y sit up taller. Definitely not used to being

130

commanded. He wore that aversion profoundly on his face and the defiance of it in his posture.

"It will be best for you both," she continued, warmth eking into her tone.

"She's fine." He pulled the tablet to him and marked off another spell.

"Dominic." She snapped at him with the sharpness of a mother chastising a child. It left me trying to figure out the dynamics between them. Nailah looked younger, late twenties, early thirties. Dominic appeared to be mid- to late thirties. Despite her initial sharpness, there was a hint of deference in the way she looked at him, a request for understanding and compliance in her expression. The disapproval lingered in her frown.

There were so many unspoken words and displays of emotions that I went from thinking there was a mentorship-type relationship, emissary, or maybe she was his moral compass and he was rejecting it. There was something else that passed between them. Compassion? Caring? Were they in a relationship? So many things passed between them, it became a rollercoaster ride that I was ready to get off.

The adage leads us to believe there's a thin line between love and hate. But there isn't. They are both intense emotions brought by feelings. Indifference is a thorn in the side. The killer of all things. The snuffing out of the fire in any relationship. Indifference was nowhere to be found in their exchange. If the dagger-sharp looks they exchanged were an indicator, hate seemed to be flickering to ignite. Or at least contempt.

"Her acquiescence was coaxed," Nailah pointed out. Coaxed by the man able to manipulate thoughts by looking at them. And moments ago, I was drowning in his eyes.

Faux relaxation and a feeling of peace. The room's abatement from poking and prodding me out of the door was an implanted thought, a manipulation.

Seething, I stood. "We're done for today and maybe... maybe forever because you're a venomous snake." I snatched my bag up and rushed toward the door. It smacked me back into the room. *You go to hell, too,* I thought, rummaging through my bag for whatever made the room prevent me from leaving. After finding a book, I tossed it, aiming for the table but secretly wishing I put too much power into the throw and that it would hit Dominic.

Aimless, I stood in the hallway without a strategy for the next step. My day off was meant to be in the Underworld, with the ambitious goal to unravel the spell and never return. With anger and Dominic's deception raining over me, I just wanted to leave. Dominic wouldn't take me and I didn't want to ask.

Should I search for Anand? Desperation had me calling his name, my voice carrying through the massive hallways.

Minutes passed with no response from him. I didn't really expect him to answer. I wasn't sure he was even in the house. Was the Underworld his home? If so, if he was easily hidden in our small store, could he be found in this ridiculously huge place?

"Yes?" Anand's mild voice spoke from behind me. Turning, I found him with one shoulder leaning against the wall, hands shoved in pockets. Disheveled hair, loose-fitting shirt, and jeans that hung low on his waist. He looked confused.

"Do you live here?" I asked.

He nodded once. A small confirmation, but the confusion remained.

"You heard me calling you?" If he had been close, I wanted to know where. Was one of the rooms on this floor his bedroom? I needed to know how to get to him.

"I'm here, aren't I?"

"Yes." A flush rose over my cheeks.

"I was in my room," he offered, putting me out of my misery.

"Is your room close?" I nudged my thumb toward the closed rooms I'd passed the other day.

"No, it's in the west wing. It took me a while to get here when I heard you call me." This place was huge enough to have wings and he heard me call him. He was on the other side of the house and: He. Heard. Me. Call. Him. Nope, not terrifying at all.

His curiosity had turned to irritation. "Luna, what do you want?"

"Take me home," I blurted.

Pushing up from the wall, he appeared reluctant as he looked past me.

"No," Dominic responded. "You'll honor your agreement to stay until tomorrow." His tone was strident and unyielding, as if he'd made a monumental concession by just letting me leave at all to resume my life.

My patience was frayed and my tolerance worn thin. Nailah eased out behind Dominic and looked between the two of us, taking in the tension. No matter how I tried to force my breathing to be calm and measured, it came out in short, sharp clips.

I held Dominic's hard-edged gaze as I marched up to him. "Don't you ever do that to me again! Do you understand?"

Dark amusement replaced his hauteur. His smirk reached his eyes as he relaxed into it. "Got it. When you are writhing in pain, I should let you be. Apparently, you enjoy it." Closing the few inches of space I had left between us, he leaned in. "That's a very interesting bit of information to know about you." He moistened his lips. "Perhaps there's more to you than just your petulance."

There was no denying the salacious innuendo. That wasn't the draw; it was the way his eyes roved over me, taking me in. Raw hunger. I piqued his interest and the darkness that dwelled in the prince.

"If you don't move, I'm going to knee you in your prince

133

peas," I told him through clenched teeth. The challenge in his smirk made me want to act on it, but knowing that guards were just a call away and Anand probably would not tolerate me doing it, I squashed the urge.

"You know damn well what I'm talking about. You ever manipulate my mind for any reason, I'm done with you and done with helping." I shoved his chest to give me more space. He didn't move. It was like pushing a concrete wall.

Nailah watched our exchange with censure, Anand with curiosity.

"Of course. Your rules. May they serve your life's interest well," he agreed. The devil was in the details and I had missed something; that was evident in Dominic's face. A tacit agreement had been made and I had missed some critical specifics of it.

Responding to Nailah softly calling his name, he turned away and strode toward her with the smooth easy confidence worthy of his position in the Underworld and his command among the supernaturals. The comfortable arrogance was likely the root of their resentment and her strained alliance with him as well.

Several minutes passed in a restless quiet. So much unspoken between them, leading me to wonder about their relationship again. It was strained and it showed.

His hand slipped to her waist and he pressed a gentle kiss to her cheek. Was that an apology? An appeal for understanding? The end of an impasse or the acceptance of it?

Anand's impassive face offered nothing.

Dominic whispered something in Nailah's ear. He was so close to her, and even if his back wasn't to me, I wouldn't be able to read his lips. Aware that Anand could probably hear it, I looked to him to see if it prompted a response. Nothing.

Nailah's look was more expressive than any words. Disappointment and frustration, but with whom or what remained a mystery.

"Anand, take me home, please," Nailah requested, stepping away from Dominic and giving me another sweeping look before turning away without another word. Had Dominic just sent his conscience away, or was it her decision to leave? I needed her tempered presence and didn't want her to leave.

Once she left, Dominic turned to me. "Let me show you to the room where you will be staying."

There was a moment of internal debate, of trying to forcibly hitch a ride back to my world. Then I heaved a sigh and followed him.

13

*C*alling it a room was an understatement. If it had a kitchen, it could easily be an apartment. Striking in blush and white, the room boasted gorgeous elaborate ceiling moldings and a king-size bed with a beautiful, tufted headboard and aged wood frame. It all seemed far too elegant for me to wear my oversized shirt that paid homage to *The Picture of Dorian Gray*—which had seemed whimsical and cheeky while packing—and shorts.

The silk-patterned chaise lounge and a chic flared-arm sofa did nothing to minimize the size of the room. One side of the room was a window, bathing the room in warm light from the garden and providing a spectacular overhead view of crimson and black flowers and a pergola with drawn curtains and delicate warm lighting giving it a comforting ambiance.

The bathroom was a relaxing oasis, the light a pale hue, making it seemed candlelit. In a world of perpetual dusk, these people seemed to appreciate light.

Aware of Dominic watching me, I gave the room just a sweeping look, underappreciating the shower stall with the stacked stone walls and overhead shower that gave the impression of bathing under a waterfall. The free-standing stone tub, I could imagine emerging from and wrapping my body in towels from the warmer, letting all the drama of the day spill from me. That was the point. This wasn't just a place to lay my head for the night, but a more subtle manipulation. Luring me into complacency.

Turning, I eyed him with suspicion. He seemed to bask in me being enamored by the room. It had its intended effect. Everything about this room was in diametric opposition to him and the situation. Soothing, warm lights, luxe and inviting furniture, the prospect of a warm shower, and even the picturesque view of the softly lit garden and pergola. Even the faint scent of lavender and chamomile made it difficult to stay enraged, and I desperately wanted to cling to my anger like a toddler gripping their favorite stuffed animal. It would serve me well not to underestimate or become too comfortable with the Prince of the Underworld.

But his words from earlier kept nagging at me. Had I made things worse, ensured that I wouldn't survive? I wanted Nailah to tell me my fate hadn't changed.

As people emerged from the shadows, placing food on the table in the pergola, I tightened my hold on my bag as if bolting out of the Underworld with it in hand was remotely an option.

"I thought it would be nice to have dinner in the garden."

Really, dinner surrounded by flowers that were a staunch reminder of where I was and who I was with? Well, okay. At least he wasn't trying to woo me.

"That would be nice."

My easy response drew his attention. His brows lifted and his depthless eyes bored even harder into me. Placing my bag on the dresser, I gave him an affable smile. *Make nice with the prince.*

"Things between us do not have to be contentious," I said.

"And yet you make it so."

You're making being nice really hard. Slow breaths. Don't knee the prince.

"I'm here to help."

He scoffed. "You're here because it's the pathway to your safety. Let's not pretend otherwise. It diminishes us both." His amber eyes danced with fire, and pulling my eyes from them seemed impossible. Was it my imagination or had the room grown hot? It felt sweltering.

"I want my prisoners returned, I want to stop a war, and I want to counter an insurrection. You play an important role in that. Make no mistake, you are a tool. It's up to you whether you will be one of use."

So that was his less than subtle way of pointing out my role in determining whether I lived or died. I started to point that out, when he swallowed the space between us and pressed his fingers to my lips. "Don't answer yet. Think about it, Luna, because your actions will determine your fate. It is in your hands."

The only thing I could think about was snapping at his finger like a rabid animal. *He silenced me. Who does that?* My face gave me away every time, and it hadn't failed this time. The prince removed his finger and turned away and headed for the door.

"Dinner should be ready in an hour. I trust you won't have any problem finding your way."

He wasn't wrong. I paid careful attention to everything, mapping out the house and observing the rooms that were kept closed and the ones where the doors were slightly ajar and anything I could glean from my vantage point. If me slowly following Dominic and stopping to get my bearings bothered him, he didn't voice it.

One hour to dinner. I took advantage of it and put on paper the Venn diagram that had formed in my head of Dominic's and his sister's magical abilities after seeing her grow claws. Any information I had to help make sense of this world and better navigate it was important. At this point, no information was too miniscule, especially discovering the magic of the Prince and Princess of the Underworld and how it intersected or aligned with other supernaturals.

Amoral and possibly sociopathic tendencies seemed to be common to all. Helena and Dominic appeared to possess forms of magic from all groups, so they were inclined toward those behaviors even more. I didn't care if my bachelor's in library science didn't qualify me to make a clinical diagnosis; this was about self-preservation. And as far as I was concerned, I was dealing with people who were even more dangerous because they shared qualities with witches, shifters, and vampires. Off to the side was Nailah, clearly an exception to the rule. Or was she?

There were holes in my information about Dominic and Helena because I didn't know the extent of their magical ability compared to other supernaturals. How much could they shift? Could they shift into any animal or were they limited to one animal or species? Did they have magical abilities like the Mors? What were their limitations in zoning or whatever they called their form of teleportation? Hopefully over dinner, I'd get some questions answered. The two most pressing things I needed from Dominic were a promise that my family and friends would be safe and the ability to navigate between this world and mine without an escort, if possible. I had a strong feeling it was possible, and he had led people to believe he'd destroyed all the Trapsens.

Dominic was waiting in the kitchen. Surprise flashed briefly on his face. He smiled, a genuine smile. That was as dangerous as his magic. Shifting my attention quickly, I looked past him at the garden, letting some of the potency ease away.

"I'm glad you decided to join me," he said. The disarming smile had settled nicely on his face and remained as he filled two glasses of wine from the bottle on the counter.

Would you have left me alone if I hadn't? Play nice. I simply smiled, took the proffered glass, and walked out of the house toward the garden. Dominic headed down a trail leading away from the food on the table on the patio. My stomach wasn't thrilled about that. Dinner wasn't just an information-seeking endeavor but also to mend my tattered relationship with Dominic, negotiate the safety of my family and friends, and lay the groundwork to enter the Underworld unaccompanied. And eat.

Him steering me through the garden pricked at the defiance in me, but I knew it was just me grappling for some vestige of control.

His steps slowed to leisurely movements. He was taking in the garden as if appreciating it for the first time. A faint floral fragrance scented the air. The slight breeze that seemed strangely oceanic had me looking around for a pond. There wasn't one. I gave a side-eye to the man who could create fire. Did he have the same ability with wind and water?

"Is there ever light here?" I asked, increasing my speed to walk next to him.

He shook his head, looked around the artificially lit area, and returned his attention to me, canting his head and giving me an evaluating look. "But that's not where your curiosity lies, is it, Luna? Ask your real questions." He stopped our stroll to continue looking at me. I had to work on keeping my thoughts from my face. It's the very reason I refuse to play poker. Bad hand, you will definitely know about it. Great hand and my beam is a sunburst.

The warm light from the lanterns made his eyes glint.

Taking a small sip from my glass, I sorted through the many questions I had.

"The hardest part is I don't know how far out of my depth I am. You have one faction that wants to reveal themselves to humans, another that will do anything to keep that from happening, and you're keeping some horrible people alive because they might be needed in case of a war. It seems like it would be easier to just let them be discovered and let humans get involved. It would take away this burden. Supernaturals would have to fall in line or deal with humans and our military," I said.

Being candid had its merits and left no room for ambiguity. I hoped he returned my candor and gave me straight answers.

He plucked a rose and handed it to me. I took it and inhaled its scent, using that time to recall what he'd done to me. I wouldn't be lured into putting my guard down.

"A vampire can create a family of hundreds in a week. At ten days old, a well-fed vampire can move faster than your bullets, can compel anyone to fight on their behalf, and can kill before the victim can fully grasp that they're about to die."

Dominic studied my face. I wish I knew what he saw because it seemed quite amusing. I inhaled his distinctive scent. His proximity crowded out the redolence of the flowers around us.

Taking my hand that held the rose, he brought it to his nose and inhaled. Moving closer, he devoured any space between us. I was standing in a black-and-crimson garden, with an ocean breeze coming from who the hell knew where, and Dominic was telling me even more horrific things about supernaturals while his face rested just inches from mine.

Focus. I stepped back and took another small sip, teetering between wanting to stay sober through the information and the need to be numb enough to handle it. When he resumed walking, I sidled up next to him.

"Shifters love rules and order, which is why they form packs and thrive best in a hierarchal system." His eyes continued to study my face. The smile still beveled his lips. "Don't think for a minute they haven't infiltrated your military, your police, your government. Although shifters are born and not created, there are more of them than you can imagine." With a sidelong look, he added, "If discord arises between shifters and humans, shifter loyalty will always be to shifters. You already know how hard it is to kill a shifter. Add their speed and strength and humans have no chance of survival against them."

We changed direction, heading toward the patio. The food beckoned me, but I continued to focus on him. I needed this information.

"And witches, what chance do you think humans have against them?" he queried, stopping in his tracks in anticipation of an answer that I couldn't give.

"They must have a weakness. Vampires can be staked and silver affects shifters. You're telling me that witches don't have an Achilles heel?"

"Ah, they do. Iridium metal prevents them from performing magic. It needs to be a cuff at least three inches wide. Anything smaller weakens them but doesn't inhibit their magic. There are some archaic spells that can obstruct it and weaken them. But good luck finding the spellbooks that contain those spells. Witches have spent much of their lives and resources wiping them from existence."

"But you have some."

I took his sly smirk as an admission. "Witches have no need to align with humans to protect themselves. Of the supernaturals, they are the most adaptive. Before technology, there was no such thing as techno-magic. Now there are witches who are experts at it. What controls your planes, missiles, bombs, and communication? Technology. Witches have the ability to control weather, time travel, and perform strong defensive magic. Seers are loosely aligned to witches, which gives them a prescient advantage. You are under the naïve illusion that humans would be a match against us. It wouldn't even be close. It wouldn't be humans against a few supernaturals, it would be against all of them. Alliances would form against the common enemy. Humans."

His hand pressed gently against my back, guiding me along another path, toward the patio. The curtains of the pergola were tied back, revealing a large round stone table with a marble top and a centerpiece of rose petals floating in a low bowl, illuminated by candles. A meal of glazed chicken, salad, roasted carrots, and an assortment of breads was laid out, along with two bottles of wine. I had no intention of drinking any more, but I'd probably get a chocolate high from gorging on the platter of decadent-looking chocolates. Forgoing the plate Dominic placed in front of me, I ate two chocolates and knew the platter was coming with me. I sipped on water between bites of food. Dominic took more sips from his glass of wine than he took bites of food.

"Do you not need to eat?" I finally asked.

"I eat."

The vagueness of his answer made me wonder if this was another thing he had in common with vampires.

"I eat food," he offered, amusement flickering across his face. He read me too well, and that was going to be a problem. Although Dominic was content with the ensuing silence, I wasn't. I hoped the two glasses of wine he'd drunk meant he'd be even more free with information, although I suspected alcohol didn't affect him the way it did humans. Perhaps it was just an indulgence that he thoroughly enjoyed.

With each sip, he made the wine seem even more enticing. I took a small sip from the glass he'd poured for me.

That pleased him.

"I'm glad you tried it. No need to be so guarded with me, Luna. As you said, we don't need to be adversarial. Our interests align, despite our motives being different."

"Exactly." I raised my glass to him, took another small sip, and set it on the table. "But you have to understand my lack of knowledge makes me a weakness, not an asset."

"Of course, Luna," he said in a cool, husky voice. Despite schooling all emotions from my face, his expression held a knowing look. He seemed unconvinced that my interest was solely in order to be a better asset. Suspicion existed between us and complicated our tenuous alliance.

"How can I make this better for you?" Dominic asked.

The BS between us was stacked high and reeked. But we ignored it and continued with our faux pleasantries, aware that the only thing that aligned us was mutual distrust and strategic maneuvering for the advantage.

"What troubles you, Luna?"

His question snapped the tendril that was holding things together for me.

"All of it, Dominic! Four days ago, I was the weird one because of my odd reading choices. I wouldn't have guessed in a million years that anything in *The Discovery of Magic* was remotely true."

"Most of what's in *The Discovery of Magic* isn't remotely true," he said drily.

"I know, but the factual information about supernaturals is even more difficult to process. The most complex thing about all the new information is you."

Amusement flashed. "Me?"

"Yep. I need to know about your magic as it relates to other supernaturals. How similar is it? You can go between here and my world, a version of what vampires can do. You can do spells, control elements, and…" Helena could grow claws and slice and dice people like a well-dressed wolverine. What she did wasn't exactly shifter-ish, but it was an aspect of it. Dominic traveled through the worlds with ease, and he possessed strong magical abilities. "Helena has claws. Do you? Can you shift like the shifters? One minute, will I be standing in front of you, a man—or whatever you are—and the next I need to give you a raw steak or doggie treat to distract you from attacking?"

His lips twitched but he didn't give in to the smile. He put down his glass. His eyes remained trained on me as he pushed from his chair and walked to me. His eyes locked with mine as his index finger elongated and the nail extended into a gruesome and scary-looking claw.

A sharp breath caught in my throat when he ran it along my neck with so much control that it was a feather touch grazing over my skin. A shiver ran through me when he leaned in closer.

"I can't shift into an animal, so no treats necessary," he whispered, his warm breath teasing my bottom lip. The solitary claw vanished as quickly as it had appeared. Once he had eased away, I grabbed another chocolate from the platter, slowly unwrapping it from the gold paper, and popped it in my mouth. He wouldn't get the satisfaction of either my fear or my intrigue.

"Continue," I told him. "I don't need the watered-down version."

He didn't immediately speak. Perhaps he was debating how much to share with me. I forced a look of impassivity and waited patiently.

"Unlike the shifters, silver doesn't bother me. My magic is strong, comparable to a Strata Three witch, but I can't control the weather and I don't possess any techno-magical abilities. I don't have seer abilities, either, which is why we employ Nailah… who seems to have a soft spot for you." His eyes sharpened on me, his lips pulling into a thin, tight line. Nailah's information sharing hadn't gone unnoticed. "I'm skilled at spell casting, but to the witches' disappointment, I do not share their weakness to iridium."

"But you do have weaknesses?"

He chuckled. "Of course, but none that I care to share."

"You can zone?"

He shook his head. "Unlike the vampires, I don't zone. I can only move between the Underworld and another location. For example, if I travel to your apartment, I must return home first before going to another destination."

"Why?"

He shrugged. The disclosure of his limitation and information was clearly a struggle for him. He took a slow sip of wine. Both of us were in a state of wary apprehension. It weighed so heavily on me, it was doubtful that I kept it from my expression.

"Go on, Luna," he urged. Averting my gaze to the garden, I tried to work out how to make my request in a persuasive way. This was a delicate dance.

"We both want this over and I just can't totally stop my life to be at your beck and call, and I'm sure you have other responsibilities as well. I believe it would be advantageous to us both if I didn't have to rely on you or Anand to travel here."

"You'd like to come to the Underworld freely, without an escort?" He seemed surprised.

"Not indefinitely. Just until the spells are undone. Then we return to our normal lives. You imprisoning the most horrible of the supernaturals while apparently pissing off the others, and me to my family, friends, job, and normal life with none of this." I waved my hand, including him in it along with the mystical garden. It was a place of unique beauty that under any other circumstances I would have found enchanting.

"Is that what you truly want?" he asked. That confirmed

he hadn't destroyed all the Trapsens; he just didn't want anyone else to have one.

My mind was winding around everything Nailah told me. Despite my suspicion that he was aware of everything she'd disclosed, I was committed to not betraying any of her confidences. I had to navigate delicately.

I nodded. Without Dominic and Anand being so entwined in my daily life, if things went into a downward spiral, I could escape. I had four thousand dollars in my savings account. It wouldn't get me far, but I could lie low enough to figure things out.

"And?" he asked. "There seems to be more, Luna." Relaxing back against the chair, he stared at me, cold wariness moving over his face. The smoldering fire in his eyes sent chills through me.

"I have every intention of helping you undo the spells, but I need to know that my friends and family are safe. No more erasing their memories—"

"I didn't erase his memories, I simply manipulated aspects of it so he would forget the ring and what you told him."

"Exactly. I want to protect the people I care about from that. Leave them out of this. I need you to make that oath to me and that whatever happens, I come out on the other side, alive and unharmed."

It was a big ask. Go big or go home. Although going home wasn't really an option.

Dominic's jaw clenched like he was biting back words. Was he about to deny the request or stop himself from agreeing?

"He won't make such a promise to you," Helena hissed, a wine bottle in one hand and partially filled oversized wine glass in the other. She had changed into a shimmering, billowy, mint-green, long-sleeve dress. The severe bun she'd pulled her hair into made her features appear sharper.

Unconstrained anger filled her eyes, and it was directed

solely at Dominic. "My brother is calculating and strategic at all times. For now, you are of use to him. Despite him finding you entertaining, it adds little value to your life. If he determines there's more benefit to your death, he won't think twice. But you don't know that, do you, Luna?" She was gifted with her brother's ability to add just the right inflection, modulation, and venom to make my name sound like a curse. Like something vile to be spat out.

Peeling her eyes from Dominic's, she finally looked at me, staring at me over the glass before tossing back the remainder of the wine. "For now, you're the queen in his game of chess. He *will* protect the queen, sacrificing anyone as a pawn to do so, including me." She put the bottle and glass on the table and yanked up her sleeves, revealing rust-color interlocking glyphs encircling both of her wrists like manacles.

Dominic maintained a chilly indifference as he leveled his eyes with hers.

"You weren't sacrificed. You offered yourself as a sacrifice by your actions," he said, then took a leisurely drink, banked fire hot in his glare.

I shot up to standing, backing away when Helena grabbed the wine bottle off the table, smashed it against the edge, and pointed the jagged edges of the bottle at him.

Fuck this psychotic family. This level of dysfunction was only acceptable in poorly scripted TV. I did not know what to do. Should I attempt to deescalate the situation? Was that even possible? Or maybe this was the time to call their father? *Hey, Lord of the Underworld, come get your terrible ass kids. One is about to assault the other. The one being assaulted doesn't seem too worried about it.*

Dominic remained unbothered, choosing to take another slow, indulgent sip from his glass.

Helena's anger was stormy and pervasive. "Return my fucking magic!" Helena shrieked, bringing the jagged glass toward his neck, which Dominic was so kindly baring to her. A taunt and a challenge.

Frozen in indecision, Helena seemed coiled for violence. Her breath came at irregular clips. It might have been the first time she didn't give in to her first impulse. That denial showed in the furl of her frown.

In helpless rage, she released the bottle at his feet. While they held each other's stare in an icy silence that stretched, I became a voyeur, gawking at a family dispute instead of having the good grace to look away.

I snapped myself out of it and started to slowly inch away from them, afraid that a sudden movement would draw her ire. Her need for violence was wound so tight, it was just looking for a target.

"As you pointed out, I protect the queen. And far too often, a princess undeserving of such protections," Dominic whispered.

The moment was forged in hostility. She glared back at me, her hatred intensified by the belief that I had dethroned her. I did *not* want her to believe that or to think she needed to wrench the position back by any means.

"I hate you!" Helena bellowed. I thought it was directed at me—after all, she probably blamed me for her magic being restricted and not her clawing her brother's face. But a declaration with such impassioned vehemence came from years of emotional connection. It could never be directed at some random stranger—despite how she perceived my part in having her magic restricted. And that's exactly who I was. Some random stranger, pulled into this complex world, who had caused cataclysmic problems.

"A pronouncement you make often when you are forced to deal with a miniscule consequence for your actions. You hate me. Okay. That dagger has dulled from overuse. Find another way to hurt me, you've exhausted that one."

She whipped around, stomping past me while Dominic

stood and began picking up the large pieces of glass. It seemed to provide a moment of catharsis.

"Luna, you may return to your seat. We have more to discuss."

We did, but we weren't going to do it then. I wanted—no, needed to be away from him.

"We can talk later. Perhaps you need some time to mend things with Helena."

"The mere fact you suggested that shows you do not know my sister," he offered with a wry twist of his lips. He was still gathering the broken glass as if there was something symbolic in the gesture—cleaning up a mess that Helena had created.

"Goodnight, Dominic," I said.

He looked up momentarily and smiled at the sight of me grabbing handfuls of chocolates.

"We'll talk later."

"Tomorrow, we'll talk tomorrow."

Before he could object, I moved swiftly toward the house, stopping at the fridge to get some water before going to my room. I locked the door and pushed one of the accent chairs in front of it. It was doubtful it would do anything to stop anyone in this house from entering, but it gave me a small sense of security. At least I'd hear it move.

Pacing the floor, I thought that despite Helena's histrionics, there was truth to the things she said about Dominic. Him being calculating wasn't a surprise, but I wondered at what point he would perceive my life as a liability rather than an asset. Unformed plans and tactics ran rapidly through my mind, but none had a high rate of success because magic, the supernaturals' world, and their rules were unreliable variables.

A ragged breath caught in my throat at the knock on the door.

"May I come in?" Dominic's voice was low, entreating.

"No."

The chair against the door slid from its position, levitated, and was eased down in a silent, sweeping movement that rendered its purpose obsolete. A silver glow flicked along the inside of the door and Dominic strolled in, hands in pockets, face expressionless, and pitfall-deep eyes sharpening on me.

"Why ask if I didn't have a choice?"

He shrugged. "The illusion of choice can be comforting."

"Anything tied to this situation has no comfort." *Including you.*

Walking farther into the room, his eyes dropped from mine. "We hadn't finished our conversation."

"I felt it was necessary for you to resolve the issue between you and Helena so your next interaction isn't a homicide."

"Helena was just venting," he offered in a tone too passive for someone who had enraged his sibling to the point of them holding a broken bottle to their throat.

"Well, it was kind of you to give her better access to those vital arteries she was aiming for."

His lips curled slightly and he lifted his eyes to meet mine, showing a primal amusement.

We fell into an uneasy silence.

"Are you two always so…" I searched for the word. Dysfunctional? Masochistic? Ridiculous? Unhinged? "Intense?"

"Sometimes Helena doesn't like me very much."

I wasn't sure she even loved him. I saw the rampant hate in her eyes and the thirst for retaliation.

"What about you?"

"Sometimes I don't like her, either."

That was fair. Three years older than my twenty-three-year-old brother, I got into fights with him that devolved into childish antics. But I could proudly report neither one of us clawed each other's face or held a broken bottle to the other's throat. Despite our fights, we still loved each other. I wasn't sure that was true with him and Helena.

"Our conversation, we never finished it," he reminded me. I wondered if he didn't like revealing that part of him or being reminded of the dysfunction of their relationship.

"Is there anything more to discuss? Based on what Helena said, you'd never make a promise to protect my life."

His jaw clenched and with some effort, it relaxed. "You would like a way to return here on your own, correct?"

This was his concession and the only thing I'd get from him.

"It would make things easier." My heart pounded at the anticipation of some freedom. Leniency in supervision would give me some options of escape if necessary.

He nodded once. "I think that's a good idea. I will make those arrangements."

When he started in my direction, I shuffled back a few steps, increasingly aware of his all-consuming presence. There was a feeling of something ominous and foreboding lurking just barely below the surface.

I held my breath, realizing they were coming at rapid clicks at his approach. He touched my hair, running his hand lightly over the loose strands that had fallen from my pony-tail, twining them around his fingers, holding my eyes the entire time. With one quick jerk, he pulled out some strands and was at the door before I could react.

"What's wrong with you! Why are you trying to bald me?"

Chuckling, he knelt at the threshold, laying the strands across it. He whispered, said a few words, and as at my home, light flashed before revealing a diaphanous wall that quickly faded.

"No one can enter, not even me." Then he was gone.

I wasn't sure if it was irritation, or the tingling from my hair being yanked out, or disappointment in myself for my fleeting moment of wanting a little more. There was a part of me curious to know what it would feel like to have his supple lips on mine. Did he have the same ardent intensity during sex? My intrigue hadn't stopped there. My thoughts and eyes had lingered over the shirt molded to what was an obviously well-sculpted chest and stomach.

Luna, I scolded myself, forcing my thoughts to the members of the Conventicle and how they had looked at him, and the cool indifference in his eyes when he bared his neck to his sister. How could I forget the malicious intent in his face when he circled me in fire? And I had to remember what Helena said about the volatility of his protection of my life. Hormones be damned. He was not the guy I should fawn over.

14

*H*eading straight to the library, the only thing that kept me from rushing back to work and ignoring the croissants I saw left on the counter for breakfast as I passed the kitchen was Anand seated at the counter beckoning me to join him.

I took it as a good sign. Riding on the high of optimism, I took my wins where I could find them. Soon I would be able to freely move between this world and mine. I hoped Dominic had agreed because he was confident we'd break the spells today. I was extremely hopeful of that, too.

Twenty minutes into working in the spellbook room, Anand seated in the chair closest to the door and engrossed in a book from the main library, keeping that flourish of hope burning was becoming more difficult. Suspicion dominated.

"Are you here as a companion, or security?" I asked, looking up from the book I'd been going through.

His lips lifted into a pleasing curl. "Companion." Despite it being a total lie, his gentle demeanor would have made a less cynical person believe it.

It only made me more curious about him and the people who lived in the Underworld.

"You're not related to Dominic and Helena, are you?"

He shook his head. Based on the blithe look that coursed over his face and gleamed in his eyes, he knew I was grasping for information and he wasn't going to offer it freely. I missed Nailah.

"Nailah doesn't live here?"

"That information you know already. I took her home."

It was my time to nod.

"I was born here," he provided, putting me out of my misery. He placed the book on the table. "My mother was once a prisoner, before things changed. My father was given the option to raise me. He declined. I grew up here with Dominic and Helena." It explained his seemingly fraternal relationship with Dominic.

"You chose to continue to live here as an adult?"

He was a man of few words, only offering another slight nod, or at least I took it to be a nod. It was such a minute movement, I wasn't sure. But that was all he provided before returning to his book. I wanted to know more about his magic. Before I could ask, he gave me a subtle suggestion redirecting me to my work. Actually, not particularly subtle. His eyes flicked from his book to mine.

"You should work on that." His tone was firm, leaving no room for debate or further questions.

Dominic attempted to slip into the room unnoticed, but he wasn't someone who could easily evade drawing attention. Anand took his arrival as an opportunity to leave. Companion, my ass. He wasn't even covert about it as he gave Dominic a "I did my job" look before leaving.

In silence, Dominic copied the spells I had found into the notebook. He scanned the findings, arranging several spells.

"Are you weaving a spell?"

He shook his head. "I can't weave spells," he provided in a

155

tight voice. He really didn't like sharing his limitations. Perhaps because he seemed to have so few, it was a reminder that he wasn't omniscient. "I'm removing each spell individually. A weaver can make a single spell that could remove them all. It's a power limited to just witches."

He waited patiently as I finished up the final book then copied what I'd found to the notebook. After several minutes of analyzing the various spells, he changed the spells around and took my hand in his. His gentleness and the warmth of his fingers on mine was a direct contrast to the clinical detachment with which he studied the markings. Something hummed off him that I couldn't quite place. Magic? Anger? Frustration? It definitely had hints of wrathful determination. It was quite apparent he didn't enjoy this part of his job. He probably delighted in the hell storms, violence, and retribution parts.

Dominic explained he wanted to observe the sigils' response to the spells, so we headed to the dungeon.

There wasn't any response from the first three spells, not a hint of a glow from my finger and nothing from the sigils on the wall. The fourth created a halo of light over my finger, matching that on the wall. The glow pulsed at a defiant beat, and there was a noticeable fading of the markings on my finger and on the wall. Smoky incorporeal figures formed in the prisons for mere seconds before fading away. Then a torrent of magic trampled through the space; small cracks formed in the glass before it exploded in a rain of shards. Covering my face, I knew my arm would get the brunt of it, but I felt nothing but the heat of Dominic's body in front of mine, the sound of shattered glass hitting the floor, and what I was sure was some against Dominic's back.

My finger ached, but I didn't feel any cuts. Nothing. Dominic didn't show any signs of injury from the spray of glass against him.

"I was able to put up a protective wall," he explained at my surprised expression. "I wasn't sure I got it up in time. That was definitely unexpected." He hooked his finger under my chin, roving over it and my neck, taking it in. Taking my hand in his, his fingers a gentle feather touch as they slid across my skin, he examined me for damage. A warm, unexpected feeling moved over me at his touch.

"I'm fine," I assured him, surprised by the tenderness of his touch. When he released me, I couldn't place the emotions that moved over his face, but there were hints of confusion and—perhaps disappointment. Was he surprised by his concern for me? I definitely was. His lips pressed into a tight line. He dropped my hand quickly and stepped back and studied the space where we'd seen a vestige of the inhabitants for a passing moment.

Preoccupied, Dominic seemed only vaguely aware of me as he made his way back to the spellbook room, leaving me trailing behind. He slowed at the sight of Helena in the library, resting back on the chaise, a book on her lap. Her dark hair was pulled back in a loose chignon, and she was wearing a delicate-looking white maxi dress that exposed her arms and the magic-restricting manacles. I wasn't sure if it was an act of acceptance or to serve as a reminder to her brother of his perceived cruelty.

There was a softness to her that belied any of the cruelty she'd exhibited before. She looked demure and innocuous. If this had been my first time meeting her, it would be hard for me to believe she was capable of cruelty. But there were still traces of something ominous and fierce in her eyes, refusing to leave despite her best effort. She was presenting a sheep, when the wolf within was rearing to attack.

That was the point. When anger, avowals of sibling hatred, and violence didn't work, she tried another tactic. Dominic gave her a passing look before heading for the spellbook room, stopping with an exasperated sigh when she called his name.

Slipping past him, I was going to continue into the spell-book room, having had my fill of drama for the day.

"Luna, please stay," she requested in a saccharine tone. Her stark change from before scared me more than if she'd attempted to strangle me again. I kept a wary eye on her approach.

"You're not having success with undoing the spells, are you?" she surmised, looking at Dominic. His jaw clenched at her statement. "You won't. The protection spell is reacting to your magic. A *deflexio* protection. No matter what spell *you* do, it will be deflected." She turned to me. "Whatever spell is being used, it's encrypting it, changing the response," she explained.

"It's responding to external magic," he said.

"Exactly."

His teeth gripped his lips in contemplation, then he slowly released them and looked from me to his sister. More silence filled the room and as looks passed between the siblings, I felt more and more like an uninvited guest.

"I'll continue to go through the spells," I suggested, and when no one objected, I went to the spellbook room. There weren't any more books to go through, but I'd use any excuse to get away from them.

I was an undesired interloper, and the room let me know. The nudge of the air was more insistent, rougher. The room was more assertive with its feelings when I was alone.

"I don't want to be here anymore than you want me here," I told it. *Great, I'm talking to rooms now. Things just keep getting better.*

Despite the revelation about the *deflexio* spell, I busied myself going over the spells, trying to make any sense of them, and help as much as I could with my limited knowledge of spell casting and magic. Being proactive and relentless were the only things I could cling to.

My eyes lifted to the door nudging open and a large raw

158

steak floating into the room with grooves pressed into it from what I suspected were teeth, since I couldn't see them.

Hi, Zareb. I let myself be momentarily distracted by the meat being unceremoniously plopped on the floor and the aggressive sounds of a dog shredding and eating the raw meat. Within a matter of minutes, there was just a bone. Silence. I wondered if he was taking a nap. A low shrill sound of shock whooshed from me when something rubbed against my leg.

Appearing next to me, Zareb leaned forward, wanting to be petted.

"Hey, Cujo," I greeted. He bristled, lifting his head until his intelligent dark eyes met mine. I flashed him a tight smile. I'd offended the massive hellhound.

"Sorry," I said, stroking his soft fur. His easy breathing and simple enjoyment were oddly comforting. His response was one of the few things that seemed consistent with my world. An Underworld hound that was sent out for scouting, enjoying the basic pleasure of being petted like a normal dog. Normal didn't last long when he eased into his invisible form, his head still resting on my leg.

An invisible hound, not weird at all. Just another day in the Underworld. Nothing to see here. Move along.

Dominic entered the spellbook room, his eyes quickly finding Zareb. When he made a ticking sound, Zareb's head lifted from my leg and he moved away, Dominic's hand reaching out to stroke his head in passing. Dominic continued to track the hound's movement toward the door, which nudged open wider. I remained focused on Dominic, looking for any changes in his eyes that would key me in to when Zareb was around. There weren't any. Another tick of sound from Dominic and the steak bone was removed.

"She's fine around her," Dominic told the animal. With the dog invisible, I wasn't able to tell his response and Dominic was a blank slate revealing nothing. I knew who the "her" was. Zareb obviously didn't trust Helena around me.

"Do you still want the ability to come here unaccompanied?" Dominic asked, closing the door after Zareb.

"Yes."

He inhaled a breath and crossed his arms with a dark, commanding primality that seemed wholly his. Helena's countenance was distinctive, too: baleful reproach, airy confidence, and predatory stealth. It was clear even when she camouflaged it with stylish clothing and flawless makeup.

Dominic moved with fluid grace, taking the seat next to me and resting back in the chair, his hands clasped on his stomach. I couldn't help but look at the way his slim-fit shirt's midnight blue complemented his physique, and the rolled shirtsleeves, his exposed well-muscled arms. It was a calculated presentation and I naively fell for it.

"Why?" His question held no curiosity. It seemed like he was asking for confirmation of something he already knew. What else had he and Helena discussed?

I'll play your game.

"As I said before, it'd be easier to continue my work. I'm just as committed to ending this as you are. Neither you nor Anand will need to shadow me. I'm sure you two have more pressing things to deal with than watching me."

"You believe you'll be safe at work?" Another non-question.

I wasn't exactly confident of that. "I don't know," I admitted.

He barely nodded.

"You don't believe I will be?"

"You're safe from the Conventicle and those under their governance."

Despite my best effort to hide any doubt, my thoughts went to the vampire attack. "Kane will honor it?"

"Kane was out of line. The Conventicle claims he wasn't

160

acting on their behalf. He never would have been violent toward you, but him attempting to circumvent our agreement was unacceptable. It has been handled." There was a hard edge to his voice.

Handled.

"Is he still alive?" It took a moment for me to get the question out, afraid of the answer. He had been staked in the chest. It seemed like a harsh enough punishment.

"He doesn't breathe or have a working circulatory system," Dominic pointed out.

"Is he still around?"

"No, but Bael is," he told me. "The shifter who attacked you," he added in response to my questioning look.

"Then I should be fine. The Awakeners won't hurt me. I die and the prisoners are returned. That won't serve their purpose if they're looking to secure an alliance with them."

He nodded but still looked unconvinced. "Understand that my sister will be here whenever you arrive unaccompanied," he reminded me.

Yes, I was perfectly aware of that. "You two seem to be playing nice," I said.

"She's playing nice because I'm the means to her getting back her magic. I know my sister well. To her, you are simply a toy she has the opportunity to break as a way to retaliate against me."

I frowned. "Toy?"

"No worries. I have no intention of playing with you." His gaze was playful, his smirk a sensual taunt. "Unless you want me to," he tacked on in a husky drawl.

"No," I sputtered. It didn't ring true or have the level of assertion to wipe away his smirk.

"Luna, why do you really want this?"

His brow hitched as he studied me. I wasn't giving him anything.

"We want the same thing. As you said, our interests align."

Nodding his head slowly, he considered my answer, but it was apparent he remained unconvinced.

"If there's a protection spell around the markings, how do we get around it?" I was genuinely curious about that, but the question also served to redirect his scrutiny.

"Magic. We have to get you your own. That should be an acceptable workaround."

It's that easy? Just get you magic and while we're at it, let's end world hunger, negotiate global peace, and develop great-tasting zero-calorie chocolate.

"Is it as simple as you're making it sound?" It might be that simple. He was magic and had an abundance of overlapping magic.

He shook his head. "Not at all. If it were as simple as loaning my magic to you, maybe."

"Why make it harder than it needs to be? Or is the idea of you being without magic for a day too much?"

"My magic will kill you," he provided with an easy shrug. "Witches crave magic and although it is against their laws—violations are met with swift and pitiless penalties—there's always one Strata Three who wants to take it to another level."

"You're that next level."

Oh, Prince, modesty doesn't fit you, I thought at his downcast eyes and his failed attempt at humility.

"It's been tried twice—and they both died. I didn't kill them," he added before I could ask or get the inquiring look off my face. "It will have to be witch magic."

"I'm human. Will it work for me? Isn't it usually witch to witch? A stronger witch taking magic from a lesser?"

He assured me with an unenthusiastic nod, but I needed much more than that.

"How do you know?"

His eyes dropped to the ring. "Because that would have killed you."

"What?" I fumbled out.

He frowned. "Magic has only been shared by other magic holders. From my knowledge, it has never been tried with a non-magical. There was no precedent that showed you casting a spell would work. You were used as a test subject. If you're able to power this magic, you'll be able to survive witch magic. It's closer to Caster magic than mine, it appears."

My frustration was solely directed at the Dark Caster. Did they have some privileged knowledge that this would work? Was I simply a guinea pig to them, risking my life without any evidence it would have been successful? Things could have gone in an entirely different direction. I could have died that day. Tamping down the panic became so difficult, I focused on things in my control.

"How soon can we get me magic?" I needed this to end and the Dark Caster found. If the desire for anonymity allowed them to adhere to some semblance of rule, then let them have it and get me out of this world.

"I just need to make the arrangements. Later today, or early tomorrow. Witches dislike being without their magic. When you have it all your life, it's as if a part of you is missing when divested of it. We will need to be efficient and strike true. I'll have all the spells in order for it."

Strike true? With so many possible combinations of spells, could we do that? The silence was stretched taut, his expression indiscernible. I wondered if we shared the same worry.

"I'd like you to stay another day," he requested.

This time, I actually wanted the same. But it was Wine-Down, and I wanted to be there for Emoni and Cameron. It would also give Dominic more time to work through the spells.

"I have to work tomorrow—and it'll give me an opportunity to travel home and back here alone."

A sly look shadowed over his face. Had I messed up his redirection? "Of course, we want you to be able to do that," he said.

Next time, try it with feeling.

———

Dominic escorted me to another room. At the door, he whispered a spell, his forearm ink illuminating, the markings awakening at his command, scrolling around his arm and realigning, causing the door to open for us. The midnight-blue room had the same unsettling feeling as the spellbook room. Strong magic thrummed through it. The ominous feel of energy that wasn't quite right and definitely didn't appreciate me being here. There were just a few books on the shelves, and they gave me an invisible push anytime I inched close to them. It only added to what was an extensive magical deterrent for the room.

The simple wooden box that held the Trapsen opened with a similar disarming process. Dominic could keep it wherever he wanted or leave it out in the middle of a room; only he could get to it.

An object that transports a person to the Underworld should look a lot more portentous than a silver, pink, and azure palm-size triangular prism. I examined the object, turning it over, exploring the barely discernable sigils etched into it. The little ebb of light that pulsed inside it.

"This is it?" There wasn't any way of hiding my disappointment. Part of me wanted it to be something grand, like the staff from *Lord of the Rings*. I'd be Gandalf, extending my mighty staff, requesting passage to the Underworld. Instead, he gave me a palm-size prism and a small pocketknife.

"What do I do with the knife?"

Smiling, Dominic took it from me and lightly pressed it to my hand, enough to feel the bite of the blade but not draw blood. He was very skilled at testing and knowing the limits of injury. The same delicate precision of movement exhibited when he showed me his claw.

"You must draw blood and close it around the Trapsen. The transport is easy. Concentrating on your intended destination is the hard part."

"If I think of somewhere else, that's where I'll end up?"

He nodded.

"One quick thought about London, poof, I'm there?"

He confirmed with another small nod, an amiable smile spreading over his lips. "No worries, I'd find you wherever you go." A look of self-satisfaction passed over his features. His hand covered the Trapsen held in my palm. His fierce amber eyes held mine, expressing the very thing that his words only hinted at. *I will find you.* Taking a step back, I swallowed.

"I know you will."

"Do you?"

I nodded, huffing out a sigh. "So we're back to this? Threats don't work on me."

He just made a sound. "When will you return?"

"I work until nine, but it might take longer. We have Wine-Down Thursday and it's usually busy afterward. We stay open longer," I told him.

"Good, I should have things arranged by then." He stepped back, giving me an expectant look. He seemed very uninterested in my solo travel from the Underworld. I expected more: him reiterating the process, words of encouragement, a reminder to stay focused. Something. But that was it. He left momentarily to get my overnight bag and handed it to me. One mini lesson and I was traveling alone without so much as a *goodbye and try not to end up in Istanbul.*

I hooked my overnight bag on my shoulder. He waited several feet from me, motionless and silent, in that eerie way of his.

Using my home as the exit point from the Underworld was too unsettling, so I chose a spot that had been used before—the alleyway of Books and Brew.

Closing my eyes, I focused on the location before remembering that I needed to prick my hand close it around the Trapsen. When I opened my eyes, Dominic's arms were crossed over his chest, giving me a view of the new reassembling of ink on his arms, looking bemused.

I got this. Pricking my finger, I put the small knife into my pocket and closed my hand around the crystal-like prism object. The electric surge of magic from it pulsed through me, my heart pounded, and my breath caught before I was plunged into darkness. *Books and Brew alleyway. Books and Brew alleyway. Books and Brew alleyway.* My focus was sharp on it because I didn't want to end up in the actual store.

Instead of the alleyway of Books and Brew, I ended up in my kitchen. I wasn't sure when that thought had gone through my mind. Obviously, my thoughts had given in to the hunger pangs.

Dominic's insistent knock came just seconds later. I knew it was him without looking through the peephole. A determined and firm knock that was wholly him.

"I knew you wouldn't end up in the alleyway," he chastised with a smirk. "Despite you saying it over and over."

Oh, you heard that? But this wasn't just about him checking on the success of my travel; it was him demonstrating he could find me.

"Thanks for checking on me," I provided, putting my speculation in my words.

"Of course. I needed to make sure you ended up where you needed to be."

We settled into the discord that existed between us. His air of smugness made it difficult not to close the door in his face.

"See you tomorrow, Luna." He turned on his heels and left.

Despite his arrogance, my elation couldn't be dampened. This could be over tomorrow. It wouldn't solve everything that was occurring in the supernatural world, but at least I wouldn't be entwined in it. The conflicting interests would eventually lead to a civil war—I was almost sure of that. I had no idea whether humans would be affected. I couldn't fixate on what-ifs, but I could address the current problem.

15

*A*nand allowed me glimpses of him. I'd been naïve to think he wouldn't be around. Dominic said the illusion of choice was comforting. He was wrong; it was patronizing. Between checking out customers, shelving books, and helping set up for Wine-Down, I played *Where's Anand* and wondered about the father who abandoned him, the imprisoned mother in the Perils, and Anand's bizarre choice to remain in the Underworld as an adult.

After approaching him with "peekaboo, I see you," one too many times—something he made apparent he didn't find humorous—finding him became virtually impossible. He slipped away and skulked somewhere, unassuming and invisible. We were back to playing hide and seek.

Making light of his ability was easier than acknowledging how scary it was. But it was more than an ability to be unobtrusive. His ability to slip in and out of view was a feat of magic. It took a lot to bring my focus back to my job and tasks at hand. My optimism was a glutton for punishment.

Books and Brew didn't have a stage, just a small section in the coffee shop's corner where Gus could sit with his guitar and Emoni could sing. It wasn't small enough for her to be heard without a mic, but having one seemed a little unnecessary. The apothecary store kept its doors open, as it usually did on Thursday. The music was soothing enough to appeal to their customers, and usually they benefitted from the increase in customer traffic.

Cameron stood next to me just outside the door that divided the coffee shop from the bookstore. Emoni's first selection was an original, written by her and Gus, his low raspy alto voice complementing the highs of hers. Concern clouded Cameron's bright smile as she watched the crowd's reception. With any other audience, it would have been well received, but our group had come to hear the covers of songs they loved, which was confirmed when they perked up at the next song: a rendition of "Brown-Eyed Girl."

It was surprising to find Peter seated at the back of the coffee shop. He gave me his small wayward smile and raised the coffee cup in his hand as if to ask me to join him. I assumed the request was to satisfy the raincheck I'd given him before. I mouthed that I was working, which was probably hard to believe since, like the rest of the employees, I had paused what I was doing to listen to the entertainment. If he'd been watching, he would have seen me indulge in a few sips of wine as well.

It seemed like Peter's request was merely polite, since he quickly returned his attention to Emoni and Gus. Maybe he didn't enjoy sitting alone. It was odd that he was. The coffee shop wasn't crowded and there were seats available in the bookstore. He seemed to be a magnet for visitors when in the bookstore, but not so much in the coffee shop. Maybe people wanted to enjoy the music uninterrupted.

Emoni's enjoyment was apparent, reminding me of her excitement during practice. The crowd wasn't their typical fans, and she could play the classics and experiment with the vocals. Watching Cameron was the most amusing part of the night. She studied the audience like it was an equation she was determined to figure out. Her eyes traveled over everyone, taking in their responses to the songs, determining which books she'd display near the register of the coffee shop, the shelf where we sold coffee beans, cups, and Books and Brew merchandise, and which books she'd put on the circular wood display that greeted customers as they entered the store.

I suddenly wondered if Cameron was just incredibly attuned to the nuances of human behavior. Could it be magic? If there were seers, what about empaths? I shrugged off the thought. Magic had spilled into my life too much. I couldn't let it tarnish this.

As Emoni and Gus transitioned into their final song, "Shallow" by Lady Gaga, Cameron beamed. Emoni loved doing the cover, not for the emotional charge but for the difficulty. She once speculated that audiences were drawn to people doing the cover in the same manner as they would be drawn to a gymnast performing a triple double or a dismount off a balance beam. They are all waiting in anticipation of an epic success or dramatic failure. Could the singer pull off the vocals starts on the C5 range where it hovers throughout, only dropping off occasionally to maintain the emotion and grittiness of the song?

I hadn't realized the stamina required to perform it, nor had I expected Emoni's faux umbrage at me pointing out that her recognizing that observation in others probably meant she did it, too. For shame.

Emoni loved the challenge and, based on the way the audience leaned forward in their seats, watching Emoni and Gus's emotionally charged performance, so did they. Emoni seemed to be anchored to Gus, their faces close to each other during the challenging parts, making the audience willing voyeurs to their exchange. Emoni knew how to play to a crowd. I wasn't sure if Gus was aware she was doing it or was drawn to her like a siren and the song like a sonnet. But part of me, that little romantic Pollyanna that dwells in us all, thought it was more than her playing to the crowd. She and Gus had a very intimate relationship, even if it only existed in the confines of music.

Cameron flashed a miscreant smile. "We are about to sell a lot of books," she said, dipping into the store with me in tow. She grabbed several Rockstar romances and grinned. It didn't hurt that the man on the cover had some similarities to Gus: soulful brown eyes, aquiline nose, intense jawline that lent to a striking profile. His hair was unruly to the point I assumed he didn't own a comb.

"A thousand lives," she reminded me, when I gave her a disapproving look. "Readers live a thousand lives," she reminded us every Thursday. She busied herself with collecting more books for easy access.

"Luna," Cameron called, handing me several more—a few fantasies, interracial romance—and told me to put them on the shelf near the coffee. It surprised me when she chose shifter romance. My brows rose in doubt.

"It'll sell," she assured me. I glanced back at Gus, trying to look for similarities in the shifters I'd seen. There weren't any. Gus had a cool gentleness to him. Shifters were raw primality. He was what people who hadn't been on the death lunge end of a shifter probably thought they'd look like.

Picking up one of the second-chance romances from the top shelf of the display tower, I cut my eye at her. "You know they were never a couple. They're just bandmates."

"I know that, you know that, but they don't." She waved her hand at the people engrossed in the exchange between the two *bandmates* that definitely gave off conflicting hints of burgeoning romance and longing of one to be rekindled.

Were people really this suggestible? If they weren't, marketing psychologists wouldn't have a job.

The biggest shock of the night was when Peter neared the display tower where I was standing and reached for the second-chance romance, snagging a string of my hair on his bracelet.

I hissed as he pulled away, my head moving forward with him. He cursed. "Sorry." He mumbled more apologies, and we attempted to quietly untangle. "I should have asked you to move. I thought there was enough space," he explained in a hushed voice, trying not to draw attention to us but eliciting another low hiss from me when he tugged too hard.

"No worries," I said, but I could still feel the sting where several strands of hair were pulled from my head by the strange barbed bracelet around his wrist. It had scraped along my hand, scratching it when I tried to help with easing him away with minimal damage.

"Nice weapon," I teased, looking at the scratch and specks of blood on my hand.

He looked at the injury, frowned, and then stared at the bracelet, a string of circles with small nubs on them that looked far less dangerous than they were.

"That's enough of this thing," he grumbled. "It was a fashion mistake I won't make again. Here I was trying to do something a little different. Add a little pizzazz to my style." He attempted to add humor to his voice, but it was heavy with concern.

Pizzazz? Come on, Peter, do better.

"I'm fine. It's just a scratch," I told him, "but I'd retire that thing."

Nodding in agreement, he removed it from his wrist and shoved it in his pocket. He hesitated, looking coy as he gave a side-eye to the book he had been reaching for.

"I need to go clean this," I said, waving my wounded hand.

Leaning in closer, I whispered, "Who doesn't love a good second-chance romance? Enjoy."

Emboldened, he stood taller, picked up that book and two more from the shelf, and headed for the register. I made my way to the employee lounge. The scratch didn't warrant a bandage, but I definitely wanted to clean it and apply some antibiotic ointment.

The combination of pleasant weather, music, the illusion of watching a potential romantic *will they won't they* moment, and decent wine at a reduced price made for a busy sales day.

"Luna," said an unfamiliar voice. A woman had moved in next to me. During a brief break in the stream of customers, I'd used the time to replace books in the coffee shop that had sold in a matter of minutes after the performance ended. I hadn't noticed the woman's approach.

The Asian woman's face brightened when I turned to face her and attempted to place her since she'd addressed me with such familiarity. I couldn't. Midnight hair pulled back from her face and crescent-shape eyes that held the same spark Madeline's had. The spark of astute wisdom, but it was beyond the years of the twenty-something-year-old woman in front of me.

"Yes?" I asked.

Flashing me a marking of a broken circle, three vertical lines with the ends curving in three different directions on the inner side of her wrist, she leaned into me. "Thank you. It's only a matter of time."

I debated whether to reveal that I had no idea what she was talking about or pretend that I did. Which would yield more information?

"Matter of time?"

"Luna, you released the only people who have a chance

against the Conventicle. Get rid of them, and we will be relieved of our restraints. We'll become the power brokers no longer restricted by their rules and mandates." She shook her head. "Why should we live in fear of being discovered by humans? They should know of our existence and…" She trailed off.

I guessed she was going to say something along the lines of "bow down to our power," "quiver in fear of our greatness," or "revere us like gods." Whether she said it or not, the portentous intentions were there in the set of her jaw, the chilliness of her eyes, and the raw malice of her words.

"I didn't do it intentionally," I blurted, not wanting to stake a claim on the hot mess, even if she did view it favorably.

Based on the reverent way she looked at me, it didn't matter. I was the initiator. A means to the end of restrictions. Did she not see the hypocrisy in venerating a human, whom she hoped to subjugate with her power and magical ability? Frustrated, I was about to point that out when she took hold of my arm—based on her expression, more aggressively than intended. She relaxed the pressure and I put a little distance between us.

Quickly I scanned the café for Anand, expecting him to show up. Wasn't this the reason he shadowed me, to prevent situations like this? Or perhaps she'd used magic to elude him. Not being completely sure how things worked in this world just complicated things.

"You can't align yourself with Dominic," she told me in a rough whisper. "He's using you to recapture the prisoners." She searched my face for some form of feedback. "We can't let that happen. Change is necessary." She took a step toward me and I moved back again, keeping distance between us, leery of the desperation on her face.

"I want the same thing as he does," I told her. She

wouldn't get false hope from me or the idea that I was an ally.

"No, you don't," she snapped, closing the distance between us again and taking a firm hold on my arm.

"Look…" I waited for her to give me a name.

"Rei."

"I know this is a cause you believe in, but can you truly expect me as a human to get involved? I just want my life back."

Desperation and determination overtook her features. Her unyielding eyes held mine.

"You are being foolish and naïve," she chastised.

Not winning me over, Rei.

Despite the rise in her voice and her aggressive posturing, we seemed to go unnoticed by the people in the coffee shop. I suspected magic was involved in keeping us unnoticed. The supernaturals' use of magic against humans didn't seem to be regulated enough. Or perhaps Rei was an exception, not the norm. I knew that the Awakeners bucked against the rules, pushing the limits and only stopping when caught and punished. Rei might have been a rogue among them, exhibiting no restraint with her magic.

"Whether you've misunderstood your role in this or not, you have done something great. I won't let you withdraw your help." Her voice had warmed, but it didn't belie her threat.

"*Let* me?"

She looked around; I felt the shift in the energy. Was she about to use magic on me or force me to go with her? I eased my hand closer to one of the candles on the shelf, preparing to use it as a weapon if necessary, watching the effort she put into calming herself.

"My apologies." It didn't sound like an apology, but a concession. She'd play nice because she had to. "Please allow me a chance to present my side—*our* side."

I thought she'd taken my silence as a tacit agreement when she retreated and slipped away. Then I caught sight of Jackson approaching. Great.

I shrugged at Emoni, who had pulled her attention from the woman she was speaking to long enough to shoot furtive death glares at Jackson's back.

I grinned at her. "I got this," I mouthed.

16

I didn't have the situation under control so much as I leaned into just evading Jackson. But it was what was needed to keep Emoni from marching over and intervening.

"Hi," I greeted him before he could say anything, and jabbed my thumb in the register's direction and the line forming. Quickly, I returned to the store before he could answer.

Him waiting for me to finish was another reminder of my underestimation of his arrogance and nonexistent sense of propriety. Why not harass someone at their job? What's wrong with that? He sat at the table nearest the checkout and waited until I didn't have any customers and no other option but to leave the area and reshelve books and tidy the store.

At least he had the common courtesy not to approach as soon as I left the checkout.

"That was a hell of a performance, wasn't it?" he remarked.

"You should tell Emoni and Gus," I suggested. "Or is this your segue to us just talking and then you peddling your 'I'm so wonderful and should be shared among the masses' speech?"

He blew out a sigh of exasperation. "Must you always be so…" He searched my face, not because he was lost for words but because he was a calculating manipulator, something else I could recognize now that my rose-colored love goggles were removed. What was his goal? A thinly veiled insult to put me on the defensive? A prick at my insecurities to unsettle me? Or would he play on my emotions?

"Cold and spiteful."

Ah, the emotion route. When narcissism and self-entitlement fail, make it the other person's fault.

"Cold? Spiteful?"

"You're throwing away our relationship because of one indiscretion. You know how much I love you and how losing you has made me feel. Don't kick me while I'm down. Is that who you are now?"

He was laying it on pretty thick. What kind of Jedi mind trick was he trying to pull? His arrogance blinded him to how contrived he sounded.

When he ambled closer, his head bowed in submission as if he were a wounded pup and I had just rejected him or— even worse—kicked him, I despised him for the dramatics. Then I despised myself just a little for the moment I allowed his performance to make me feel guilty.

"Three years and it's gone and you're ready to say goodbye to it. All of it."

"No, not at all. We had a history. Some good times that I will remember fondly and some bad times that I'll remember, too, and take as lessons for future relationships. But we're over. To be honest, it's not just the cheating. That shone a light on the flaws in the relationship that I'd ignored. We need to let the relationship stay over. Not just for me, but for us both. Move on."

"Lulu." I hated that name and had told him numerous times. "Don't do this to us."

"You would rather me be miserable in a relationship with you, so that you can be happy?" I asked, though he'd never admit it. He'd have to be a special type of ass to openly admit that he would not have a problem with that.

"You weren't miserable. It's a protective mechanism. I made you happy. And you know that. That was always my goal, and I succeeded in every way." His heavy-lidded look used to work, so of course he'd try it now. He made it sexy, and I fell for it time and time again. He attempted to follow it up with a kiss. The gentle ones he used to give me. A feather touch with the promise of so much more. It had worked before, enhanced by my love for him. But not now. I shoved him back.

"You know this isn't about us getting back together. It's about you winning. This is just *you* wanting *your* way and nothing else. You want me happy, go away."

"As you wish," Rei said. Jackson's eyes glazed over; his body became rigid before collapsing to the ground. Dagger in hand, Rei started driving it toward his chest.

"Stop!" I yelled, not caring who heard, but there wasn't anyone to startle. I took a quick glance into the coffee shop. Empty. Almost. One person remained: a man standing just a few feet away. His round face and stern appearance matched his short, stout body. The eyes were keen with predatory alertness, like the others. Scoping his prey. Shifter.

How had I missed Cameron and Lilith leaving? Or the absence of customers? There was no way I was so engrossed in my conversation with Jackson that I missed people exiting the store, and Emoni wouldn't have left without telling me, and we never left anyone in the store alone. The witch must have used a spell to compel them to leave.

My theory was proven when four non-humans joined the shifter. Two of them were vampires, for sure. I suspected one of the new arrivals was a shifter. She had the nuanced ferocity that I'd come to attribute to them. Predators in their own right. I wasn't sure what type of supernatural the fourth new arrival was. Perhaps another witch.

"Don't kill him. Please."

My heart pounded and my mouth dried as I tried to make sense of what was happening.

"Luna, we owe you a great deal. We know what you've done. What you have sacrificed to make this happen. I want to convince you of our cause and our appreciation."

What terribly wrong version of the story had they heard? Willing? Not at all. Sacrifice? I was at the point of bartering anything to get out of this web I was caught in. Was this part of Rei's swaying me that supernaturals should be revealed, unimpeded by the rules that kept them from using their magic against humans, doing things like this without consequence?

"Luna, it is as you wish. What would you have me do with him?"

As I wish. I wish you not to be an ex-boyfriend-killing sociopath. Why is death always the first option with them?

She waited for instruction. What to tell her? *No to the killing or hurting him, but can you cast a spell to make him less of an insufferable ass,* seemed really inappropriate. I knelt down and pressed a finger to Jackson carotid's artery; I found a pulse. The beat was steady but slower than mine. Was this his normal or a result of him being in this state? Would it continue to slow until it stopped?

"It's just a sleep spell," she assured me. "I can wake him or do whatever you wish me to." A cruel smile feathered across her lips. *This is not how to ingratiate yourself to a person. This is not normal. Be more normal.*

"Wake him and let him go," I said, watching the thrill from the anticipation of violence eke from her face. It wasn't the violence she wanted; it was domination.

180

She scoffed. "Let him go? It's not that easy, Luna. He knows. Right now, those are the rules." She bristled, her voice tight with irritation. "But it doesn't have to be that way. That's what we're fighting for. Our acknowledgment and place in this world. No longer will we have to go through such extremes to hide our existence or be penalized anytime we risk exposure."

"Don't hurt him. Get him out of here, or all talks are over. I'm leaving." I had bargaining power and I had to wield it to help Jackson out of a mess that I was moored to.

With a sound of contempt, she nodded in agreement and looked in the vampires' direction. A woman started toward us, her auburn hair a stark contrast to her limestone-fair skin. She possessed an overwhelming presence, despite her slight build. Her movement toward us was done with the ease of someone floating through the air. I glanced at her eyes but refused to hold focus with the vampire as she attempted to hold mine. As if it was instinctual. Compel the human, get them to do your bidding.

With the vampire at Jackson's side, the witch whispered a spell, and a brilliant silver light moved over Jackson's face. He eased up on his elbows, like he'd been awakened from a deep sleep. Confusion was all over his face at me standing a few inches away, the stern-faced witch in front, and the vampire's tranquil features that vied for his attention. Which he surrendered to easily. Transfixed by her eyes, he was lulled into complacency.

Her brusque, stilted voice didn't sound melodic or entrancing, but Jackson was enchanted by it. Enthralled by her. I remembered that feeling—and hated subjecting him to it. Forcing him into a faux need to please her and follow her wishes without challenge. Even if it was her simple request that he go straight home and remember that it was a lazy day for him.

Attentive to her directions, he stood when commanded

to, walked out the door, and didn't look back, just as she had instructed. He obeyed, without any signs of being controlled by someone else, which seemed the most worrying thing about vampires and their ability to compel. How did you determine if a person was acting of their own volition or at the behest of a vampire?

"This is why living in the shadows is ridiculous. He should know who we are, what we are capable of, and leave us the hell alone. Spending our talents hiding, making sure the simple little humans don't know of our existence is foolish. We're giving them power over us. Over us!" the vampire hissed. Nothing about her voice was beautiful or lyrical, despite the hold it had over Jackson. It was arctic, cold and sharp as a blade.

"It's always power with you all, isn't it?" Anand acknowledged, moving from the shadows, a blade in hand, taking in the five people in the room with the disinterest of looking at common nuisances.

The witch stood and squared her shoulders. Her lips furled as she placed a laser-sharp focus on him.

"Abandon this Awakening absurdity and walk away unscathed," Anand urged.

"Or you can stop following Dominic and the Conventicle's restrictive and insidious rules and join us. Why should we be hidden from humans and forced to accommodate them? Why are we required to bow to their whims and not the other way around? Why are you complicit when the most powerful of our kind are being jailed to satisfy the Conventicle's ego and flaunt the control they have over us? We don't need regulation and anonymity," she challenged.

"Rei, this misrepresentation isn't befitting of you. Own your belief and your true desires," he told her. "You believe revealing magic will put you on top of the food chain. That you'd be allowed to be openly reckless without consequences. You all want exemption from governance and rules under the false belief that it will be liberation. It won't. It will lead to a great deal of violence and everyone vying for domination."

He closed the distance between them, forcing her to adopt a defensive stance despite her shifter and vampire allies spreading out to surround him. She was clearly a powerful witch, and the others were undoubtedly just as formidable, but faced with Anand, apprehension and fear lingered in their postures. Forcing them to be reactive. He had the lithe, calm assurance of a person who thrived on adrenaline and danger. Surrounded by predators and powerful magic, he carried himself as if he was a wolf surrounded by lambs.

"How is that different from what we have now? The Conventicle making and enforcing the rules."

"Rules? You mean, not using magic on humans, not stealing magic from other witches, and not killing other supernaturals. Are those rules too hard to follow?"

Rei tutted. "They break them all the time."

I wasn't totally convinced that the world knowing about supernaturals was a bad thing. We could learn to coexist. Were the Awakeners the bad guys or the good guys? I was getting a stress headache trying to figure out who the good guys were and where I stood.

"Most of the time it's fixing issues that arise as a result of you and your ilk being reckless and trying to reveal yourselves."

"I don't care. It's time for new rules and governing."

"You don't like the rules? Fine, let me put you out of your misery."

Rei's eyes flicked from Anand to Helena, who had taken up a position next to him. She was dressed in slim beige slacks she'd paired with a burgundy draped crisscross tank that revealed another network of markings twining up her arms, similar to Dominic's. The magic-restricting marks were still in place. Flawlessly shadowed eyes with thick mascara, liner forming a peak at the end, cherry-red lips, and defined cheeks highlighted by blush. She'd pulled her tresses back in a severe ponytail. She looked as if she was going to an event and not a potentially violent ambush. But this was Helena; maybe she might consider this an event.

Rei swallowed, stepping back, her lips moving ardently and her hands circling around each other. A blast of spherical magic launched from her like a rocket, smashing into Helena and dissipating over her body.

Rei's breathing became more ragged as she shuffled back a few more steps, more aggressive magic springing from her with no effect. Her face was panic-stricken as she looked at her companions. The vampire was the first to react. A lightning strike movement placed him just inches in front of Helena. A self-satisfied smile traveled over Helena's lips as he looked down at the stake embedded in his chest. His shock barely registered before the blade she held in the other took off his head. Instead of a body, there was just a splattering of dust piled on the floor and the bloodstained stake.

I swallowed the scream. Rei's lips furled into a snarl as she made quick slashes in the air. Books flew from the shelves like a whirlwind, whipping around the room and striking at Helena and Anand, who used their weapons to slash and hit them. Another slash of Rei's finger, and the pages of the books ignited. Fire blazed, books launched, the strain of the effort heavy on Rei's face.

The room was pure chaos at Rei's hand as Anand and Helena dealt with the flaming books being hurled in their direction and chairs being magically flung at them.

"Animal," was all I blurted as one of the shifters morphed into a bear without breaking stride. Seeing the quick change from human to beast was shocking, no matter how many times I witnessed it. The bear pinned Anand to the ground.

Anand delivered blows hard enough to make the animal huff and growl in pain.

Too preoccupied with fighting off the flaming books and warding off flying furniture, Helena couldn't help Anand or counterattack.

The supernatural that I suspected was a witch cupped his hand, and a whirl of white, blue, and black coalesced. His brow furrowed as he concentrated, making it bigger. As black overtook the sphere, the room clouded over. His face showed strain as he directed the sphere over Helena. She gasped for breath, her color waning. The witch had found a workaround by affecting the environment.

Even feet away from Helena, I could feel the results of the oxygen-removing spell. She clawed at her throat. I moved back toward the wall, keeping my distance from the magic. I needed to distract the witch, break his concentration. Grabbing one of the few items still intact, a heavy Dungeons and Dragons light, shaped like a die, I hurled it at the witch, hitting him on the side of his arm.

The oxygen-siphoning sphere shuddered a few feet away from Helena, but not far enough to prevent its effect. The heavy mug I lobbed at him next hit a diaphanous field, rebounded, and pitched into my hip, sending me stumbling back. Recovering with a groan, I looked for something that could pierce the field and found Rei on the other side of the room providing protection for the oxygen-siphoning witch. She shook her head, a silent request for me to stay put. She wouldn't kill me—that was some comfort—but the throb in my hip was proof she would hurt me.

The shimmering field that covered the witch flickered and dropped, and the mug I hurled smashed into the side of the witch's face. He stumbled to the side, and the sphere shuddered then vanished. Running out of objects heavy enough to throw, I searched for more items and found the source of the breach in Rei's field.

Dominic.

He had pulled Rei against his chest and held a claw at her jugular. I turned back to find Helena standing over the manacle-subdued, oxygen-siphoning witch. There was a naked man where moments ago a bear was fighting Anand. The man wasn't moving, not even a faint rise and fall of his chest.

Rei's eyes were calculating, glancing at the claw at her throat then cutting to the two remaining allies in the room, who were doing their own assessment.

Amid all the violence and pandemonium, it was hard not to think of Cameron. The damage was extensive, with areas empty of books, partially burned books strewn throughout the store, the registers on the floor, and several bookshelves smashed.

Her store was in shambles. She'd lose income. How would the destruction be explained? The cameras? Was this being seen on her phone real-time? How would they handle her knowledge of them?

Dominic's expression was stoic as his eyes met mine. I wasn't sure if it was his presence or tempered anger that had increased the room temperature by several degrees.

One of the shifters watched Dominic as he took in the damage.

"Is this what you all want?" Dominic asked, directing his attention to all the Awakeners in the room.

"No, but it seems to be what you want," the lone shifter growled. I knew the tell now; he was about to shift.

"You do it and I'll kill Rei," Dominic told him. "Then my sister will kill you and this little stunt will be for naught."

More evaluation took place. I felt sure they were speculating whether this cause was worth their life. They'd lost two already with nothing to show for it.

"Helena." Dominic nodded at her and she moved aside, allowing the magically neutered witch to stand.

186

Dominic released Rei, I assumed as a sign of good faith or to show that she was not a threat to him. He hadn't restricted her magic.

"Has there been any contact between Roman, Celeste, or Vadim?" He directed the question to everyone in the room.

Their jaws clenched in a mutual demonstration of allegiance. Dominic inched in Rei's direction.

With ire, she squared her shoulders and met his gaze. "You won't get any information from me. Are you afraid you'll feel the sting of Roman's claws, or is it Celeste's magic that you fear? You have no immunity to it, do you? I hope it's Roman's claws that get you both." She snapped her head in Helena's direction.

The tight air of contention filled the room. She'd struck a nerve—pointed out their weakness.

The front door of the store blasted open, and strong magic flooded in with the group of seven people who entered with practiced efficiency and military precision. Magic reminiscent of when I was in the room with the Conventicle burst in. Powerful. Heavy. And undeniably hostile.

Friend or foe?

I could see the lack of recognition on Dominic's face before the woman at the front of the group fired three gunshots at him. He darted to the left, barely missed being hit by bullets that blew the plaster from the wall. Dominic returned fire. A menacing red glow of magic pummeled into the woman's chest. She crumpled to the ground. Dominic was moving faster than the other people could target him.

Rei realized too late that despite their attack on Dominic, this new group weren't allies. She was ensorcelled in a bubble, blue and white intermingled, giving way to smokey black. Her oxygen was being choked off as the magic-wielding newcomer efficiently pulled it from her. Rei collapsed, her face distorted by her struggle. Her lips were losing their rosy color and her face blanched. Small lines formed across her eyes from broken capillaries. Dead.

The vampire was locked in a frozen state. I could only assume this was necromancer magic. Power over the dead. The vamp wore his helplessness with a tight-lipped scowl. I didn't avert my eyes fast enough to miss his demise by beheading. This wasn't an idealistic group of people like the Awakeners; they were trained assassins. Magically powerful and brutally efficient.

The assassins' precision seemed to unleash something in Helena. The vampire body hadn't become dust on the floor before Helena had its assailant's head twisted at an odd angle that no one could survive. Anand was a whirlwind of movement, lithe and deadly. I still hadn't been able to determine if he was immune to magic, or so swift that no one could use it against him.

I chanced a glance in Dominic's direction. A thrown ball of magic breezed over my shoulder, barely missing me as I dove to the floor. My head hit a toppled bookcase. I was a little dazed, but I fared better than the wall with the hole punched through it. That could have been me.

Scrambling to my feet, I grabbed a piece of the metal wizard collector's item and threw it at the magic wielder, hitting him in the head as he prepared for another strike against me. Shock and anger took over his face.

Running out of items heavy enough to be of use, I searched around while moving in a zigzag to prevent being in his line of sight. I whipped around at the sound of footsteps behind me. I threw a charred hardback, but the shifter dodged it. Her menacing approach was measured and taunting. I kept my eyes fixed on hers, looking for the spark that seemed to light their eyes before they changed. If the others were so efficient with their magic, would this shifter be just as skilled at changing without the identifying precursor?

Anand lunged at her, knocking her to the ground and holding her down in her partial shift to tiger.

I continued to ease back, taking myself out of the cross-fire, hoping to melt into the background. My mind was rampant with thoughts. They'd killed the Awakeners. Were they there to also kill Anand, Dominic, and Helena?

Convinced they wanted to kill me, too, I scanned the room for an escape route. There was an emergency exit to the left of the store and another exit leading to the alleyway in the employee lounge. From my position, they were an equal distance apart, obstructed by toppled bookshelves, bodies, and debris. I chose the employee lounge.

Before I could run, I felt the intensity of eyes on me. Two pairs turned in my direction. Helena saw it a moment before I did. One of them, a man in his mid-fifties, moved toward me. The cold gleam in his eyes and the cruel curl of his lips belied his gentle, paternal appearance. How often was his lethality underestimated by his appearance? With a slight flick of the man's hand, I slammed back into the wall. His magic held me firmly against it. I strained, trying to tear away. His hands were rigid in front of him.

Was Helena afraid to challenge him? Why was she just standing there doing nothing? Out of my periphery, I saw Dominic speeding toward the man, whose chest caved in from the impact of Dominic's punch. Dominic was just a blur as he twisted, avoiding the knife hurled from the center of the room. Without losing his speed, he sent what looked like a fiery arrow in the attacker's direction. Dominic was the embodiment of puissance and violence. It worked to my advantage at the moment, but I was witnessing his unre-strained power, what he could do. This was why the Conventicle feared and hated him.

The affable-looking man gurgled out a strangled gasp for breath that wouldn't come. His struggle to hang on to life seemed to take too long, the shock of his demise slowly registering on his face. Helena taking a knife to his throat seemed like a mercy killing. She chose that over dealing with the man standing near her, who shot a sphere of magic straight at me. I dropped to the floor and flattened my body against it and watched as it hit the illuminated wall that surrounded me.

The shock of his failure registered briefly before Dominic was behind him. He wrenched the man's head to the side, and the man dropped.

My breath came at short shallow clips. The violence was horrific. Dominic was violence. Period. A powerful reminder of my goal: do whatever was necessary to untangle myself from him and this world.

Dominic stepped forward, examining the cocoon of magic that surrounded me. He pressed his hand against it then quickly jerked away. Amber seized his eyes, and his face strained as he tried unsuccessfully to dismantle it. After several attempts he was joined by Helena, who circled it, examining it, and jerking back at the pain from touching it.

"This isn't witch magic."

Dominic grimaced. He was searching the destroyed room, moving quickly throughout the space, opening doors, moving anything large, when the cocoon of magic fell.

Left in the room was just Anand, who was on the phone, Helena, who stayed close to me, examining the space where I'd been enclosed in magic, and Dominic, who kept searching through the store for something or someone he hadn't revealed.

I was preoccupied with picking up broken ceramic pieces. Engaging in the useless act of trying to clean up. I had to do something, no matter how futile.

"Your arrogance will be your failure," Madeline said as she entered the room with several other people. Her gentle tone was diametrically opposed to the harshness of her scowl.

Startled by her presence, I was again unnerved by the ease in which they navigated the world undetected.

My eyes followed hers as she took in the state of the store: the bodies, the blood, the evidence of extreme violence. Then her eyes rested on the trash bag I was holding and the pieces of broken ceramic in my hands.

"Leave it. We will handle that," she instructed me. She directed the rest to Dominic. "Zana will take care of the cameras," Madeline told him, shooting me a harsh look before nodding to a woman with a purple pixie cut, shorts, an oversized shirt with strategically placed rips, and an ankle-length cardigan. A crescent moon and stars tattooed her neck, and the boredom with which she walked through the store was in stark contrast to Madeline's intensity.

Moving her hand in rhythmic circular motions, Zana whispered an incantation as she moved through the space. The same iridescent glow flitted over the room where I knew there were cameras. She was precise and methodical. Techno-witch. Once she'd gone through the store, she went through the coffee shop and all the surrounding stores.

"Is she erasing them?" I asked Dominic.

"No, she's changing what will be shown."

"If Cameron already saw it, she'll know it was changed."

He shook his head. "She won't. Zara's the best techno-witch because she leaves no evidence," he admitted quietly.

"Or rather, there's an illusion or compulsion spell with her magic. We're just pawns whose minds you manipulate on a whim," I spat out.

He stood taller, his hand shoved in his pocket, ignoring my barb.

"What about this?" I waved my hand around. "You can't just make this go away, magic it away with illusions and manipulations. These are real things that were destroyed. Real consequences because of this. How much more do the people I care about have to suffer because of the super-naturals?"

"That's enough, Luna," he snapped.

"Enough. Yes, I've had enough."

Anger had clouded all rational thought. I marched off, needing to get away from reminders of my predicament and another attempt on my life. I was furious at the supernaturals treating our lives and minds like game pieces to be manipulated at will to win whatever game they were playing.

The thrum of magic that brushed against my skin as I stared out the window seemed foreboding, now that I knew what it was. Before, I'd ignored the breeziness of air, viewed a slight fluctuation in the energy as innocuous—just my mind playing tricks on me, a stuffiness in a room that needed to be ventilated. There was something quite ominous about an area that was usually bustling around this time of day, now that no one was around. I didn't believe in coincidences. Magic. It was all magic, and I hated it. I just needed to fix the situation. How?

Fixing the situation consumed me as people entered the store and left, and I took in more magic-drenched air. Watching the orchestrated removal of all evidence of super-natural existence left me awestruck. The cleanup crew. The people behind the machine who had done this so often, it was a methodical and efficient system.

Dominic's placid face of indifference confirmed this was just another day for them. Murder a bunch of people, destroy a store, set books on fire—no problem, I got you covered.

Repulsed, I went outside, several feet from the store. Stared at the markings on my finger.

"Undo," I whispered.

"Luna."

I turned to see Jackson, who had been compelled to go home. I wondered, like the witch's curse, whether the compulsion broke when the vampire died. He eased toward me, the arrogance and self-assurance muted, genuine concern and curiosity filling his eyes.

"Can we talk?"

"About what?" I asked. *Magic? Because if you remember it, hell yeah, let's discuss it.* I was desperate enough to even collaborate with him. He'd become the lesser of two evils.

He shrugged. "I don't know, you seem like you could use someone to talk to," he said. "Let's get a drink."

Alarms went off. Apprehensive, I took several steps back. "Maybe another time."

Something was off and I couldn't put my finger on it.

He grasped my arm. "It doesn't have to be a drink. Coffee?" He pointed in the direction of the Starbucks a few blocks away. His grip tightened at my attempt to tug out of his hold.

"Is everything okay?" Dominic asked.

Jackson released my arm.

"Everything is fine." The contempt Jackson had for Dominic was the only thing consistent about him. "You know where to find me, if you need me," Jackson entreated. Hints of desperation lingered in his voice as concern flooded his eyes.

Dominic pressed his hand to my back. Warmth crept along it, and I stayed in place as Jackson warily backed away, his shoulders drooped.

Things were indeed a mess if I was contemplating going to Jackson for help despite something being noticeably off about him. For a brief moment, I thought he could provide something Dominic couldn't. Not quite safety—maybe a neutral zone? Or perhaps it was just familiarity. That's what it was. Despite his recent unsavory role in my life, the weirdness going on with him, he was a version of normal, and nothing I was experiencing was anywhere near that now.

I wanted somewhat normal, even if it was in the company of Jackson.

17

I navigated from my world to Dominic's massive estate in a fugue state, unable to get Jackson's look of defeat out of my mind. It was as if he'd failed to stop an accident. Despite his unsettling mien, his insistency was protective. Even Helena's searing glare as I passed her in the home's entrance, arms crossed over her chest, couldn't pull me out of my state and my debate over whether I should have left with him.

She extended her arms to her brother, showing him her magic-restricting sigils, her lips a thin tight line. "Remove it," she demanded.

Helena sneered at Dominic's hollow and dispassionate expression as he approached his sister.

"You're not nearly as clever and sneaky as you believe yourself to be. Your slow reaction wasn't for deliberation; it was to provide him the opportunity to kill Luna. The second one, you weren't aiding me; it was a chance for him to finish where the first one had failed," he said in a low, carefully controlled, rough voice. "They nearly killed Luna, and that was your intention." He turned on his heels, striding past me, leaving me in her crosshairs. Her features wilted into a sullen look of disappointment before it snapped into anger, which she directed at me.

"Don't you dare be smug," she snarled. She had definitely misread my expression. Not smug. Shock. I had given her the benefit of the doubt. I knew in the moment of fighting and chaos, it was hard to prioritize and errors in judgment were inevitable. But they hadn't been errors—they were opportunities for my assassination.

Her movements were like the strike of a serpent, quick and deadly as she devoured the space between us. Refusing to cower, I squared my shoulders and met her blazing, spiteful eyes.

"Don't be too confident in Dominic's protection. He only seeks to capture and destroy the only person whose magic rivals ours. This is not an act of altruism. It's ego-driven and nothing more. When he finds you have no value to him and aren't a means to a satisfying end, he'll go nuclear." Her nails swiped across my neck. I knew she wished she had her claws. "Then there will be no more Luna."

Stepping away, I said, "You mean, magic that rivals *his*. You no longer have magic." Turning from her, I kept looking forward, feeling her hard stare boring into me. I didn't care about her or her hate-laced glares. If she attacked me, I was going to fight dirty. I wasn't above using the tried-and-true windmill tactic. I was bound to land at least one good blow.

Dominic hadn't waited for me, which was probably best. I needed some time alone to process everything. Making my way to the room where I'd stayed before, it surprised me to find Dominic seated in the chair, legs spread, deep in thought. His eyes slowly moved to mine. The raw depths held a level of unrestrained violence and calculating intensity that supported Helena's comments.

He rose from his chair like a numinous wave. Not only had an attempt on my life been made, but one on his as well.

I pointed to my overnight bag, which I hadn't considered

when we were leaving the store. It had the Trapsen and the knife in it. Placed in my locker, I didn't fear it would be taken. If found, it would probably be by someone who had no idea what it was. But I felt better knowing that a pathway to the Underworld was no longer in my locker—secured only by a padlock. And since Dominic had it, not one vulnerable to supernatural lock picking.

"My bag," I said, hoping to start some dialogue because him motionlessly watching me was off-putting.

He nodded, not offering anything more of an explanation.

"What's going to happen to Books and Brew? There's no way magic can fix that."

I'd seen the height of it, but illusions could only go so far. Could magic replicate the scorched books, renew the destroyed display shelves and bookcases? Or the blood, vampire dust, and fog of powerful magic I was convinced lingered in the room?

Dominic had settled into silence as he stood in front of me. It ticked on so long that I didn't think he'd answer.

"This isn't the first time we have had to handle something like this. It will look like a random act of property destruction. There will be recompense for loss of income. The store will be back to normal in three or four days."

"How much of this efficiency will be a result of mind manipulation and compulsion? Making people perform for the magical puppet masters."

He blinked once, his fiery amber eyes an abyss that was hard to pull from. "Do you have other options? If so, do tell."

The fact that I didn't frustrated me even more.

"You wear your thoughts on your face," he told me.

"Good, then you know how exasperating and overwhelming all of this is."

He closed the distance between us, putting me face to face with him. The continued silence, taut as a stretched rubber band, remained between us. When it snapped, would I be verbally sparring with the Prince of the Underworld?

The light touch across my cheek was a contrast to the intense, painful-looking scowl that did nothing to diminish his appealing features. It enhanced it—a cruel beauty.

"Does it hurt?" he asked. "The bruise," he added, answering my confused look. I shook my head; it had just merged with all my other aches and bruises. With the adrenaline gone, I felt them even more.

"Why didn't you leave with him?"

"As if that was a choice. Remember, I only have the illusion of choice."

His finger moved from my cheek and was resting against my hand. Warmth slithered around me, his intoxicating smell enveloped me, and I let myself be submerged in the depth of his eyes. Searching for answers that he wouldn't willingly offer. He was a mass of contradictions. Raw power and violence but capable of gentleness. A fuse just waiting to be ignited but stalwart tolerance with Helena, and even with me.

"I wouldn't have stopped you," he admitted.

"Really?"

"It wouldn't have stopped the plans I have, but if you needed to be with him, I wouldn't have stopped you."

"I don't think I will ever *need* to be with him."

He let the surprise show on his face.

"It's time for him to be out of my life. Today was a lot for me, and it would have been nice to have a little normal. But something was off with him."

Dominic moved back to the chair, canted his head, and waited for me to continue.

"I'm not sure what it was." I explained about him being compelled by the vampire and my suspicion that it had been broken by the vampire's death, and about Jackson's return to the store.

"You are correct. Just as a spell is broken when the caster dies, the same happens with a compulsion from a vampire."

"He just seemed odd, and I don't know why he'd return to the store."

"Someone made him do it. The Dark Caster was there."

"The wall," I concluded. "It was the Dark Caster who erected it, which was why you couldn't break it."

He confirmed. "Your boyfriend—"

"Ex."

"Your ex, could he be the Dark Caster?"

"If he had magic, there's no way he would have kept it a secret. He would have been found immediately. His ego couldn't handle godlike powers."

Dominic gave me a faint smile. His swift movements were as off-putting as Helena's. A frown beveled the corners of his lips as he looked out at the garden.

"Tell me about your boy—*ex*-boyfriend, Jackson."

Since I'd never given him Jackson's name, I knew he had all the information he needed. The general information.

"Why?"

He turned to look at me, his eyes lazily traveling the length of my body, lingering over my lips before they met my eyes. "Because I asked."

"Technically you didn't ask, you sort of ordered me."

"Consider it a question."

"Then phrase it as one. Give me the option to decline."

He chuckled and returned to admiring the view. "It is rare that I ask and even rarer for me to be declined."

"I'm overjoyed to be giving you such a rare experience."

Abandoning whatever held his attention outside, he flashed a roguish smile, making me wish I'd phrased things differently. "Rare experience," he said. "Intriguing." He approached me in a slow, easy stride. I focused on the light splatters of other people's blood on his shirt and how comfortable and oblivious he was with it.

"Will you tell me about your ex?"

I shrugged. "I'm not sure what you're looking for. I can assure you that there's nothing magical about him. And if there were, he'd be leading the Awakeners and you wouldn't be able to keep him from letting people know he's a special little being."

The love goggles were nowhere to be found. I'd loved Jackson's confidence, but with clear vision, I could admit it had descended into self-aggrandizement. "Why are you curious about him?"

"Knowing him, I get to know you better."

That caught me by surprise.

"You want to know me better. Why?" I sputtered. I had no chill in me.

"Helena was right. I find you intriguing. And the reason the Dark Caster chose you even more perplexing."

Join the club.

"What drew you to a man whom you clearly don't seem to like? The ending of your relationship is new, your dislike of him, but there are hints of residual feelings. He's pursuing you, but you lack interest and don't show any signs of rekindling the relationship. That speaks to a betrayal, and he's seeking forgiveness."

"He's not seeking forgiveness. It's acquiescence that he wants."

His eyes narrowed on me. "You're too nice to be aggressively rude enough to force him away," he surmised.

"I'm plenty rude, he just has a high tolerance for it."

Dominic continued to scrutinize me. He ruminated over my response to the point I felt uncomfortable under his intense gaze.

"Did Rei try to persuade you to go with her?"

Keeping the conversation between us seemed moot now that she was dead. I eyed Dominic's bloodstained shirt again.

"Yes. The irony of her wanting to protect me from you—a

lowly human she wanted to subjugate once the supernaturals were revealed."

"You seem to want humans to know of our existence."

He waited patiently as I considered his statement, still acutely aware of his light touch on my hand. His magic seemed subdued enough to ignore.

"No, I don't," I finally said. "I just don't want us to be victims of your whims. Your anonymity makes us easy targets."

"Do you think knowing would give you an advantage?"

It was a rhetorical question, but I still felt the need to answer it.

"Not an advantage, but it would arm us adequately."

"How?"

"I don't know, if you wake up a little foggy headed, it might be a vampire, so you won't think it's you. Laws can be put in place to better regulate the supernaturals' use of magic."

"You think human laws will be obeyed by people far more powerful than them? A vampire could compel your politicians. Spells could manipulate outcomes. Shifter and vampire strength could dominate any human. But humans will attempt to regulate how we deal with things, muddling our system."

Frustrated by his interrogation pointing out the holes in my solution, I moved back from him, shoving my hand through my hair.

"Your system doesn't work either," I snapped. "Kane tried to compel me to injure myself and he's part of the Conventicle. He blatantly ignored—"

"Kane was handled," he reminded me.

"I know, but he still went against the wishes of the Conventicle. And what about the people who killed Rei and company?"

As he pointed out the holes in my suggestion, he needed to see the flaws in theirs, as well.

"That, I'm not sure. They wanted you dead."

"You, too."

"Many people want me dead. I'm not sure if my death was a bonus or an objective. You were definitely a target. I have no idea what their part is in this. It needs to be investigated."

Did he just flex about people wanting him dead? *Hey, Prince, that's not a good thing!*

"Why didn't you go with Rei?" Satisfaction lifted one side of his lips. "Despite your apprehension, you've chosen a side."

I shook my head. "No," I admitted. "I'm an unwilling participant. Our goals align. You want the prisoners back and to find the Dark Caster. I want the markings removed and out of this world. That's the crux of the matter."

"Ah, so you haven't determined I'm the good guy."

My mouth dropped open and I snapped it shut. Perhaps it was the fatigue and the assassination attempt, or the fact that I was firmly in "I don't give a fuck territory," but I said, "I definitely don't think you're the good guys. I'm not sure you're even the somewhat okay guys. It's debatable whether you're even the barely humane guys. You take lives effortlessly."

His face had been pitiless, totally lacking any mercy or remorse.

"They were trying to kill me and you. I defended us. What should I have done—ask them not to do it?" His mocking annoyed me. "Or do you have a death wish, Luna?" he tacked on, derision heavy in his voice.

He was right. But it still felt wrong. Like there should have been an alternative.

"People are killed all the time in your world. Does it bother you?"

I nodded. "But the difference is, I'm not there or hanging out with the murderers."

He nodded slowly as he regarded me. I wondered if he could mute the searing intensity of his gaze.

"The prisoners aren't responsible for their escape," he said, seeming to be in need of a subject change. "Our speculations were wrong about them being involved. If they were, you wouldn't be with me. If they knew you were the only person keeping them out of the Perils, they would have found a way to you. They're lying low, because they need to figure out things just like I do," he speculated.

This wasn't the time to point out there wasn't really a "we" in this when it came to finding out the truth about the prisoners' involvement. Whereas he seemed to desperately need the why of the situation, I was firmly in camp how. *How do I untangle myself from this situation?*

His finger glided over the light shadow of a beard as he was drawn into further speculation. My interest remained piqued by Rei's apparent hope that he encountered Roman. More specifically, Roman's claws.

"What effect do Roman's claws have on you?"

He diverted his eyes from me, moving his attention to the wall behind me as he deliberated.

"His claws are poisonous," he eventually said, crossing his arms over his chest. "Even to us. Weakens us and mutes our magic."

"For how long?"

"Until it's out of our system. The last time, it was about thirty-six hours. I was unable to return home, use my magic, or fight at my normal level," he admitted. There was a reluctance to his confession and a hitch in his voice. Was he embarrassed that he'd been clawed, or that he had vulnerabilities? It humanized him and dampened his intensity. I closed the distance between us.

My voice was low and entreating as I continued the questioning, learning more about his world. If I was forced to live in it, I wanted to know everything about it. Whatever my expression revealed to him, it caused him to relax.

"Dark Casters' magic can affect us, even with my immunity to witches' magic." He gave me a knowing smirk. "But that's information you already know."

Well, I upheld my promise. I hadn't revealed that I knew the information. I wondered if Nailah had confessed. Based on the self-satisfied look on his face, he was speculating and I had confirmed it.

"Go on," I urged.

"Their spells I can break, but their magic can be used against me."

"Some witch magic as well."

He nodded. "Atmospheric and some elemental. If it rains, it rains on me as well. Snow, I get chilled. And if there's a cyclone, I can be swept into it like anyone else."

His eyes narrowed on me, searching my face. "What are you thinking, Luna?" He might not have added the "Little" to it verbally, but the taunting gleam in his eyes had.

I had a speech about how they arrived at the average and pointing out that for five-six to be the average, there had to be people significantly shorter and that there were scores of people shorter than I was. Emoni, at close to five-eleven, would just look at me with a combination of amusement and a trace of mockery, urging me on. "That's right," "You tell them," "I'm with her and the Lollipop Guild." On the opposite end of the height spectrum, Emoni didn't seem bothered when people commented on her height.

"I thought you said I wore my thoughts on my face. You tell me."

"I'd like to hear it from you."

"These reveals make you seem—approachable. Real," I admitted.

"Real?"

"Normal. Like other people." These were all wrong

descriptions. So. Very. Wrong. But telling him that he seemed less of a larger-than-life figure, insurmountable presence, or ethereal force, although true, seemed hyperbolic.

"It shows the many dimensions you have. Like everyone else."

Self-assurance bloomed over his features, in the fire that banked in his eyes, his supple lips, and carved features. "But I'm not like everyone else."

That was apparent.

"Can bullets and blades hurt you?"

"They hurt," he offered in a level voice.

They hurt. Well, Prince, they hurt everyone, but will you die? "That's nothing notable. I think they hurt everyone."

"I'm very difficult to kill." He leaned toward me, a hint of a warning.

It wasn't even a fully formed thought—just a fleeting moment of me knowing I had other ways to protect myself against him and Helena. One freaking passing thought. A half thought. Not even a complete thought.

"Tomorrow, we'll get you magic and you'll do the spells and this should be over for you."

"But not for you?"

He shook his head. "There are other players involved and I need to find out who they are. What their endgame is. Those people who came after us—after you—weren't the Conventicle guards and they aren't allies of the Awakeners. If I figure out their objective, then I'll know how to deal with them."

"Perhaps they're just the ruthless arm of the Awakeners," I tossed out but quickly added, "but that wouldn't explain them killing Rei and the others. If they were allies, they wouldn't have tried to kill me. If anything, they're more aligned with the Conventicle."

He nodded, then frowned. "Unless there's about to be an attempt at a coup. Perhaps they don't like the agreement the

Conventicle has with me. That may be why killing me was a bonus." Looking down at the blood splatters on his shirt, he added, "I should shower and change."

Had he only just noticed that?

I had to drag my eyes away from the exposed warm, olive-colored skin, the sculpted stomach muscles, and the light trail of hair leading into his pants when he tugged his shirt from his pants, examining the crimson stains on the bottom of the shirt.

"Do you need anything, Luna?" he asked, dropping his shirt.

"What?" I wasn't leering. I know I wasn't. It was just a casual perusal. *Of the Prince of the Underworld, Luna*, I scolded. *The Underworld*.

That should have been sobering. I blamed my gawking on everything that had happened today. My body still hummed from the adrenaline rush. The highs and lows. The attempts on my life. That was all. I'd be ogling any moderately attractive man. That was my story and I was sticking to it.

"Food, drink, a platter of chocolate?"

I nodded. I hadn't eaten since lunch. "Food—definitely. Vodka in a Big Gulp cup, and I'd take a small tower of the chocolate you had earlier." I planned to take that home with me. It was expensive, decadent, and the type of chocolate I couldn't afford to treat myself to.

"Very well. I'll see what I can do about the Big Gulp of vodka. We usually only have wine."

I shrugged; my taste in alcohol wasn't very discerning. I wanted something to take the edge off and to make sure it didn't involve being naked with the prince.

"Very well."

He left, but there was a smugness to him. His teeth gripped his lips.

"Meet me in the kitchen in an hour."

18

*A*fter a half-hour shower, I headed down and found Dominic seated, with an empty plate off to the side, a different notebook than our original in front of him, and sipping on wine. He gave me a once-over: the damp hair pulled into an untidy bun, loose-fitting *Dorian Gray* t-shirt, threadbare leggings, and fluffy ankle socks. I wasn't going for sexy but wouldn't have known that from the look Dominic gave me. He seemed most intrigued by my t-shirt, giving it a long, languid look.

In a black, soft-looking cotton t-shirt and age-worn jeans, he was the most casual I'd seen him, but he still possessed the refinement of someone wearing a bespoke suit. The edges of his exposed tattoos shimmered under the halo of the warm yellow lights.

"No Big Gulp," he said, "but we had enough to make you a French martini."

I took a small sip. It was really good.

It wasn't until the smell of the steak, caramelized potatoes, and tomatoes skewered with mozzarella hit me that my stomach started growling uncontrollably. Since he hadn't waited for me, I tore into the food.

I drank the water provided instead of the martini. Looking up from my plate, feeling the heat of embarrassment inch its way up my neck and cheeks, I said, "I was hungrier than I thought." I wiped my mouth with the napkin and took a sip of martini. "Thank you."

He smirked and pushed the wrapped chocolate toward me. It wasn't a tower, but a small pyramid.

Unwrapping one, I popped it in my mouth, convinced that the wrapping had actual gold in it so I wouldn't crumple it.

He slid the notebook over to me and I looked at it. The spells were sectioned into easily readable chunks. Dominic was committed to us striking true.

"I have divided them into the ones most likely to succeed based on the response of your markings and in the dungeon. Most are educated guesses, but I believe what was hindering the success of the spells was my magic."

Perusing the spells, it was really difficult not to be overtaken by the hope forming. Once the spells were reversed, I could work on damage control because I wasn't convinced there wouldn't be some fallout from what happened at Books and Brew.

"Is it just you and your family here?" I asked after I moved the notebook aside.

Dominic seemed comfortable with silence. I saw it as a missed opportunity to learn more about this world, and him.

"Anand, the guards, and staff. The guards are resident here, as are some of the staff. We have humans—indentured."

"Enslaved," I corrected.

He shook his head. "Contractually obligated. Presented with the option to work here for money, or a favor. I'm sure the number of people willing to give up a short period of freedom for money, opportunities in your world, a new and better life, doesn't surprise you."

Dominic's jaw was set, awaiting new questions, but I had

none. Money for ten years in the Underworld. Five years to return to our world with the job of your dreams, home, and spouse.

I only had one question, but before I could answer he said, "We never offer immortality. We respect the limits of life."

I hadn't hidden my look of apprehension and disgust.

"Anand was born here?"

He nodded, his focus intensifying. It wasn't as if I was ever surreptitious about gathering information.

"His mother was a witch?"

He shook his head. "A wolf shifter—a dangerous one. I suspected a hybrid with a witch. Her bite was dangerous to both vampires and wolves."

It was like pulling teeth. "His father?"

"Not a shifter or a vamp," he offered. His voice held a hint of finality, trying to end the discussion.

"Then what?" I asked.

He leaned forward and studied me. "Will knowing his background affect your life in any meaningful way?" he asked, his words acerbic, his tone curt.

"No, I'm just curious about him," I explained. I'd provoked a protective response he had for Anand. That was interesting. "He just vanishes into the background, or maybe he's camouflaging himself. Is that shifter magic? Vampire magic? Some type of illusion magic they can perform?"

"Except for Vadim, changing into an animal is the only magic shifters can perform. Vampires can zone and compel. But I've already told you that." Coolness drifted into his expression and made its way to his eyes. "Perhaps, if you want to know more about Anand, ask him."

The long draw he took from his glass punctuated the end of the topic. He relaxed back in his chair. "Tomorrow you'll have magic." A flutter of excitement moved through me.

"We'll come here to do the spells. It'll be best to see the response to it," he told me. "I'll need the Trapsen back."

"Of course, it's not like after this is over, I'm going to traipse back to the Underworld." I still couldn't believe how casually I said that. As if it was just another destination on the map. Underworld.

Was that disappointment in his expression?

"This might be our last night together," he whispered, seduction and invitation heavy in his voice.

"It doesn't have to be." *Um, it damn well better be*, screamed killjoy Luna. And I really needed to listen to her.

When he leaned forward on the table, I felt the pull of his presence, the dark sensuality that marked his presence, and the invitation. He exuded raw sexuality, and whatever he was doing beckoned me. Naughty thoughts crept through my mind, and I had to work hard at squashing them.

Dominic was luring me into his web of seduction, and I was willing to fall prey to it in a manner I was sure many others had before me.

"Unless it fails." Helena wore her cruel smile proudly as she approached the table. Ignominy wafted off her like a fragrance. "Then you'll have no other choice, Dominic, but to go to extremes. Not only is the Conventicle losing patience, but there are others involved. You'll be forced to be practical, which is what you do best." Her eyes were merciless as they bored into him and then turned to me. Was there any love between them? "Allow yourself the pleasures of his seduction. Let him have you tonight. If the sounds of passion I've heard from others are any indicator, it will be enjoyable for you."

Gross thing to acknowledge about your brother, but do go on.

I swallowed. My eyes flicked to Dominic, who, immune to her cruelty and antics, watched his sister with a casual indifference.

"You can fuck him tonight. Take your pleasure from it.

But know that he'd roll from atop you and slit your throat in the process." She provided a vivid portrait of Dominic's ease of violence and indifference. And the images that resurfaced about earlier only reinforced it.

With a great deal of effort, I kept disappointment or shock from showing. I wished I could've found the audacity to look her in the face and say something like "If I'm going to die, it might as well be under a hot guy." It would have shocked the smirk off her face. But I couldn't be that cavalier about dying. I wanted to live.

The expressionless look Dominic directed at his sister was a reminder of the casualness with which he approached murder and violence. He was a person who honored his promises, but he'd never promised to not kill me.

Backing away, I kept a careful eye on them both. Before I could turn and leave, I glimpsed Helena's look of victory and Dominic's indecipherable expression that made her air of triumph fade. For a long time, they held each other's gaze. The taunting defiance that she'd reveled in dwindled into apprehension. She swallowed hard and closed her eyes briefly. Had she managed to finally cross the line?

He dragged his eyes from her and let them follow me as I walked away. He didn't stop me from leaving, nor did he deny her statement.

———

Sleep didn't come easily. Helena's incendiary words stayed with me. Holding on to the optimism I shared with the prince was becoming increasingly difficult. My tossing and turning stopped when someone knocked at the door. I didn't answer.

"I know you are awake. I heard you." Had he been standing at the door, ruminating on the acceptable way to say "I know murdering you is my last-ditch strategy, but can we push that aside and be friends?"

I rolled out of the bed, marched to the door, and yanked it open.

"What!" I growled. I sounded formidable. If words had the power some people claimed they did, they would have ripped his head off.

He didn't speak for a long time, his eyes traveling the length of my body and settling on my lips, as if he had a hard time believing that level of anger came from them. Then they met my eyes.

"My sister was out of line."

"Did she say anything that wasn't true?"

He answered with a sigh. I took it as a tacit confirmation.

"May I come in?"

"Do I have a choice?"

"Yes."

"Then no."

He nodded. "I need the Trapsen."

Closing the door in his face felt better than I could have ever imagined. I went to the dresser where I'd placed the Trapsen, grabbed it, opened the door, and shoved it into his chest. He took hold of my arm and pulled me into him. I could smell his scent intermingled with the redolence of wine and feel the firmness of his body.

This dude has killing you as an option if things don't work out tomorrow, I reminded myself and cursed my hormones. They had lamentably poor self-protection instincts.

"The only way you don't survive this is if I don't," he whispered. "That's my promise to you." He inched in closer, his lips warm, his breath breezing across my lips. "Okay?" he breathed. It was such a featherlight touch I wasn't even sure it was a kiss.

He released me but I kept the miniscule distance between us.

"Okay?" he repeated.

Relief flooded through me and lifted a burden I hadn't realized had weighed so heavily on me. Perspective changes judgment. All the things that I considered questionable about him—propensity for violence, power, calculating strategist, and arrogance—were things that would ensure we both came out of this victorious.

"Goodnight, Luna," he said before walking away. I watched him until he disappeared around the corner.

"That is his oath, not mine," Helena clarified, her voice acrid with disdain. I turned to find her just inches from me.

I pointed to my face, devoid of any emotion. Fatigue made it easier to maintain. "This is my 'not giving a fuck' face. Sorry if it looks similar to my 'your little act is getting tiring, so get a new spiel' face."

Without giving her a chance to respond, I walked back into the room and slid a chair in front of the door. I had given Dominic the Trapsen, not the knife. Helena would feel the blade if she came in.

19

*I*t took a while to take in the spacious living room from the entryway where the elevator had deposited us. To my disappointment, our destination from the Underworld didn't put us in the alleyway of Books and Brew. I wanted to see the end results of their cleanup work. And Emoni's five texts asking me to call her and checking in on me didn't ease my concerns despite Dominic's assurance that everything had been handled. His version of "handled" differed greatly from mine.

"I'm fine," I texted. "You?"

"Have you heard about the store?"

Throughout the day, I had gone over how I'd handle this if asked, but now faced with lying to my best friend, it was more difficult than expected. *I'm protecting her,* I reminded myself.

"Yes, Cameron left a message. Store vandalized." I added an angry emoji. "Sometimes I hate people."

"Me too."

I was about to send a message when Emoni's ringtone sounded. Her calling set off alarms. She definitely preferred texts or video calls.

"Luna," she rushed out as soon as I answered.

Dominic appeared to be busying himself, straightening up things in an already immaculate kitchen. He managed to change the spice rack from one side of the stove to the other. The kitchen looked like it had never been used and the spices were for staging purposes only.

"Are you okay?" she asked, concern drenching her voice.

"Yeah, why?"

"Your *ex*"—the word held the same level of disdain as if she'd said "jackass"—"was in the coffee shop today, urging me to talk to you." Knowing how Emoni felt about him, Jackson approaching her probably made the situation seem dire.

"I'm fine."

"Are you with Dominic?" Calling him by name and not referring to him as the handsome man from the coffee shop meant that Jackson had done more than just urge. He probably gave her a Jackson version of the encounter with Dominic and the events of yesterday, if the Dark Caster or the Conventicle crew hadn't spelled him to forget.

"No." That lie hurt. "But I've hung out with him several times. He's—" I looked Dominic straight in his face, because he'd given up pretending he wasn't listening to the call and was leaning against the wall, arms crossed over his chest, wearing a crisp, tailored olive-green shirt that complemented his eyes. Making me aware of his enviable long lashes. Perhaps I'd purposely ignored them in my effort to dismiss his allure. Why force people into the Underworld? I was sure he could just entice them into following.

"He's not as strange as I imagined. Rather interesting, and of course anything Jackson has to say about him is fueled by jealousy."

Silence.

"Do you have plans today?" she asked.

Yep, I'm getting magic, undoing a spell so I can recapture pris-

oners from the supernatural prison in the Underworld. Then I plan to sit in front of my TV, watch the lightest, funniest show available while shoving chips and M&Ms in my mouth, and mainline margaritas while devouring tacos. What about you?

"Nothing much, why?"

"Can you stop by the coffee shop for a few minutes? I… I… I'd like to see you. Please."

It was a strange request, but the anxiety and urgency in her voice made me want to do whatever was necessary to ease it.

"Of course. I'll see you in an hour," I told her when Dominic mouthed a time.

"Great." Relief flooded her voice.

After I disconnected, Dominic was expressionless. The peach glow from the sun through the floor-to-ceiling windows that made up one wall of the apartment created a halation backdrop against his figure.

Pulling my eyes from his, I took in the curved white leather art deco chairs that wouldn't look out of place in a museum. They were for looks, not function. The clean lines of the wood coffee table. The large artworks hanging on the neutral walls. The rug was the only thing in the living room that looked comfortable. I leaned down to touch the soft material. I could see a sitting room to my right that was just as pristine.

"Helena and I share it. The bedrooms look more lived in," he admitted.

I looked at him suspiciously, not missing the invitation in his statement.

"Can you take me to the coffee shop, or should I call a Lyft?"

"I'll take you. I think it's a good idea for us to stay together until this is over."

As I followed him down to a garage with a silver BMW

sedan, black Audi R8, and a Range Rover, he turned to me and said, "It's private—came with the apartment."

Emoni's eyes brightened when I entered the coffee shop. There weren't any customers, so she came from behind the counter and hugged me.

I pulled from her hold and studied her. Hugging was another uncharacteristic thing.

"Can you believe this?" She waved a hand toward the bookstore, where the door was closed and there looked to be a team of people repairing things. The display shelves and books had been moved to the coffee shop, along with whatever saleable items had survived.

The items took over a small section of the coffee shop but didn't seem to bother the few customers. With coffee in hand, they perused the additions while Lilith stood behind the register, waiting to help them with their purchases.

"I wonder why the bookstore was the only store hit," Emoni mused with a frown.

"What?"

She looked at another barista and mouthed for her to cover. Turning back to me, concern creased a frown in her face, giving her a stern appearance. Her thick, tightly coiled curls were worn back off her face with a Puff Cuff; she looked younger.

"This might sound ridiculous… You know what, I'll admit it's bananas, but Jackson said that Dominic's obsessed with you. He thinks Dominic vandalized the store so he could have more time with you. Jackson's convinced that you've been spending all your time with him." Once it was out, she covered her face. "Ugh, it sounds even more ridiculous saying it out loud." And she let out a mirthless laugh, spreading her fingers to look at me through the spaces.

"I have spent a lot of time with him. He's interesting." Not a lie.

"And hot as hell," she added.

"I'm not going to deny that." I grinned, still unable to shake a suspicion that she might have been compelled, as Jackson had been. But no, this was Emoni, a sardonic quirk in her lips, expressive eyes, and that charismatic presence that allowed her to get away with snarky and poorly veiled insults to "faux coffee lovers."

"I just wanted to make sure you're okay," she admitted.

She led me to a table a few feet from Peter, who had taken over a table in the corner of the store, legs out, books, papers, tablet, and an uneaten sandwich and muffin in the middle of the table, making it uninviting for anyone looking to share.

Shaking my head, I jerked my chin in his direction. "Someone is definitely an only child."

"Or a self-centered ass."

"Possibly, but he seems nice enough. Just weird."

She looked unconvinced and moved her attention to the window. "It's nice out. Let's go for a walk. Catch up. I feel like we haven't talked in so long."

Familiarity eased in. We took many walks around the eclectic neighborhood to people watch, admire the unique fashions, take in the smell of food from the restaurants, and make predictions about whether the dog spa, hemp bakery, or 'I really didn't think this through" store would be around the next year.

"Sure."

Dominic was seated outside on the patio of the restaurant across the street from the coffee shop. Unless she was looking for him, he'd go unnoticed. Based on Emoni's line of questioning, it was good that I'd suggested he stay away.

"This way," she said, pointing away from the main street, through the alleyway. "We always take that route. Let's go down Kern Way. I want to check out that new coffee shop," she said when I hesitated.

Okay. Her smock was still on; she was going to broadcast her reconnaissance efforts.

"Tell me about Dominic," Emoni said as she pointed at our destination, the coffee shop signage of a steaming cup of coffee next to the name Café Intermezzo. Would it appeal to Americans, or would it be considered pretentious?

"I don't know a lot about him. He's broody and standoff-ish." Not a lie.

"So he doesn't think you're a witch?" she teased, turning to look at my expression.

"He changes the subject when I steer it toward that. He believes I am, but I think he knows the absurdity of it." Lie. But I didn't know what to tell her, and the guilt of lying to protect her left a heavy pit in my stomach. Emoni didn't seem to notice any change in me, and the conversation quickly moved to her asking if I liked him. I gave a very unconvincing no. She let that lie slide. It was more complex than just a simple no. I couldn't like the Prince of the Underworld. But denying my attraction to him was ludicrous.

The ardency of his promise to make sure I survived this had changed the way I saw him. I doubted he made many promises that involved protecting a life. Rather, he was definitely the type of person to make vows to take a life in the most painful manner possible.

Letting all thoughts of Dominic slip from my mind, I realized how much I'd missed being with Emoni, talking, the normality of it.

"The owner of the Kingmakers would like our band to be regular," Emoni told me after we got a coffee from Intermezzo. I wasn't sure if the sneer on her face was from all the shop's designer coffees and super sweet desserts: frosted cookies and muffins, fudge and candy. "This isn't a coffee shop, it's a bakery," she complained under her breath after the barista gave us a judgmental eyebrow cock at our black coffee order and rejection of pastries.

"Really."

"It was the woman I was speaking with at Books and Brew after my performance."

There was a hitch in her voice. Apprehension. Where she should have been excited, she wasn't.

"She booked the band for twice a month," she admitted. The heartache was so heavy in her voice, I stopped walking and looked at her. "And me and Gus on Wednesdays, as a duo."

I blinked once and made my face emotionless. A blank canvas to give her what she needed.

"Does she want you to do covers, like you two did at Wine-Down?"

She nodded. "On Wednesdays, twice a month. She believes it will be a good fit with the Wednesday crowd. You know how I feel about covers. It's fun occasionally but I need to do my own music. Songs that I wrote and I let her know that."

"And?"

"She agreed if I'd do a mix."

"What are you thinking about doing?"

She guided my elbow as we took a different route back to the coffee shop, one with noticeably fewer people around.

Taking a sip from my coffee, I waited for her to speak. She seemed to be having an internal debate.

"A few artists have been discovered. Performing without the entire band seems like a betrayal," she admitted. "Gus is on board—he doesn't see it that way." She rolled her eyes. "But maybe she saw something in just the two of us performing that I missed. The two of us might find more success. It will give us an opportunity to write more songs for the both of us. Two days a week, I'm turning my back on my band."

She shrugged and blew out an exasperated breath. "I'm twenty-six and unfortunately—" She frowned the rest of her statement; we'd gone through this a thousand times. She was always pointing out that her race, age, and "exotic" look might limit her. I wasn't sure about the others, but her looks definitely would not hold her back, but it wasn't the time to point that out. Her biggest complaint was that people were placed in boxes and artistic expression was limited for a myriad of superficial reasons.

She looked at me earnestly. "It's a great opportunity and could open doors for me." There was still a hint of hesitation. "What should I do?"

I gave her the impression of thinking about it for a long time, although the moment she asked, I had the answer. "I think you should do it."

Something snapped against my back, pushing the wind out of me as I fell face forward onto the ground. I quickly rolled onto my back, spilled coffee soaking into my shirt as I moved. Four supernaturals sped toward me. A vampire was to my right. Her finger under Emoni's chin, she drew Emoni's eyes to hers.

"Thank you, Emoni, for bringing her to us. Forget that you saw Luna today. You called her and she said she's visiting family. Return to the coffee shop."

She continued instructing Emoni, implanting a new situation in her mind. She wouldn't remember our conversation or seeing these creatures. Anger and fear warred in me. I didn't want them exposed, I wanted them gone.

I scuttled back on my butt, trying to put some distance between me and the supernaturals, and looking for anything I could use as a weapon. Nothing. My coffee had spilled. My phone was in the car.

Stopping the vampire from further compelling Emoni had to be my secondary objective. I wanted her to forget this.

We had navigated to where factories and businesses had

been converted to industrial-looking lofts. No one was around. Even if anyone wanted to come outside, magic would be preventing them.

One of the four, a shifter, approached, his cold, predatory eyes fixed on me. I was cornered. He was about to shift, when his head snapped toward the vampire who had been staked. The vampire's dusted body speckled the air. It was the first sign of Dominic's presence. His claw sliced the vital arteries in the shifter's neck. He collapsed to the ground, covering his neck, waiting for his preternatural healing to kick in. The silver blade Dominic shoved into his stomach would make that more difficult.

No longer under the dead vampire's compulsion, shock cut Emoni's scream off. Open mouthed, her eyes widened at the violence before her, at Dominic's violence. I hurried to her.

"It's okay," I soothed, but it only made her direct her disgust to me.

"Luna, what the fuck have you gotten yourself into?" She wouldn't let me get close to her, shuffling back several feet for every step I took toward her. I felt the magic against my back, heard the violence of a gasp being cut off, and if I hadn't already seen variations of what was taking place behind me, I would have been able to imagine the brutality from what was playing out on Emoni's face.

Wind gathered, whipping in the air, its cyclonic pull tugging us toward it. I looked over my shoulder. The remaining supernatural—a witch, her fingers whirling around. Emoni and I ran, fighting against the growing force. Before we could get any distance between it and us, the small cyclone disappeared and the elemental witch collapsed face forward on the pavement.

Emoni had no problem with her scream this time. It resounded like an alarm. I launched at her, slapped a hand over her mouth. "Stop. Please. It's okay. It's okay."

No part of this was okay. And nothing in my voice made it seem that way. She had seen the violent underbelly of the supernatural world. She was an unwilling pawn in an attempt to assassinate me. This was so many shades of wrong, and I didn't have the skill to make it out to be anything other than the massive clusterfuck that it was.

Her scream became a soft whimper against my hand as tears gathered in her eyes and spilled, wetting my hand. I knew the feeling.

Dominic was on the phone; I assumed requesting a cleanup. Who knows, maybe he was feeling a little peckish and was ordering a pizza.

"What's going on?" Emoni breathed out in a weak voice once I removed my hand.

"It's going to take a while to explain."

"You can't do it here," whispered Peter, who had managed to sidle up next to Emoni, a protective hand on her back. I wasn't happy to see him because he'd be another person pulled into the damage control process. I wasn't sure what they'd do to him to clean up the situation. Whatever he witnessed hadn't rattled him to the extent it had Emoni. Perhaps he missed the violence and display of magic and only saw Emoni's response.

"Let's get away from here," he urged, still in a whisper, but it was enough to carry to Dominic, who was removing identifying information from the fallen assassins and looking at their faces as if committing them to memory. His head snapped up and he stood quickly, racing toward us at full speed.

Emoni and I looked back and forth, trying to make sense of it. Dominic's face. It was twisted into a cruel and wrathful sneer. Emoni focused on the sphere of fire forming in Dominic's hands. She missed the yellow illumination of magic and the innocuous mask fall from Peter, the Books and Brew book nerd. His eyes darkened several shades and the otherworldly feeling I had felt when ensorcelled by magic wafted from him. Feeling it again made me recognize there had been hints of it when I spoke to Jackson outside the store.

I whipped in his direction. "It's you!" I moved back.

"I really didn't want you to find out this way," he admitted. His hand reached out to the air, smoothing the fire that Dominic had launched at him. When he returned an offensive-looking sphere of gray and white that looked like oxygen-siphoning magic, Dominic darted out of the way. Clearly, he wasn't immune to Peter's magic.

I grabbed Emoni's hand, pulling her closer to me. And once she was next to me, I moved to put my body in front of hers. Peter wouldn't kill me, but I wasn't sure what he'd do to her.

The footsteps were barely audible. It was the whip of the sword through the air that announced Anand's arrival. Peter grimaced, turned, and hurled a string of white illuminated magic at Anand. It smashed into him, sending him careening back several feet. Peter concentrated. The magic wove around Anand. His body relaxed to the ground, his breathing noticeably shallower. He was killing him.

Dominic's claws were exposed on one hand, so he used the other to toss fire at Peter, ending with a rapid fire of magic pelts. Peter responded with disinterest, his hand reaching up and snuffing out the magic as if it were merely a nuisance.

Something pulled his focus. He grumbled his disdain, turned in my direction, smiled, and vanished. Reappearing behind Emoni, he whispered something, pressing his hand to her throat. She choked out a gasp before collapsing to the ground.

Flashing Dominic a taunting smile, he said, "You can't save her and come after me." Then he disappeared again.

Anand rolled to his side, lethargic but alive. He'd lost his grace of movement as he lumbered to his feet. "The repellent has been broken. It needs to be restored," he told Dominic.

"It's up again," Madeline said from a few feet away, showing her dissatisfaction at the sight of me and Dominic.

Dominic didn't care about her displeasure; he was debating whether to go after Peter and he wore the indecision on his face.

Cradling Emoni in my arms, I called out to him. "Help her," I demanded, my words sharpened by my anger and his clinical assessment. He'd found the Dark Caster; he could go after him. She was one life lost to catch the big bad. "Now," I snapped.

Reluctantly, he kneeled next to her. He examined her and frowned. Shaking his head, rage flooded from him.

"A *necri*," he explained to Madeline.

Her face contorted to the same look of disgust and contempt. "It is used to simulate death. A difficult spell to perform and one of the few that are illegal with no exception."

Peter wasn't abiding by any of their rules, the very thing the Awakeners wanted the freedom to do.

Watching the unhurried and measured way in which Dominic undid the spell, I knew it was dangerous. Like defusing a bomb. I wasn't sure how long it took. It felt like hours although it might have been minutes. My heart was beating so fast it had to be distracting.

When the veil of death lifted from Emoni, a silver light unwinding around her, she sat up. Apprehension filled her eyes. She attempted to scoot back away from us when Dominic called her name. It was an unearthly, captivating sound. Melodic. It wasn't just Emoni being urged to hear its lure and respond.

Madeline stepped back, preoccupying herself with removing all signs of the assassination attempt. Her efficiency was a reminder that they did this all the time. Too many times.

Tears formed in my eyes, watching Emoni be bespelled, as Dominic manipulated her memories to make her believe she saw me today and we had coffee in Books and Brew. She then followed him to Café Intermezzo, where I was sure he'd *manipulate* more thoughts to explain her standing in front of the café.

The only solace I could find was that at least we knew the identity of the Dark Caster.

20

*D*ominic watched me pace back and forth in the ridiculously sterile apartment that felt like a luxurious hospital. It lacked the warmth of a home. The gray wood floors, lifeless neutral walls, and light streaming in from the window all seemed so much harsher now. I knew the room hadn't changed; I had. The world looked irreparably different.

"It had to be done," he assured me for the third time, but it was more than just Emoni that bothered me; it was speculation about Peter. The Dark Caster had been under our noses the entire time. Watching me, commenting about the ring that covered my markings, knowing damn well why it looked different. He had chosen me, out of all the people he had encountered, and I wanted to know why.

Dominic finally blocked my pacing, looking down at me. "What is this helping?"

"Thinking. It's helping me think." It wasn't. Moving was just giving me a distraction.

"In less than an hour, we'll meet with Emmanuel, get the magic you need, and then this will be over for you, Luna."

"Will it?" I challenged, putting all my frustration and

anger into it. "Assassins came after me. Once the prisoners are recaptured, I'll no longer be at risk of assassination, but what's to stop you all from using magic against me—against us? From where I stand, the enforcement of the law against using magic against humans seems really lax. And the level of magic allowed to protect you all from being discovered is awfully broad. How do we stop being compelled by vampires?"

"Don't look them in the eyes."

Well, thanks. That was the same information Anand had given me, which simply infuriated me.

"If we don't know they exist, we can't even take that simple measure."

The Awakeners had a valid argument: Supernaturals needed to be revealed. Give humans a fighting chance to protect ourselves. But they wanted to be elevated to some royal status. Not live as equals but our betters. The Conventicle and their acolytes wanted to cling to the shadows, but from what I could see, they weren't sufficiently enforcing supernaturals' limits of magic on humans.

"And the attack yesterday. Who are they? What's their ideology? What are their goals? How can you enforce your rules on them when they don't seem to have any allegiance to anyone?"

"I'm still looking into leads. I think it's an uprising—a coup in the making."

Once I was dead, the people attempting the coup could persuade those who wanted to maintain the supernaturals' anonymity to switch their support to them. After all, that was the group that got things done. Would they be better or worse than the Conventicle? The assailants from the attack wanted me dead, so even if they were better at controlling the supernaturals than the Conventicle, I still couldn't root for them. At least the Conventicle wasn't actively trying to kill me.

"Luna, you're out of this after today. I will work on behalf of humans' best interest."

I wanted to believe him. Even more when his warm hands rested on my hips, amber eyes entreating me to do so.

I couldn't. He worked on behalf of his own interest. I needed to work on behalf of mine. It would be great if we had a common goal, but I didn't see that happening.

Not every bar has the welcoming vibes created by music loud enough to be heard from outside but not be overwhelming and an exterior that welcomes you in to have a drink and good times. Two harsh lights that wouldn't be out of place in an interrogation room were at each end of the single-story dingy blue stucco building. Dirt and discoloration from age obscured the signage. The inside looked dim, and if it weren't for the number of motorcycles parked outside, I would have thought the building was vacant.

"So, this is where Emmanuel hangs out?"

Dominic nodded, apparently not sharing my concern. It wasn't just the grim building; it was also that the bar wasn't on the main street, it was thirty miles from the city, and the only other business establishments were several miles away. They could be as loud as they wanted here without disturbing anyone. Which meant no one could hear screams for help.

"He doesn't have a home where we could have met?"

"Of course. He wanted to meet here."

"That didn't strike you as odd?"

"Doesn't matter either way to me."

He got out of the car and when I stayed put, still eyeing the place, he came to my side and opened the door.

Ignoring his extended hand, I hopped out of the car. *I got this. Just a powerful witch I'm borrowing magic from, at a bar way off the beaten path, where screams won't be heard. Easy-peasy.*

I had to stop reading mysteries and crime novels.

The inside was just as poorly lit as I expected, and all eyes turned to us. Well, Dominic, dressed in a crimson shirt, granite-colored pants, and leather shoes, with the messy coiffed hair and rugged low beard of a man who belonged in a posher bar than this. Even with his sleeves rolled to the middle of his forearms, showing the arcane symbols and intricate designs that were understated compared to the tats of the bar patrons. Most wore short sleeves or tanks, showing off an impressive and beautiful tapestry of colors. Others were dark with portraits of predatory animals: wolves, panthers, and snakes.

All eyes remained on us, the interlopers. Dominic traipsed through the bar with airy confidence, people parting for him instead of him having to weave around them. Pulling my shoulders back, I stood taller, trying to put on the same airs. It's easier to do when you have magic, claws, and preternaturally fast and precise movement.

Dominic slowed until I was next to him, a hand well placed on the small of my back, momentarily redirecting my attention from the crowd to the tinge of warmth that spread over my back at his touch.

He leaned in and whispered in my ear. "It's fine. This is just a power move by Emmanuel, to unsettle us."

"He succeeded. I'm unsettled." I would've preferred to meet at a restaurant. Maybe an ice cream shop. Nothing menacing in a Coldstone Creamery.

Staying close to Dominic, I tried to present the same level of confidence he radiated. I thought I was pulling off the "don't screw with me vibe" in its entirety. *I will knock you out with my phone. Squash your man grapes and elbow you in the tatas.*

I was grabbed by the waist and slammed back against a

firm chest covered with a softer layer of fat. A rough beard rubbed against my cheek.

"You don't seem like the type that goes for the pretty boys," the alcohol-laced breath whispered in my ear. Before I could raise my foot to smash it into his and ball my fist to punch him, the hold he had on me relaxed.

Dominic was no longer in front of me. He was behind the man, hands clamped around his throat and knife held at his jugular. The stout man huffed out a breath through clenched teeth. His eyes were ablaze with anger, but as the knife bit into his skin, flight and fury shadowed his face.

"I'm the nice one. You touch her again, I'm going to let her at you." Dominic continued to hold the man, looking far too confidently at people who were now armed with blades and guns. One was scarily close to Dominic's temple. He eased his hostage around, using him as a shield. What lingered in his eyes was calculating, cold, and dangerously unsettling.

"Let him go and there won't be any trouble," said one woman with a gun trained on Dominic. The implication was there wouldn't be any trouble for Dominic and me, but her voice didn't hold the confidence that she believed it.

His lips kinked into a mirthless smile, his voice rough and hinting at unspeakable levels of violence. "We're just here to visit Emmanuel. You don't give me any trouble, I won't give you any."

"Release him," the woman demanded.

The grin firmly in place, Dominic said, "Of course. Your wish is my command." No semblance of humility was in his words.

You convinced me you're a jackass. He was quickly next to me, urging me forward, not even giving the crowd of people the courtesy of looking back. Taking his lead was hard. Unable to hear footsteps over the music or see movement because of the low lights, I was alert. I'd had enough violence to last a lifetime.

"I'm the mean one," I teased in a whisper once we were down a hall and the door closed us off from the bar.

"I have a feeling you can be quite brutal when necessary."

I was *so* brutal that a punch from me only evoked laughter from him. "Don't you forget it," I told him.

"Don't think I could."

After three abrupt knocks on the first door in the hallway, a gravely baritone invited us in. The office was sparse. A half-filled bookshelf in the corner, and a rug presumably intended to add a decorative flourish but that seemed to deliberately collect dirt. At one time it was probably a nice rug, cream, rust, and hunter green complementing the pine-green walls. One wall was covered with pictures of restored motorcycles. With the man seated at the desk proudly posed in front of them. Or maybe he was just some weirdo taking pictures in front of other people's bikes.

"Emmanuel."

"Dominic," the man responded just as brusquely. He was of an indeterminate age, shorn dull mousy-colored hair highlighted with gray or silver. His square jaw gave his face a blockish look.

The man kept his arms crossed over his chest, exposing large arms. Not defined but they could probably deliver a lot of power. Stern, watchful eyes paid close attention to me and Dominic.

"I see you made it without incident," he said, a hint of humor in his voice.

Dominic shrugged. The tension in the room was pulled so taut, it was only a matter of time before it broke. Had I been in any room or met anyone who liked Dominic?

"So this is Luna," Emmanuel mused, taking his legs off the desk and standing. Just a few inches shorter than Dominic and with a broader build, but Dominic's presence still over-powered the room.

Emmanuel moved closer, regarding me carefully, his eyes traveling over every inch of me. My ring covered the markings, but his knowing look felt as though he could see beyond it.

He reached out to touch me. Dominic grabbed his hand and pushed it away. "I never told you her name."

"Ah." A flush fell over his parchment skin. "She's sort of a celebrity," he admitted.

Dominic narrowed his eyes. "What do you know about her?"

Emmanuel returned to his chair, plopping down in it and returning his feet to the desk. He linked his fingers behind his head. "You seem so hostile these days. Perhaps you need a partner." I wasn't sure if he was offering his services or subtly telling him he wanted to deal with someone else.

"You know damn well that I have a partner."

Emmanuel's brow hitched. "Do you? You're not referring to Helena, are you? She's not a partner so much as a rabid creature that should be put down."

Helena was no longer involved, but I guessed that wasn't widely known. Probably the prospect of having to deal with her worked to Dominic's advantage.

"That's your one and only time. Helena has nothing to do with this. As I said on the phone, I need to call in my favor. I need to borrow magic."

"For her?"

Dominic's head barely moved into the nod.

Emmanuel looked at me thoughtfully, trying to suss out something. "I heard she's responsible for releasing the prisoners from the Perils." Although his question was directed to Dominic, he kept his eyes on me. I remained expressionless, trying not to give anything away.

"I loan her the magic and that will satisfy my debt," Emanuel confirmed.

Dominic gave a slight nod.

"Well, I think I need to clear out the place. Don't want anyone interrupting us." Emmanuel eased past me. I didn't need to follow his movement to feel his gaze on me.

Looking around the office, Dominic's face remained indecipherable. Emanuel's voice was faint on the other side of the doors.

"Will this hurt?" I asked.

"It shouldn't."

"That wasn't a definitive answer."

"Because I don't have one. I've never borrowed magic before. I've seen magic taken from someone and they didn't look to be in pain as it was done, just pissed off."

"Like your sister?"

"I didn't take her magic, it's just restricted," he corrected.

It still pissed her off.

Time ticked by. Dominic moved to the desk and grabbed a pen and piece of paper, scribbled something on it, and handed it to me along with the key fob.

"If I tell you to leave, go to this address. The emergency exit is out this door and to the right, okay?"

I nodded, taking the items. "Dominic, what's wrong?"

His eyes narrowed at the door. "Nothing yet."

I shoved the paper in my pocket, palmed the key fob, and continued to wait for Emmanuel. Ten more minutes passed then Dominic scrutinized the door and mouthed for me to go.

I ran.

Halfway to the exit I heard pounding feet and saw seven people flooding through the door, a silver-blue sphere of magic being released into Dominic's chest. The woman in front stood in frozen disbelief when there was no effect. Swallowing a gasp, I hesitated for one moment before darting for the car. Hauling myself in, I started the car without adjusting the mirror and reversed, guilt and panic washing over me at the sight of newly arrived cars and more people spilling into the bar.

Once on the main road, I could think more clearly and my internal debate persisted. Out of the rearview mirror, I glimpsed another car turning into the bar's parking lot. I couldn't leave him.

Chuffing and huffing drew my attention, and I was startled to find Zareb had made himself visible.

I cursed under my breath, one hand going to my chest. "Are you trying to kill me? How did you get in here?" *Great, I'm talking to hellhounds now.* But if he could travel from the Underworld, answering me wasn't terribly unrealistic.

Zareb's response was a low rumble in his chest.

"I can't leave him," I repeated aloud.

The hound nudged my shoulder as if to tell me to keep going, but I swung the SUV around and headed back to the bar, parking it facing out so I could make a quick exit if necessary. In the trunk I found an emergency kit. I rummaged through it until I found three flares, and I snatched up the wrench. The only thing I could think to do was throw in the flares, hope they hit something flammable. If nothing else, it would be a distraction. If I had the Trapsen, I could notify Anand. Worst case, Helena.

A bloodied body crashed through the door and landed, his right arm twisted in a manner that wasn't anatomically possible without a break. A clawed creature stood over him. It had Dominic's features, clothing, and body, but there wasn't anything human about him. This wasn't the refined, coolly subdued man that I reluctantly found sexy as hell. This was an animal. A beast of the Underworld. His eyes blazed like fire, his magic thrashed the air, and blood—I was sure other people's blood—coated his clothing.

Lips furled, he hissed at me. "Go!"

My feet were planted, eyes wide, horror-stricken, when he used his claws to slash the man's throat. The spurt of the man's blood jolted me into action. I ran to the SUV. A hand grabbed my hair and tossed me to the ground. My hand held onto the wrench but the flares dropped. I made a half turn and smashed the wrench into the person's wrist. They released me with a shriek of pain. I rolled to my feet and swiftly turned and delivered another hit to the head.

Magic cracked into my back, sending me sprawling. Pain, awful pain, seared through me. Relief flooded me when I wiggled my feet and they moved. I scrambled back up and saw the magic thrower on the ground, fending off something I couldn't see. Zareb.

I ran for the car, opening the back passenger door.

"Come on, Zareb!" I screamed. He waited until the attacker had stopped moving. The man was still breathing, but he hadn't come out on the winning end. His shirt was shredded, blood trailed from bite marks, and he was curled in a protective ball, his hands covering his face.

The hound brushed past my leg as he jumped into the car, making his body visible once in. I rushed to the driver's side and we fled.

There was no way I was going to where Dominic had instructed me. After I was far enough away that I couldn't see the bar, I pulled over. Taking out my phone, I searched for hotels. I'd stay at one for a few days and figure the rest out later.

Zareb's warm breath, grunts, and chuffing made ignoring him hard.

"Go home," I told him. Hard, primal eyes leveled on me before his nose nudged my shoulder.

"No," I told him. "Go home," I repeated.

He pulled back his lips, exposing razor-sharp teeth. My eyes slid to the wrench on the driver's side. I didn't want to hurt a dog, no matter how menacing he looked. And he really looked menacing. His powerful build, the amber glow of his eyes, and the ferocity of his stare made him look absolutely like a hound of the Underworld.

"Are you going to eat me if I don't do what Dominic said?" I asked in a half-hearted tease.

He showed teeth again and nudged me harder. Apparently, I hadn't moved fast enough, because his mouth covered my arm, his teeth exerting enough pressure to demonstrate how quickly and easily he could get to me and the damage he could cause.

"Point made."

Taking out the paper, I put the address in the navigation and drove. Zareb settled back. In the rearview mirror, I saw the attentive eyes on me.

"I'm going," I ground out. I wasn't going to get magic from Emmanuel, and I had no idea what the next step was.

21

The home leaned into the modern farmhouse design, unlike their apartment. The apartment was him. Sleek lines, modern décor, and a tad pretentious. This was homey, nice, and simplistic. A beige, oversized sofa that looked like a cloud. Blankets peeked out from a soft woven basket. A double fireplace separated the living room from the kitchen.

The kitchen had simple white appliances, light wood cabinets, and a large island in the middle. Light hardwood floors and a round table completed the room. Large sliding doors looked out to acres of land. Whereas the other homes we'd passed had cattle and corn and soybeans, here there was just verdant grass. The scent of pine wafted throughout the house.

The hellhound plopped in front of the door leading to the garage, where the car was parked. "I don't plan on leaving," I said, rolling my eyes.

For an hour, I sat in the same place on the sofa, staring at my phone. I texted with Emoni, who was home; nothing about our interaction suggested she'd remembered anything from earlier. I was grateful for that, but knowing the reason still left the heavy weight of guilt.

Dominic walked in with the same wrathfulness in his eyes. "Make yourself at home, I'll be back." His eyes moved away from me and he disappeared down the hall.

Initially, I didn't move. I just wanted to figure out the plan. But, restlessness getting the best of me, I started roaming, starting in the opposite direction Dominic had gone. Nothing was exceptional about the four-bedroom farmhouse. A small sitting area, a library with a few books on the shelves, a small office with an open laptop. The last door was where the house deviated from anything I'd seen. My breath caught at the sight of chains affixed to a rune-covered wall. Swords and blades hung on the opposite side of the room. In the corner was a massive cage.

"Don't make yourself at home there," he said from behind me. "Close the door, Luna."

Startled, I turned to find Dominic wearing just a pair of sweatpants, all his ink on display, inching over his shoulder, the left side of his chest, and twining around his arm, ending at his wrist. The scent of his woodsy soap. Disheveled hair, misted skin, devoid of the savagery that I witnessed, although it lingered in his eyes, posture, and tense muscles. When I didn't move to close the door, he did. His lips lifted into a lazy smile, which took a lot of effort.

I still eased away from him. He didn't have to worry about me making myself at home anywhere there was a room that clearly was designed for torture.

His forehead creased. "What were you planning to do with the road flares?"

"Save you?" I squared my shoulders and stood taller.

Amusement curled his lips and lit his eyes. "How?"

I shrugged. "I had flares and a wrench. There wasn't time to coordinate a proper extraction rescue—so I had to keep the plan simple. I just knew *something* or *someone* was going to get hit or burned."

His lips twitched. He was fighting a laugh. "That doesn't seem like a viable plan at all."

"Fire and metal? Did I really need an elaborate plan? Burn and hit. No one's thinking I'm innocuous with those things at my disposal," I shot back. And that wrench helped me. Definitely a confidence booster.

"Ah," was his only response. He licked his lips, his eyes aflame with a wicked delight. "There's nothing innocuous about you, Luna."

His lips pressed against mine, hot and commanding. At my response, he pressed me against the wall, the kiss becoming increasingly voracious. Deft fingers slipped under my shirt, kneading my skin. A shiver coursed through my body when his nails grazed over my skin. Dominic's body was heavy against mine, and my body heated at the awareness of him hardening against my leg.

When he pulled back, I exhaled a breath and tried to focus on anything other than his hands that made me want more. More of his hands, more of his lips, and all the places I wanted to feel them. *Prince of the Underworld,* I reminded myself, but logic didn't prevail with him standing there shirtless and in sweats that hung off the crest of his hips. Corded muscles, warm olive skin, intricate tattoos, and raw sexuality.

I put some well-needed space between us. "You can just thank me," I teased.

He moved closer, devouring the distance. One hand rested on my waist. I could smell the scent of his soap on him, feel the heat of his body. It wasn't me; his body was abnormally warm. In the cool room, it was welcome. Bending down until his mouth was inches from my lips, he whispered.

"Thank you for your help, Little Luna. I wouldn't have

survived without you." His lips were so close, the warmth of his breath tickled my lip.

"You're very welcome." *You're not the only one who can sound insincere.*

He hadn't moved, and I was acutely aware of everything about him. Him grinning at me urged me to put more distance between us. He seemed unsettled. Frenetic energy that he had difficulty controlling reverberated off him. Based on the way he was looking at me, I knew what he wanted to do to subdue it. His expression promised something sinfully delightful.

I forced every off-putting image I had of him to the forefront, including the room I'd just seen. It wasn't enough. We needed a distraction. We had one. This crapshow of a situation.

"Is Emmanuel still an option for magic?"

He shook his head. "He betrayed me, but they were the ones to kill him. I was able to retain one of the attackers and talk."

Translation: I kept one alive and forced him to speak.

"And?"

He looked grim. "Emmanuel had joined the Awakeners. When he was supposed to clear out the bar, he contacted them. They were to take you but were intercepted by the cadre from yesterday."

They had done this so long, everything they did was a PR spin.

"They murdered the Awakeners," I simplified. "Who are *they?*"

"The new Conventicle. They seem to have grander plans than the current members. One being getting rid of me, taking over, and having a 'comply or die' rule for anyone who doesn't abide by the laws of anonymity. They see the current Conventicle as weak. Me as unnecessary."

"So they plan to take over the Underworld?" I was incredulous.

The current system wasn't working but the new Conventicle was ruthless. Would they protect humans and how magic was used against them? Their success meant death for me. It was a hard place to be, wanting to protect humans and rooting for a regime change and rooting against them to save my life.

"So, what's next?" I asked.

"You still need magic but it will have to be from a different source."

"Do you have someone in mind?"

He nodded. "Madeline."

"Oh, so going the implausible route."

"She'll require a great deal of coercion and diplomacy."

"I don't think you're using that word right."

His lips quirked into a half-smile. "Which word?"

"Diplomacy. None of you all are using it right. Diplomacy is a delicate dance requiring negotiation and finesse. You all are all 'do what I say or you die.' That's a threat, not diplomacy."

He shook his head. "Threats won't be necessary. The Conventicle will need my help to ward off the coup. She either helps or I'll let the new members take over and I'll work something out with them."

The thrill of the challenge darkened his eyes. Either way, he was confident he'd end up on top. Whatever showed on my face caused him to cast his eyes down, and when he lifted them, they were softer, gentle, not flaming with desire for violence and subjugation.

My eyes dropped from his to the markings on his body, finding the markings on his chest that were like the new ones on Helena. Without thinking how creepy and invasive it was, my fingers traced the intricate pattern.

"This is why the witches' magic doesn't affect you?"

He nodded.

"Can I get one?" Although an admirer of body art, I'd never had the desire to get my own. But if this could keep me from being susceptible to the whims of the supernaturals, I'd do it.

He shook his head. "You don't have magic."

"That's the problem. You all do. That puts us at a disadvantage. We can't even protect ourselves from magic with something like this." I hadn't moved my hand from the tattoos. His muscles tensed under my touch.

He frowned. "I wish I could change that for you. I can't. Luna, we have to return the prisoners and defeat the Dark Caster."

"Peter," I offered. It still felt peculiar associating his name with something so dangerous. But undoing his magic was a priority.

22

*M*adeline sat in the chair where I'd first encountered her. Her eyes, and the eyes of everyone in the Conventicle, pierced me with wary annoyance. Either they had the good manners or the self-preservation instinct not to say it, but they seemed to be wondering why I was still alive. Madeline had refused to meet Dominic without them present, which worked out. He was able to tell them about the plans to take over the Conventicle. They didn't seem worried enough about that, but they did seem worried that the attack on Dominic ensured that he'd be involved.

His request for Madeline's magic garnered more of a reaction than the news about the coup. Nothing about these people made sense. They all seemed to share the shock of his request, unable to understand why he wasn't taking the easy way out. End me, break the spells.

Madeline's look of abhorrence overshadowed them all. As if she were a queen requested to do menial labor.

Canting her head, she blinked hard once. "I'm sorry?" Clearly, she must have heard him wrong. He could not possibly have asked her to share her wondrous magic with a mere human. She blinked again, waiting for him to repeat his request.

"We have the spells; we just need magic. *Your* magic to invoke them. My magic can't be loaned to her."

Madeline reacted to that as though it invoked a terrible memory. Had she known someone who attempted to take his magic?

For someone who wanted the prisoners returned and the coup against the Conventicle handled, she was taking a long time to respond. I wasn't the only person who thought this because the impatience in the room was palpable.

A waifish Hispanic woman with loosely curled midnight hair and deep golden skin with cool undertones curled her lips back, revealing sharp canines. Vampire. I assumed Kane's replacement. "A decision needs to be made, Madeline," she drawled.

"Fine. One hour and I must be present the entire time. The moment the prisoners are returned, my magic is returned as well. I don't want your human to get any ideas."

His human. Nothing about my snarl was human, and it sounded so close to a growl that Lance, the shameless shifter, found it humorous.

"Just once, an exception will be made, and you can travel to the Underworld," Dominic conceded. "Shall we?" He turned, heading for the door without looking back, expecting Madeline and me to follow.

"No," I said. He stopped and turned to look at me. For just a moment, he wore his shock on his face before erasing it, leaving him expressionless. A blank canvas. The tension remained in his posture. He crossed his arms over his chest, giving me the full weight of his stare. Hard and penetrating.

"I have some requests," I told him.

Everyone looked surprised except for the tattooed seer from the first meeting. With a smirk on his face, he rested back in his chair, clasping his hands behind his head as if preparing for a show.

"You all need to stay hidden," I demanded.

"We are," the vampire provided, becoming less invested in the conversation with each passing moment.

"But you're not. You all aren't known to us, but you're very much present in our lives." My eyes flicked to Dominic. "You compel us, manipulate us and our memories." I looked at the vampire. "Feed from us." I looked at each of them, giving them my full attention. "Use magic to corral us and influence our lives. Whether or not you are seen, you affect our existence. That needs to stop now." Emboldened by images of Emoni's fear-stricken face, I knew I had to do something.

I looked at each one of them, giving them the full weight of my condemnation. And they responded with offense—definitely a result of being reprimanded by a human.

"You have rules to keep and you have a concerted effort to ensure that, but when you are discovered by humans, we suffer the consequences. That stops now."

"And if it doesn't?" one of the shifters asked in a dagger-sharp warning, leaning over the table, predatory eyes homed in on me. Drawing up taller, I met his ire. Whether it was magic I wasn't aware of or the sheer intensity of a shifter's glare, it was difficult to hold. Sheer defiance was the only thing that kept me doing it.

"Nothing. I'll go home, learn to live with the markings on my finger, and you all live with three powerful beings who have a thirst for revenge. Beings who will eventually get word that they're at no risk of being imprisoned again. They won't have any qualms about being discovered. That will nullify Dominic's involvement, leaving you all to deal with the coup. They've demonstrated the ability to be quite efficient with their violence. I suspect you'll spend most of your time trying to stay alive. And the Awakeners? You probably won't have to worry about them. They'll be cleaned up in the sweep as the others eliminate you all. Their 'comply or die' policy will ensure that."

"Are you threatening us, human?"

"Is it a threat if I plan to do it?" I challenged. "I'm negotiating on behalf of the humans. If they are safe, I'll do what I can for you all as well. If not. . ."

Dominic still had the cool, implacable look that made it difficult to read him. If he hated me for this, he wasn't letting it show.

"You aren't doing a good enough job. Perhaps there should be a change. You're biased—and the dissenters don't fear you enough to follow your rules. Make a situation that will force compliance."

Oh, so that's what it feels like to have the searing glare of powerful supernaturals on you.

"She's not wrong," Dominic offered, but I couldn't gauge how he felt. Was this a concession he made so I would help return the prisoners, or did he approve of the changes I proposed?

"You put her up to this!" Madeline snapped.

He held his hands up. "I assure you I didn't, but she sees what I've been telling you all along. Your leniency has led to this coup attempt. They see you as feckless. To be frank, you have been. I'm not. The threat of my reprisal and them being taken to the Underworld is a far better deterrent. I have an army. Return to the old ways, lift my restriction. I guarantee you won't have as many situations to clean up. Nor such casual slipups."

I didn't say that. The old ways seemed really violent with harsh penalties. There had to be a middle ground. But perhaps harshness was needed right now.

I shrugged. "I don't care how it's done—I just want it done." Sounding more callous than intended, I said, "I don't want us to be victims of your whims. We shouldn't have to suffer for your failures. If Dominic's involvement promotes better compliance and protects us, then do what you must."

Dominic nodded and looked to the members of the Conventicle, who didn't seem sold on the idea.

Madeline bristled. "So your sister can return to her reign of terror for the most minor offences."

"No, that rule will stand. My sister will have no jurisdiction."

They continued to debate, becoming hostile at times. I remained silent. Nearly an hour later they had come to some resolution, but contention remained in the air and amplified when Madeline retrieved a piece of illuminated paper.

"Do I have your permission to make the changes?" she asked the Conventicle.

They nodded, and she passed the paper around, each individual placing a blood-pricked finger on it. With a swipe of her hand over it, the paper was erased. Feeling like I'd been pulled into a gothic version of *Fantasia*, I watched a magic-controlled pen scroll over the paper, scribbling out the new terms. I'd made this happen. Flushed with pride, I realized that in a room full of powerful supernaturals, I had prevailed. One point for Team Human.

Madeline was smug as she negotiated going to the Underworld to watch the spell casting, whereas Dominic still hadn't made it known how he felt about the changes. Was he indifferent, or aware that he now had more responsibilities and that the actions of the supernaturals fell on him? Instead of guarding the worst of them, he'd be responsible for holding all rulebreakers accountable.

Madeline's response to the estate was more subdued than mine. She gave it a sweeping look and followed behind Dominic as he entered the house, with the same greeting he'd received on my first visit. The guards lined the walkway, and as soon as she was through the door, two flanked Madeline.

"What the hell?" She halted. "What is happening?"

"Go with them, we'll be with you in a moment," Dominic said in a level, neutral tone. She seemed just as confused as I was when Dominic took me by the elbow, guiding me down a hallway that I had missed. Or perhaps it hadn't been visible. The pitch-black hall made it impossible to see what was in front of me. A faint hint of sulfur and smoke permeated the space. Magic pulsed off Dominic at an erratic pace.

"Dominic," I whispered. He turned to me. His eyes glowed. Roaring amber and bright gold like an active flame held my gaze until I pulled my eyes from his. He threw open a door to reveal more darkness. My heart pounded. Interrogation. Torture. The air was thick with his emotions and my fear.

"I need lights," I told him.

"You don't need light, I'm right here." Heat wafted off him.

"Lights," I demanded.

He held a ball of fire in the palms of his hands.

"Little Luna," he whispered.

"Oversized Dominic," I shot back. No alliteration, but I made my point as I split my attention between looking at the two sources of light—his eyes and the fire in his hands. But the fire garnered the bulk of my attention. I took slow, cleansing breaths, hoping to calm my racing heart. He squelched the fire, making the room dark again.

A chuckle reverberated in his chest.

He blinked, eyes muted. When he whispered a spell, the warmth of his breath breezing against my lips made me painfully aware of how close he was to me. Embers of light were floating around us, enough for me to see his face. He tilted his head, dark amusement playing over his face.

"Do you know what you've done?" he asked softly.

Shoulders squared, I looked at him defiantly. "I've protected the humans. We aren't your playthings. You don't get to do as you want with us."

His eyes darkened. "Playthings?" Another deep rumble of laughter filled the room. He shifted; his lips brushed against my ear as he spoke. "I'd love nothing more than to play with you. Only you," he whispered. "But we don't have time."

A shudder raced through me.

"Oh."

Great response, Luna, you eloquent orator. "You're okay with my request?"

His finger languidly traced along my jawline; heat was blazing off him. "Okay? It was needed, but if I had broached the topic, it would have been more forceful, weakening the already tenuous relationship I have with them. My hands are clean in this. I'm very satisfied. Very."

His lips covered mine in a ferocious kiss, his tongue a sultry caress. Pulling away, he nipped softly at my lips. His tongue slowly laved over his bottom lip, soft, sensual, and inviting. Showing me the many ways he'd like to play with me. Panting, he stepped back, letting me catch my breath. My eyes dropped to his growing interest. I was grateful for the dimmed light, hoping it obscured my flush.

"We should go," he suggested. Neither of us moved.

Eventually, he moved to the door, leading me back into the darkness. He held my hand as he guided me down the dark hallway.

"I'm not sure if that's how you usually thank people, but I think most people would be fine with a gift card," I said.

He made a sound that might have been a laugh. Not much effort was put into it. "I'll remember that."

His hand slipped from mine. Once we approached the lit hallway, all humor had left his face. Helena was right: Dominic was concerningly calculating. As I followed him to the office where Madeline was waiting, she must have noticed my concern and my flushed face. I must have looked regretful because she seemed smugly pleased as she gave me a narrow-eyed look of rebuke. As if she was telling me to know my place and not intervene in supernatural business.

In the dungeon, Madeline couldn't take her eyes off the notebook of spells. "May I?" she asked.

Dominic had made some more changes, numbering the spells he wanted me to try first. He didn't hide his reluctance. Looking down at the spells, he handed her the notebook but stood close, observing her keenly.

"These aren't spells I'm familiar with. I'd love to read the source." Her fingers were running along them as if she could absorb them by touch. Madeline was looking at the spells longingly and furtively, glancing around the room for the spellbooks. I was sure she'd try to take them if she could. Her covetousness was on full display.

"No."

Her head snapped back at his terse response. She dropped her voice. "You understand my coven's predicament. We must explore all resources to stop Celeste. If she dies, so does my coven, taking out the strongest of witches. Far too often we've helped you. This is your opportunity to return the favor."

"Perhaps if you spent less time trying to remove my immunity to your magic and restricting my ability to navigate between your world and the Underworld, you would have discovered a way to counter the spell."

Madeline blanched and swallowed, taking several cautious steps back. "Let us continue," she said, glancing at me. Anything to ignore the knowing look Dominic was giving her. As she approached me, my anticipation of experiencing active magic overshadowed my fear about it.

"Your hand," she instructed. Her lips twisted into a rigid moue before taking out a knife. She clasped my hand even more firmly when I tried to jerk it away.

"I need blood, Luna." My name was said with the same disdain she said human. Why blood? It made me more amenable to having my hair plucked. She pierced the skin with no care for gentleness. The throbbing kept my hypochondriac mind from going into overdrive.

Her hand clasping mine was painful against the cut.

She invoked the spell and its effect was undeniable. A little shock to my finger culminated into a bolt of magic that rampaged through me, knocking the wind out of me. Madeline clenched my hand harder as I struggled to pull away. My ragged breaths filled the room and I closed my eyes, fighting back tears. I opened them only when Madeline released my hand. She'd slumped into herself, her eyes showing the same weariness as her posture.

Magic frenetically coursed through me. My body felt too small for everything that thrived in me. I wasn't sure if it was because I was human or wasn't used to having magic. Or maybe it was the way Strata Three magic felt. It was like trying to contain an enraged bull in a backyard.

Dominic moved quickly, handing me the notebook of spells and then placing the vellum in front of the cylinder he'd used to track Peter. I rushed the spells out in a long string of sentences. The marks on my finger glowed, slowly unraveling, reluctantly tearing from my skin. I didn't care. I ignored the pain and continued.

The black ink spiraled and landed on the paper with each completed spell. Heat wrapped around my finger with the fourth spell; it clung to me and held midfall, resisting its fate before finally dropping to the paper. When the last spell was invoked, Vadim, Celeste, and Roman were enclosed within the newly repaired cells. The sigils on the wall were gone, and the prisoners were glaring at me and Dominic.

The vampire, Roman, slid a finger over his bottom lip, removing the rivulet of blood from whomever he had been feeding from or changing. Dominic stepped closer, a taunting smile on his lips.

"Welcome back."

Vadim launched at the glass, drawing back his lips and exposing his teeth like a wild animal. Celeste was the only one who held her rage, probably clinging to the fact that imprisonment would be the lesser punishment, since her death would be the end of Madeline's bloodline. As long as she lived, so did they. It wouldn't help her with being imprisoned, but it guaranteed her life.

Madeline didn't even give me a moment of celebration before she had the knife to my hand, ready to do the spell to return her magic.

"Give her a moment," Dominic demanded. If a moment was five minutes, then that was all she was willing to give. She snatched her magic back with the voracity of a starving person who had just been handed food.

It didn't bother me; I wanted it gone. My finger was red from the spells being removed, but it was the end. I was done. With the vellum rolled up, Dominic and Madeline left the dungeon with new determination. His was to find Peter; hers seemed to be to gain access to Dominic's spellbooks.

"I want to go home."

***

My home felt more welcoming than I could've imagined, even with the Prince of the Underworld in it. I kept looking at my unmarked hand.

He moistened his lips and ran fingers through his hair.

"What happens to Peter?" I asked.

"I find him and he will be imprisoned. Indefinitely. He's a menace, but I need to find out why he released the prisoners.

It makes little sense. Was it just for the chaos?" He considered it again. "Do you want to question him when he's found?"

I shook my head and searched for the right words. Searching wasn't really necessary. I knew what I wanted to say. It was figuring out how to say it nicely that was the problem. "It won't change anything. I've learned a valuable lesson. The world of magic isn't for me. I don't belong in it. I'm not even equipped to survive in it."

"You survived fine. I'd even say you are a force—"

"No." I shook my head. Everything that I had encountered rushed to my mind. "I survived with you protecting me, and luck. It's a dangerous world, far more than I can handle. More than I want. A simple, non-magic world is what I want. My world."

He nodded slowly, understanding showing on his face. Whatever existed between us, I didn't want to explore. A relationship with him was a relationship with magic and the Underworld. While magic was being pulled from my skin and different magic was coursing through my body, it hit me harder than ever how much I wanted to be removed from it. Look at it from the rearview mirror and give it a well-deserved middle finger.

His eyes dropped to my lips as I moistened them. They lingered, and when he looked back at me, fiery eyes revealed his thoughts. He wanted to explore things—me. I didn't. The complications he came with weren't worth it to me.

"Luna." It was a low, sultry entreat. "It doesn't have to be complicated."

"But it would be. I don't want that. The magic, violence, clandestine meetings, complicated politics. I like my human existence."

"I know how to separate the two worlds. I've done it all my life."

"Yes, two worlds of the supernatural. Not my world —exclusively."

Without needing further explanation, he knew. His wasn't a human world. He lived in the parallel world that existed with the supernaturals. They were just mirror images of one another.

He leaned down, his lips pressing lightly against mine in a chaste kiss. He cut it off abruptly, as if he feared it would heighten into more.

"Bye, Little Luna," he whispered against my lips. Then he left before I could respond, which was just as well because that simple kiss had me rapidly rethinking my decision.

This was for the best.

23

*N*ine days without magic or the Underworld, and my life had slipped easily back to normal. The mundane days of reading, going to work, and the excitement of Emoni's new life. My guilt about her mind being manipulated had lifted, and Reginald only occasionally gave me a concerned side-eye. Jackson hadn't been around, and I was fine with that. Torn between checking on him and leaving things as they were, I decided to give it a few days. I didn't want to encourage him.

Most peculiarly, the supernaturals slipped away. I knew they were around, but the ability to sense their presence, feel their enigmatic energy, faded. I contributed my enhanced senses to the markings. Show me fangs, and I'll know you're a vampire. Knowing what a shifter looked like before he was about to go beast mode was something I would always remember.

It was the tenth night of my separation from Dominic and magic when I woke up with a start, pressing my hand to my chest out of habit, to prevent the book from falling to the floor. Only there wasn't a book, nor was I on my sofa.

I jumped up from the bed, my eyes trying to adjust to the

dim light. But I didn't need light. The flutter of magic against my skin, Dominic's peppery scent inundating the air, and the frosted glass in front of me. I was in a cage—no, a prison. A prison in the Underworld.

"I'll be damned, he did it," said an unfamiliar voice. I assumed it was Roman or Vadim. Although it could've been another misbehaving supernatural.

I yelled. It was a rough, heart-wrenching sound of desperation.

No response. I called Dominic's name, and there was a low female chortle. My scream was so loud it obscured his name. Despair kept me going. I became a siren that no one could ignore. But they did. My vocal cords felt raw.

I was readying to abuse them more when the light brightened in the room. A surprised Anand appeared in front of the prison door.

"Luna," he said, his eyes wide at the sight of me. He parted his lips, but the words just didn't flow. A strange understanding moved over his face that made my heart drop to my stomach.

"The human is here." In the ten days of not seeing me, Helena had conveniently forgotten my name, or my name no longer had value.

I could feel him before he approached, feel the wash of magic and power suffusing the room. And something else. Rage. It was palpable as he got to the cell.

"What the fuck?" His eyes darted around the room, but it was a limited space. "What happened, Luna?" Dominic asked.

"What happened?" Helena taunted. "It is not a coincidence that you found Peter so easily yesterday. It was strategy. He wanted to be caught."

Helena's sinuous movements were slow and purposeful as she approached the enclosure. "Tell me, Luna, how have you helped the annoying Dark Caster this time?"

I shook my head and looked at my finger and all my exposed skin for markings or sigils. Nothing.

"I haven't read any magic books or picked up anything. I've been very careful," I said.

Dominic opened the cell, easing me to him. He started to lift my shirt but stopped. "May I?"

I bobbed my head, too shocked to say much. Just hours before I was on my sofa reading a book and now, I was in a prison in the Perils being physically searched by the Prince of the Underworld. Fear and confusion overshadowed any modesty, so when he asked if he could see my legs, I wasn't discreet. I just dropped trou, exposing the full length of my legs for him to see. My shirt covered most of my panty-clad ass, so I didn't care. I needed to figure out how Peter had snared me into the supernatural world again.

"I don't know what happened," I admitted, pulling up my pants after he'd completed the body check.

"How could he do a *temporalibus* with you? He'd need to use a body conduit."

"Body conduit?"

"Blood, hair, intimate clothing item."

Suddenly in need of support, I stepped back until I felt the hard, cool glass of the cell against my back. He had it. When we got entangled during Wine-Down Thursday. What I'd thought was an accident had been a carefully orchestrated plan.

"He had it," I admitted and told them what led to him having both a dab of blood and my hair.

"There's no need to keep him alive," Dominic asserted angrily. "No information I can get from him is worth it. He's too dangerous."

Helena hadn't taken her appraising gaze off me. I had the distinct feeling that she considered me a co-conspirator rather than an unknowing accomplice.

"Luna, I think you should stay here for a few days. Call

out sick or whatever you need to do. I don't want you to be placed at risk of any harm," Dominic said.

Any more harm. Peter had found a way to have me replace him in the Perils—how much more harmed could I get? If he'd done this with such ease, there was more danger out there.

"Let's get a few of your things and come back here, okay?"

Words didn't come easy; things had just devolved to me nodding. When he extended his hand, I took it, finding comfort in its warmth.

Dominic's traveling from the Underworld was always done with such ease. If it took effort, it never showed on his face. This time, there was a slow migration of confusion, concern, and then outrage. He couldn't leave. Dominic looked at Anand.

Anand attempted to travel from the Underworld. His irritation gave way to fear. His breathing hastened, and it seemed like he was about to have a panic attack. Then they looked at me. Helena couldn't be tested. Still wearing the marks of her magical restrictions, she no longer had the ability to travel from the Underworld.

Helena's gaze went to me, slid along the cells in the dungeon, and to her brother. Her eyes were deep with thought. "Every time you encountered a Tenebras Obducit, you returned exhausted and often injured, but not this time," she pointed out, speculative. "This time was different."

Dominic frowned. "He was distracted and in the middle of performing a spell."

"Without putting up a protective field, a trigger to notify him of trespassers, or a magical minefield? A practitioner of his status wouldn't be so careless. You even admitted his capture was easier than expected," she said.

Dominic's teeth gripped his lips. I figured he was either taking in his sister's observation or reviewing Peter's capture because he released his hold on his lips. "He's arrogant," he offered in explanation. "It caused him to be overconfident and careless."

Helena shook her head. "I don't think so. You're arrogant and often overconfident but never careless. I suspect the same is true for him. I do believe you've met your match, brother. I don't think it was ever about the prisoners," Helena said thoughtfully, her hard gaze on me. "It was about her. He used *your* human to release the prisoners. Now he's used her to escape and imprison us here. The most pressing question is why. Why Luna?"

Good question. Now we were the prisoners in the Underworld.

MESSAGE TO THE READER

Thank you for choosing *A Touch of Brimstone* from the many titles available to you. My goal is to create an engaging world, compelling characters, and an interesting experience for you. I hope I've accomplished that. Reviews are very important to authors and help other readers discover our books. Please take a moment to leave a review. I'd love to know your thoughts about the book.

For notifications about new releases, *exclusive* contests and giveaways, and cover reveals, please sign up for my mailing list at McKenzieHunter.com.

McKenzieHunter.com
McKenzieHunter@McKenzieHunter.com